Falling For Ken

LAUREN GIORDANO

PUBLISHED BY:
Harvest Moon Press

FALLING FOR KEN

Cover Design and Interior format by The Killion Group
http://thekilliongroupinc.com

DEDICATION

To my beautiful daughters who have taught me the true meaning of
the words *unconditional love.*
And to Dan,
best friends for thirty-three years . . . and counting.

LOVE UNDER CONSTRUCTION . . .

Site contractor Kendall Adams is going broke and the guy who was her only hope of saving her company has just tumbled into the project. To avoid getting sued and maybe sweet-talk him into paying, she'll do . . . just about anything.

With no family to rescue him from the hospital, injured executive Harrison Traynor's choices are: 1) an indefinite stay or 2) risk being 'nursed' by the angry, amber-eyed beauty he's on the verge of bankrupting. But falling for Kendall was never in the blueprint.

Flings with sexy enemies don't usually lead to happily ever after. And the anti-prom queen *never* ends up with the football stud. Will Kendall risk her heart when loving Harry was never in the specs?

CHAPTER 1

For the tenth time that afternoon, Kendall Adams peered out the window. Oblivious to the roar of earthmoving equipment just yards from the construction trailer, her gaze centered on the lone man trekking across the arid wasteland. In twelve months, the site would transform into the anchor store of an exclusive mall. Today, it more closely resembled the surface of the moon–endless acres of red clay broken only by gaping craters the size of city blocks.

"What's your plan, Kenny? With the Specialty guy?"

Startled, she discovered her foreman leaning against the doorjamb. *Beg for mercy?* The looming meeting with Specialty Construction was life or death for Adams & Rey Contracting. As the Adams part of that equation, Kendall's fate lay in the hands of the Traynor brother crossing the site. "Guess I'll sweet-talk him."

When Jimmy's leathery face creased with a smile, she caught a flash of her daddy– the rare times he'd ever smiled. "No– seriously."

If things weren't dire, she would've laughed along with him. More likely to throw a punch than a kiss, the image of Kendall Renee Adams sweet-talkin' anyone was downright laughable. But with her bank account indicating they were about a month away from running out of money, she was willing to try anything.

"You sure Specialty got our pay applications?"

"Claire says she's called a hundred times." Kendall's stomach twisted. "Three months work out here . . . and Specialty hasn't paid a dime."

With Specialty responsible for the whole project, one of them damn Traynors was about to read her the riot act. A & R's piece was the sitework. And her piece was making a muck of things. Mechanical breakdowns, equipment theft . . . all normal headaches she had no problem taking ownership of. But Specialty deserved some heat as well. Dammit– if they'd just pay up, half her problems would go away. She'd still have plenty to keep her from sleeping at night, but her imminent financial ruin would temporarily slide to the backburner.

This business grew tougher each year. She hated the arguments, the threats, the tiresome hoops she jumped through just to get paid what they were owed. Barring a miracle or a last minute lottery win, Ken was prepared to throw herself on Traynor's mercy. Her daddy and Linc Traynor went way back. If she had to swallow her pride for the sake of her crew-

"Girl, you're gonna have ulcers by the time this is done." Jimmy scowled. "Everyone will survive if it ends, Kenny. It's not your job to take care of these boys."

Too much like a real father, talking with Jimmy would only lead to tears. "Can we discuss this later?" Worse than meeting Traynor would be the call to Ken, Sr. Explaining to her father why, after a scant three years under her leadership, Adams & Rey would be shutting down.

The news would probably kill the old man.

As bearer of the news it just might kill her, too.

∾

Harrison Traynor strode toward the gaping hole in the earth, one hand raised to shield his eyes from the glare. The harsh smell of diesel lingered around the huge machine he cautiously approached. His hardhat weighed heavy in the afternoon sun.

The burly equipment operator paused mid-scoop when he caught sight of him. Jumping to the ground, a plume of dust rose around him. "Help ya?"

"I'm looking for Ken Adams." Competing with the idling equipment, he raised his voice. "I'm with Specialty Construction."

"Kenny's expecting you." He jerked his thumb toward the far side of the site. "We just moved the trailer down the road a piece. You'll have to walk."

Hoisting his briefcase, Harry began the long hike across the rock-strewn site. He faced a huge decision. Adams & Rey had been in business thirty years– nearly as long as Specialty. But talk around town suggested A & R was on shaky financial ground. Harry would determine whether the rumors were true.

The other buzz surrounding the legendary site contractor– that he slung a shotgun like a western movie cowboy– he hoped to avoid confirming. Passing busy crews on thundering equipment, he resisted the urge to blot his forehead on the sleeve of his now damp suit. Ahead, a lone construction worker left the trailer, starting toward him, his angry strides creating a swirling red haze.

He studied the man approaching. Adams was slighter in stature than legend suggested. Determined to set the right tone for what was sure to be an awkward meeting, Harry extended his hand. "Harrison Traynor. Are you Ken Adams?"

"I am."

Though belligerent, the whiskey-soaked voice was suspiciously female. Harry might be a little slow on the uptake, but eventually, he could puzzle through just about anything. "I'm the CFO at Specialty. I was looking for-" He rechecked his file. "Ken Adams? The owner?"

"And I said you're lookin' at her."

Removing her sunglasses, the diminutive woman's eyes were an unusual shade of amber. Despite a vague whisper of familiarity, her expression suggested she'd enjoy nothing better than working him over with a tire iron. "Have we met?"

"No."

"I assumed I was meeting with . . . your father?" His question met with stony silence, Harry persevered. "Okay. I thought it best we meet in person regarding your progress."

She didn't blink. "You got a check for us, Traynor?"

Her hardhat covered what was clearly an even harder head. "I'm prepared to discuss an advance on your next draw . . . once we reach an understanding on our expectations."

"Advance? How about payin' us for all the work in place?" She waved expansively toward the nearest crater.

"Why don't we continue this conversation inside?" Nodding toward the trailer, Harry ignored the beads of sweat trickling down his spine, unsure whether it was heat or the proximity to the edge of a damned canyon. Though he'd avoided thinking about it, a glimpse at the height made his stomach tighten with familiar dread. The only path to the trailer ran along the rim of the cavernous hole. Despite knowing the path was wide enough to travel on, his stupid heartbeat accelerated anyway.

Her eyes shooting sparks, Ken stood her ground. "If you don't have the money you owe, there's nothing more to discuss."

"Miss Adams . . . we're concerned whether you'll complete the sitework on time. I've received calls from several suppliers saying you're overdue paying them." By the tight clench of her jaw, her silence spoke volumes. "You signed a contract with Specialty," Harry reminded. "The agreement includes an expectation of performance."

"That contract also included timely payment," she shot back.

Dropping his briefcase in the dirt, he tugged his jacket off. *Why the hell had he worn a suit?* Rolling up the sleeves of his formerly crisp cotton shirt, his temper eroded in the heat. They were twenty feet from air-conditioning. Why couldn't they go inside and cool off? Despite her immunity to the smothering humidity, twin spots of color rose in Ken's cheeks. For some reason, Harry was cheered by the tiny chink in her armor. "You still have a skeletal crew out here. Where are your men?"

"How the hell can I pay them when you're holding my money? How much more do you think I can float?"

Her rusty voice scraped Harry's edgy nerves. Dust clinging to him, he was hot and sweaty. And staring into that damn gaping hole in the ground was making him lightheaded. The longer they stood there, the more he fought visions of plunging over the side. He'd had just about enough of the annoying little wasp zinging around him with her irritating voice. At this point, her old man and his shotgun would be preferable.

"If you're experiencing financial problems, tell me now so we can help," he suggested, loosening the silk tie suddenly strangling him. "We can't afford you going bankrupt midway through this dig. The steel's already ordered and the concrete crew is waiting on you to finish."

Take that, Wasp. Winning a chunk of the huge mall contract had been a coup for Specialty. Though his cousins might be the building experts, he alone was responsible for making sure Specialty remained profitable on the deal. Harry wasn't about to let anything go wrong.

Fury heating the gold flecks in her eyes, Ken took a step closer. "You think you've got trouble now, Prettyboy? Three months without any payment means I'm filing a lien Monday. If I shut this job down– you'll be dead in the water." She advanced on him. "And, just so we're perfectly clear– this job is two days *ahead* of schedule. So, you can shove that concrete crew up your ass-"

Three months? What the hell was she talking about? Harry's temper spiked. "We've paid you everything you're owed through the end of last month."

"You're a damn liar, Traynor."

Despite her belligerent stance, her words didn't match his records. "I have the proof right here." More alarming than her accusation was the catch he heard in Ken's voice. Hell– she was choosing *now* to go all female on him? "Can we *please* move this to the trailer?" He lifted his briefcase, hoping she'd accept his not-so-subtle hint. "I'm willing to review your contract and each pay application," he offered. "Line by line if that's what it takes."

"I can't imagine your daddy would be proud of what you boys are doing to us."

That did it. Upset or not, the she-troll was *way* out of line. "If my father was alive, he'd be *damned* proud of how we conduct business, Miss Adams. And Linc is still active on the board of directors," he pointed out, his voice chilling over the insult. "If it wasn't for him cutting you a break, we would've had this conversation last month."

⮾

Kendall shoved fisted hands in her pockets. *Great job, Ken– insult his dead father.* Would she ever learn to control her mouth? Her daddy was right. Trouble seemed to follow her like a starving dog. Until meeting Harrison, she'd hoped to reason with him. Despite Jimmy's misgivings, she could be persuasive. Sometimes.

But thirty seconds into their conversation Ken realized she'd rather grab Traynor in a chokehold than play nice. He was rich and arrogant. Gorgeous. And way better dressed than she could ever hope to be. A volatile combination when she was staring at a mountain of unpaid bills, a lazy, narcissist partner her father had foisted on her, a crew who expected money for their long hours and two demanding pets with high expectations.

"Alright. Let's go." How could she make him understand there'd been an error? Specialty owed her serious money. The bigger question was whether she could convince Harrison of the truth before she was forced out of business.

Despair swamping her, she trudged back to the trailer, uncaring whether he followed. Halfway there, the yellow caution tape fluttering in the breeze caught her gaze, reminding her of problem number seventy-eight she'd yet to address. The damned fence had been designed to withstand a Category 4 storm. Yet somehow, several bolts had managed to loosen up overnight.

"Yo– Traynor." She spun around to warn him. "Careful near the guardrail. I noticed today-"

Surprised to find him dogging her heels, the grim determination in his eyes was coupled with– apprehension? When she stopped abruptly, he nearly plowed into her. Forced to sidestep around her, he moved the wrong way.

"Be careful." Reaching for him at the same moment he tripped, Ken sucked in a horrified breath as he stepped dangerously close to the loose rail. Her eyes snapped the terrifying images as the tassel on his expensive loafer snagged on the barbed wire and he lurched into the fence. "No-" Her heart contracting with fear, she watched the rail give way under his weight. Witnessed the briefcase leave his hand and become airborne. Lunged to pull him back as the fencing collapsed and he plunged into the yawning hole of the mall's underground parking garage.

A terrifying lifetime passed during his plunge to the bottom. Her scream mingled with his shout of fear moments before the fencing crashed down upon him. Only her tortured breathing broke the desolate sound of absolute silence.

❦

Minutes felt like hours as Kendall's heart catapulted from her chest. *Now. Now. Now.* She needed to get down there. The more people who gathered at the edge, the more helpless she grew. Everyone was just *standing* there. "Jimmy– where's the ambulance?" Before he could respond, she slipped into the harness, cursing her trembling fingers. "I'm not waiting."

"Kenny . . . you can't-"

As close to fainting as she'd ever been, Kendall skirted around her foreman, clipping herself to the rig line. "I have to help him."

Scaling down the side of the crater, she forced herself to move methodically, resisting the urge to freefall to the bottom. Thoughts flooded her panicked brain. Her company was nearly bankrupt. What if she'd killed the guy with the money to save her? *How could she think about money at a time like this?* "Lord– if you're listening, I'm sorry. Please let him be all right."

Unclipping from the line, she hurried on legs that wanted to fold beneath her. Dread coursing through her, she approached him. A groan caught in her throat when she viewed the damage to a body that until five minutes earlier had been damn near perfect. Harrison's left arm lay at an awkward angle. *Probably broken.* Spots of blood leeched through his cotton shirt in several places.

He appeared to be sleeping. Swallowing a shiver of icy fear, Ken stepped closer, confirming the rise and fall of his chest through the torn designer shirt. Moments later he groaned. His lashes were coal-black spikes against the chalky paleness of his skin. From her vantage point he appeared almost boyish, tousled hair marring his perfect features. "That pretty face survived intact," she muttered. Engulfed by remorse, she was mortified by her words. *What was wrong with her today?*

"That's a relief. I wondered whether GQ . . . still want me."

When his eyes fluttered open, Kendall instinctively shielded his face from the glare. "I'm so s-sorry. I don't know where that came from."

"Ken?"

"Please forgive me?" Hearing the rasp of fear in her voice, she fought to steady it. Melting down wouldn't help him stay calm. Conscious of his emerald gaze following every movement, she brushed away some of the dirt.

That had to be good, right? His being aware of her? "You probably shouldn't move," she warned when he would have rolled. "Ambulance is coming. How do you feel?"

"Like I . . . tumbled off the side of a mountain."

Kendall sat back on her haunches. "I think your left arm is broken."

"It feels that way," he said through clenched teeth. "Good . . . thing I'm . . . right-"

"You've broken it before?" Gently, she ran shaking hands over the rest of him. Each time he winced, a jolt of anguish stabbed her chest.

His lips tightened. "Football. Reason why– switched to soccer."

She skimmed down his legs. "It doesn't seem as though anything else is broken, but I can't be sure."

"But my face is okay?"

Her glance was sharp. "Dammit, Traynor. I said I was sorry."

Harrison attempted a smile that twisted into a grimace, skin pulling taut over his cheekbones in an effort she recognized as a battle for control over pain. Pain appeared to be winning. She made a consoling sound in her throat. "Where does it hurt?"

"Hell– everywhere."

On impulse, she nearly grabbed his right hand before thinking better of it. What if that was broken too? Instead, Ken laid a hand against his forehead. Her fingers bumped against his wallet lying in the dirt near his head. Scooping it up, she tucked it in her pocket. Of their own volition, her fingers returned to his dusty hair. The thick, black strands were surprisingly soft.

"S'Okay. Don't need-"

Groping to recall her first aid training, all she could remember was CPR. Since Harrison was breathing through rather perfectly formed lips, he clearly didn't need mouth-to-mouth. Dragging in a steadying breath, Kendall attempted to control her rising panic.

"Damn, Traynor, I feel responsible." Unsure of where she could touch without hurting him, she stroked his cheek until she heard the soft wail of sirens in the distance.

"It's not like you pushed me." He paused for several beats. "Right?"

She played along, pretending not to notice the thread of anxiety in his voice. "I solve all my contractor problems by dumping them into foundations."

Aware of his gaze, Ken tried not to wince at the sight of his battered body. It wouldn't help him to know how afraid she was. "Won't be long now. I bet you'll be up and movin' before the weekend's out."

"Hope so."

Traynor was deathly pale. *Where were the damn paramedics?* When his eyelids fluttered shut, her heart plunged to her stomach. "Harrison?"

"Mmm?"

"You got big plans this weekend?" Panic seeping into her voice, she asked out of sheer desperation, unsure whether she should force him to remain conscious.

"Got something in– mind?"

"I think I'm supposed to keep you awake, so tell me what you're doing this weekend," she ordered.

His eyes jerked open at the command. "Working. Always work," he muttered.

"Friday night and no plans?" Overhead, she heard the painstaking progress of the rescue crew. Keeping him awake was better for her guilty conscience. The silence had gone on too long, filled only with his shallow breathing and the snorting sound of equipment rumbling above their heads. When a shower of pebbles fell from above, Kendall threw her body over his, careful to keep her weight off him. Her insides liquefied when she thought of another possible worry. *Please– not a cave-in.*

Eyes closed, Harry's eyebrows scrunched in thought, oblivious to their impending doom. "Too much to do. Jake's– honeymoon. Jeff . . . vacation. All gone."

"So, you're in charge?" She could kiss off any hope of a financial reprieve. Traynor hadn't been in a giving mood when he arrived. Kendall could only assume his tolerance of her had deteriorated over the last several minutes.

"Guess so." When he attempted a weak smile, she experienced the uncomfortable urge to place his head in her lap. To do something– anything to alleviate his discomfort. But her daddy always said she had a knack for making bad situations worse.

Brushing dusty strands of hair from his forehead revealed an evil-looking gash she hadn't noticed earlier. Her stomach clenched in anguish.

"Dammit to hell. Is there *anywhere* on you that isn't hurt?" Her bottled-up remorse exploded in a wave of helpless fury.

"If I apologize . . . for falling, will you . . . stop yelling?"

Tears filled her throat and spilled from her eyes. "I'm so sorry, Traynor. If I could trade places with you, I would."

His eyes fluttered open at the croaky sound of her voice, searching through the haze of dust. "I hear them-"

Harrison's sharp groan of pain sent fear chasing down her spine. Swiping her tears, she burrowed through the rubble to grab his hand, forgetting it might be broken. His skin was cool and clammy. Hell—what did that mean? Shock? "They'll be here soon." Relief coursed through her when he acknowledged the pressure of her fingers with his.

"Ken– can you do . . . something for me?"

"Anything . . . just tell me." Amazed, Kendall watched as he fought to stay conscious. His voice had dropped to a whisper and she leaned down to hear his next words.

"Could you loosen your grip? You're crushing my hand."

His head pounding, Harry discovered it hurt to breathe. Over the roar in his ears, he heard an argument escalating. Forcing his eyes open, he glanced around. Hell– he was in an ambulance? He must be worse off than he knew.

"I need to go with him-"

"Ma'am– please step back."

Ken hadn't released his hand. She'd loosened the painful grip, thankfully, but he'd been aware of her presence the entire time. Even as he'd passed out– and again when he lurched awake while they carried him from the hole. Unfortunately, it didn't sound as though she would be leaving him anytime soon.

"Jeez– let her come." The *only* thing Harry wanted was to get the hell away from that crater. The sooner he made it to a hospital, the sooner they'd patch him up and he could drive back to Stafford.

Blissfully, it was quiet for a moment before Ken's smoky voice issued several orders to her team as she hoisted herself into the ambulance and they were underway. When her fingers slid between his, Harry was surprised to realize he'd been expecting them.

"Your name is really Ken?" She had freckles. A spatter of them across her nose.

"Short for Kendall." Her gaze had switched to the scenery flashing past the window in a blur of green and brown.

He hadn't thought he liked freckles. Now, he wasn't sure. Harry frowned. Was it possible he had a concussion? There wasn't a spot on his body that wasn't throbbing or bleeding. Maybe he was hallucinating.

Several minutes passed before she spoke again. "We're almost there."

"Doesn't change . . ." He frowned, trying to remember what he'd been about to say. "We still . . . your contract." When her eyes widened in surprise, Harry again experienced a flash of familiarity. *That color*.

"Let's worry about getting you patched up."

He wondered whether guilt had caused her change of heart. "Where's– briefcase?"

"The boys were bringing it out of the hole. I'll get it for you tonight, once you're squared away at the hospital."

"Thanks." His fingers twitched against hers and Harry experienced a strange flicker of comfort. She was one of the most prickly females he'd ever met. Ken had been belligerent, demanding and insulting prior to his nosedive through that fence. Yet, she'd been the first person into the hole to rescue him. Since then, she'd been surprisingly human. "Thanks for coming with me."

"When I nearly kill a man, it's only polite to cart him to the hospital."

He felt the strangest urge to smile, but damned if he knew how that could be possible. "Where's the original Ken?"

"My dad," she admitted. "He retired to Key Largo three years ago. I'm the only Ken left."

"You run the company?"

"I've worked for A & R since I was seventeen."

Their conversation ended when the ambulance arrived at the emergency room. Releasing his hand, Ken stepped aside while the attendants hustled him inside. The last Harry saw of her was a shaky smile of encouragement and a shy little wave. He was left to wonder whether she'd be waiting when he was finally released or if he'd have to hitch a ride back home.

∞

Every instinct urged Kendall to follow him through those doors, but her brain jerked the reins. Lord's sake, she'd nearly killed the man. Fighting the urge to cry, she found a seat in the waiting room. Sinking into the chair, she closed her eyes. When an hour ticked by with no word, she approached the window for a status report, her heart thudding like a freight train.

"You're with Mr. Traynor?"

Nodding, she crossed her fingers. The clerk didn't need any ugly details. "Any news? Can I see him?"

"Not yet. But since you're waiting, you can complete the insurance papers." Slamming forms onto a clipboard, the harried woman passed it through the window.

"But-" Kendall sighed when the woman turned to answer the phone. After several minutes, she gave up. The slender bump in her pocket reminded her she held Harrison's wallet. It lay there, beckoning her to rifle through it.

Not rifle, she corrected. Rifling was when you didn't have an actual reason. Rifling was snooping. Releasing a gusty breath, she withdrew the leather fold.

Reviewing her mental list of the contents– there had to be at least one picture of the skinny supermodel Harrison was most assuredly dating. Probably sporting a thong, she amended. Guys like him didn't date average women like her. Kendall had grown numb to the inevitable feeling of failure at being a woman. But she'd learned the hard way that jeans and boots were suited for digging in the dirt. And it was more important to gain her crews' respect than to attempt lookin' cute (which was hopeless anyway). She ran a construction company– not a damn nail salon.

Summoning her courage, she removed the insurance card. Every thirty seconds, she snuck a peek at the doors, certain Harrison would burst through them and catch her snooping. She was relieved to return the forms a few minutes later, his wallet safely returned to her pocket. Back in her seat, she couldn't help wondering about the photo she'd spied. Harrison and his cousins, posing near the ski lift during a day of skiing at some fancy resort.

"Ma'am? Mr. Traynor is asking for you."

Startled from her thoughts, Kendall eyed the nurse with apprehension. "Is he okay?"

"The doctor says he'll make a full recovery."

Releasing a shaky breath she hadn't realized she'd been holding, she trailed the nurse through doors leading to a corridor that smelled strongly of antiseptic.

"He'll need some recuperation at home for a week or so," the nurse continued.

She bit her lip at the news. When the pain meds wore off, Traynor would be seriously ticked– probably at her.

"This way, Mrs. Traynor."

Mrs.? Kendall followed her into a brightly lit examination room. "I'm not-"

"Baby, is that you?"

Sweet Lord– a head injury. Any intelligent words she might have summoned died in her throat. Nearing his bedside, she ran her gaze over his battered face, the angry stitches standing out in stark contrast against his bleached skin. His beautiful mouth twisted in a grim line when he tried to smile. Harrison's eyes fluttered open, revealing recognition of her and a strumming pain that hadn't been quelled by drugs.

"Harrison? Are y-you– are you all right?" She glanced at the nurse hovering near the door. "Is he alright?"

"Baby, come here. I can't see you under these bright lights."

Baby? Sweating now, she swallowed a sob of fear. *A brain injury.* Adams & Rey was about to have their corporate ass sued off. "Is that better, Tray– I mean. . . Harrison?"

"Kenny, bend down so I can talk to you." An IV'ed hand reached for hers.

She shot a nervous peek at the nurse.

"Go ahead," she encouraged. "The doctor will be a few minutes."

Nodding, she closed the gap between them, surprised to catch a faint whiff of a mouthwatering, woodsy cologne. Only a Traynor could freefall into a pile of dirt and come out smelling great. When the nurse finally left, she released a worried sigh.

"Have they examined your h-head yet? I think you may have hit it harder than we thought-"

"Ken– listen up." Harrison's eyes snapped open, shocking her with the sudden clarity in his gaze. "They want to keep me here until a family member can take me home."

"You fell two stories and landed on your head. That's probably not a bad idea."

"I don't *have* family available," he shot back. "If someone doesn't take me home, they'll make me stay indefinitely– like . . . maybe until Jeff gets back next Wednesday."

A mental light bulb went off and she chuckled with relief. "*That's* why you were asking for me? For a minute there, I thought you'd lost your marbles."

"I already told them you're my wife. You have to back me up or they *will* think I'm confused. Tell them you're taking me home and you won't let me out of your sight," he ordered. "Otherwise, I'm stuck here."

"No offense Harrison, but maybe this is where you belong for a few days. You don't look so hot."

"Like *hell*." His pain-filled eyes shot daggers at her. "I've got casts on my wrist *and* my ankle, thanks to you. And stitches in three places." He struggled to sit up before falling back against the pillow. "You *owe* me, Ken. For the next few hours– you're my wife, got it?"

Based on his mood, the honeymoon was clearly over. "Think about it," she urged. "You're lucky the fall didn't kill you-"

His expression hardened. "You're gonna sign me out of here and then you're gonna drive me home and help me inside."

Was it possible she'd met someone more stubborn than her? "You've got broken bones and you're in serious pain-"

When the door swished open a graying man entered, white coat flapping behind him. "What have we here?" He scanned the chart briefly. "Once your x-rays come back, we can probably release you . . . but you're not to move out of bed the next three to four days."

"Are you sure it's safe? He suffered a serious fall." Kendall ignored smoldering glares from the invalid.

"He's got a goose egg on his head." He reviewed the chart. "Possible slight concussion. His spine is in remarkable shape, all things considered. Other than a couple broken bones and a few stitches-" He nodded to Harrison. "You were lucky today."

"Yes, sir."

The doctor swiveled his attention back to her. "If his headache doesn't improve noticeably in three days, or if it worsens- get him back here. For his broken bones– call this orthopedist next week." He handed her a card. "Crutches will be awkward with only one working arm, so use the cane instead. Keep his casts dry."

He tugged a pad from his pocket and scribbled a prescription. "One pill every four hours for the next three days, then only as necessary for pain." He glanced from Harrison to her. "I don't want him out of bed for forty-eight hours. Then– only up for brief periods for two more days. That'll give him a jump on healing. Any questions?"

Probably several hundred, if Ken were allowed a moment to think. "W-what about- Do I need a visiting nurse-"

The doctor smiled over her worried expression. "He looks bad, but he's in decent shape. You should be able to take care of him."

"But-" Traynor's hand tightened in warning.

"I'll feel *much* better at home. My wife will take great care of me."

The doctor swung his gaze back to her. "You'll keep him quiet, young lady?"

Forcing a smile, she answered Harry's vice-like warning with one of her own. Oh, she'd take care of him, alright. "I'm sure I'll have no trouble at all."

CHAPTER 2

Harry hurt everywhere. After three excruciating hours, his x-rays were finally read and all the damned paperwork signed so he could finally be discharged. Three hours for Kendall to locate some guy named Jimmy on his barstool at the Hickory Pub and confirm her truck had been delivered to the hospital. Three hours for the pain to worsen. Whatever shock he'd been in after the fall had long since worn off.

There wasn't a damned spot on his body that wasn't battered, broken or bruised. But he couldn't risk a pain pill yet. If he did, Ken would likely abandon him. She'd confess to the doctor she barely knew him. In his drooling state, he wouldn't be able to argue. They'd wheel him into a noisy, sterile room and he'd be trapped for the weekend– or longer.

But damned if he didn't want a pill. Or five. Jesus, he felt like hell. He eyed the pharmacy bottles in Kendall's hand. If he could just get to the truck . . . He'd allow himself *one*. To take the edge off. Despite the mother-huge headache assaulting his brain, he ran through the list of tasks to be accomplished before he could collapse into bed.

He had to get home. He had to get *into* his home. Christ– he had to find his briefcase containing *the keys* to his home. Harry bit back a groan. His mind wandered over the logistics. Did he have any food? The way he felt, he wouldn't be leaving the damn condo for several days. Of course, the way he felt, he probably wouldn't be eating anytime soon, either. Could he even make it up the stairs to his bed?

"You okay?" Ken's croaky voice interrupted his disjointed thoughts.

Glancing down at the cast on his ankle, Harry regretted it as a wave of dizziness threatened to topple him on his ass. Praying he wouldn't throw up all over her, he blinked owlishly and sucked in a few cleansing gulps of cool night air. Through clenched teeth, he answered. "I'm fine."

"You look like hell."

Kendall had the bedside manner of a truck stop waitress. She would be the one snarling at you to hurry up and order– while she sloshed coffee down your pants. Harry had trouble imagining what it would be like to endure her presence for an extended period of time. Her voice alone was enough to make him wince.

Next to his wheelchair, he sensed her smoldering. She'd been second-guessing him all evening, badgering him to stay at the hospital. And he was damn sick of it. She'd gotten him into this mess. She'd damn well help him out . . . whether she liked his plan or not. Risking a slow turn, he was thankful when the movement didn't cause cymbals to crash in his head. Her golden eyes glowered at him, more with concern than anger, he acknowledged. But all bets were off once they were alone. She was gonna blast him.

By then, she'd be stuck with him. Adams might be belligerent, but she wouldn't leave him for dead by the side of the road. *He hoped.* Ken held her silence as the orderly strapped his battered body into the passenger seat of her ramshackle truck. As the orderly rolled the wheelchair back to the building, she pounced.

"I should have my head examined for letting you talk me into this."

Wincing at her shriek, Harry resisted the urge to unload on her. "Any civility I possess was exhausted several hours ago. If you *must* speak, please whisper. My head is ready to explode."

"I knew this was a bad idea," she said through clenched teeth. "You need to swallow one of those damn pills and lay back against the headrest."

At least she'd lowered her voice. "I'm counting the seconds until I can do that, but I have to drive myself home."

"We've been at the hospital for seven hours." She snorted in disbelief. "No way am I driving out on that construction site in the dark. We'll end up in the bottom of another crater."

Forcing his eyes open, he bit back a groan. God– even the parking lot lights were too bright. "Fine - then you've bought yourself the hour drive back to Stafford."

"Listen up, Prettyboy-"

Her amber eyes turned molten in a heartbeat. *Big mistake.* Prickly Ken was apparently dangerous when poked.

"You're coming home with me," she announced. "You're gonna get in bed without arguing and you're gonna stay there until I decide you're well enough to leave." She stared at him, a fierce scowl on her face. "You got that?"

"Like *hell*. Holding me hostage wasn't part of the plan."

She had the gall to laugh. "You're the one who said I was responsible, remember?"

"It was my fault I-" Suddenly, Harry didn't have an ounce of strength left to argue. He was too busy fighting the nausea rising in his throat.

∞

Braking for a traffic light, Kendall heard his stifled groan. Risking a sideways glance, his face was etched with agony as he swallowed convulsively. Traynor was approaching the limits of his endurance.

"I promised the doctor I'd take care of you." Sensing his ripple of shock, she hid a smile. If it were possible, Harrison Traynor was even more stubborn than her daddy.

"I am *not* staying with you, Ken."

"Harrison, honey . . . we married in sickness and health," she drawled. "I mean to honor my vows."

"I said that so they'd release me." His head tilted drunkenly when he turned to glare at her. "I can take care of my-" Slumping back against the seat, he clutched his head a moment later when she jostled over uneven pavement. "Dammit– you'd better pull over. I'm gonna throw up."

Kendall slowed the truck, edging to the side of the deserted road. Harrison barely made it out the window before he started retching. Afterward, he rested his face on the frame, gulping in shaky breaths of the cool night air.

"Death has *got* to be preferable to this."

"Think you're finished?" Harry startled, unaware she'd jumped out and rounded the truck. When he nodded, Kendall peeled off her sweatshirt and doused a corner of it with bottled water before running the wet cloth over his forehead. His hair was streaked with dirt and perspiration, his forehead patched together with stitches. Splashing more water on the shirt, she gently swiped the back of his neck before lifting his chin and cleaning his face with the rest of the bottle.

His eyes closed, dark lashes swept his ghostly face. Kendall was caught by a wave of sympathy for the excruciating pain she knew he suffered. "Let's get you home and clean you up. I'll drive as slow as I can, okay?"

"Jeez– I'm pathetic." He sagged against the cushion.

"I think you're bordering on superhuman to endure what happened today." She re-fastened the seatbelt around his slack frame before heading back around the truck. When he started shivering, she slid him a worried glance before turning up the heat. How the hell would she get him upstairs to bed?

By the time she arrived home, Traynor's soft breathing told her he'd either passed out from pain or fallen asleep from sheer exhaustion. Ken swung down from the seat and headed into the darkened house, in need of a few minutes of preparation before she could haul him inside.

Wincing at the chorus of barks that began the moment her key turned in the lock, she prayed Lurch had been able to hold it for so many extra hours. She'd endured enough messes for one night.

"Let's go outside, pal." Scrambling through the house, she snapped on lights as she headed for the back door. Jerking it open, she released a relieved sigh when Lurch bounded into the backyard. Taking the stairs two at a time, she ran to her bedroom. There, she flung back the comforter on her bed before heading for the bathroom. She emerged with a stack of clean towels and two extra pillows. Harrison needed sleep most of all, but eventually he'd want to be propped up. Tossing his prescription on the nightstand, she returned to the stairs.

Time for the hard part. She propped open the door before crossing the front porch and heading for the truck. Harrison was still asleep when she neared the passenger side. Hating the thought of waking him, his participation was unfortunately necessary.

"Harrison? Can you hear me?" He grunted a response when she swung his legs out. Grabbing his cane, she slung it over her arm.

Hoisting him around his waist, she gently tugged him to his feet, then quickly dove under his arm to support his weight before he pitched forward.

"As soon as we're inside you can go back to sleep." Kendall panicked for a moment when Traynor slumped over her. She didn't want to calculate how much weight she was trying to prevent from crashing to the pavement.

"Harry, wake up." After only a minute, she was perspiring from the effort to hold him upright. Groaning, he finally took some weight on his good leg. She waited until he was awake before handing him the cane. "Can you help me get you inside?"

"H-how far?"

"Not far," she lied, glancing up. The turret room window glowed invitingly out of reach. She tried to block out the vision of all those stairs. When they reached the top of the porch steps they collapsed by mutual agreement.

"God, Ken– can't I just sleep out here? Roll me inside in the morning."

Panting for breath, she lay beside him on the porch, staring up at the moths fluttering around the light. The scent of honeysuckle wafted over her like a thin summer blanket. From her vantage point, she noticed the porch ceiling needed painting again.

"I might join you, Traynor. If it takes this long to get you upstairs, it'll *be* morning before we get there." Turning, she found him watching her, his vivid, green eyes red-rimmed from fatigue, yet quietly assessing her in the dark. He'd gone from comatose to alert in a matter of minutes. "You ready yet?"

Squeezing his eyes shut, he cursed under his breath.

"I'll take that as a 'yes'." Biting back a groan, she stooped to grab his cane. If every muscle in her body was aching, she could only imagine how Harry felt. She staggered with him through the foyer, their movements reminding her of the three-legged race she'd won in second grade, and used the momentum to launch up the stairs for the bedroom.

Ten minutes later, she hobbled with him to the foot of the bed and sat down. Before she could remove his arm from around her, Harrison collapsed back on the mattress, taking her with him. They lay side by side, out of breath and drenched in perspiration.

"Please tell me I don't have to move again."

"It's only three feet to the pillow, but we'll wait until your pain pill kicks in." When he didn't respond, Ken allowed herself the luxury of one satisfying moment before the awkwardness of their situation began to unnerve her. She had the gorgeous, hard bodied Harrison Traynor in her bed– one muscled arm still wrapped around her. As fantasies went, this was about as close to perfection as she would ever achieve.

And she was too exhausted to enjoy it. As her eyelids drooped, the irresistible lure of Traynor's force field of body heat demanded she move, lest she fall asleep beside him. She still had work to do. It was probably a blessing when Lurch began howling at the back door.

"I hear a wolf." Traynor's voice slurred with sleep. She rose quickly, retrieving a long overdue pill from the bottle. When he murmured, she slipped the pill between his lips, holding his head up while he swallowed it with water.

She would've undressed him and tucked him in, but Lurch continued to whimper. Cursing, she strode from the room. The last thing she needed were angry calls from the neighbors. Lurch bounded inside, hovering by his dish until she noticed it was empty.

"Sorry, Sweetie." After filling his bowl, she set out clean water before filling the cat's dish. Like magic, Wink appeared, stretching her slinky frame and yawning as though oblivious to the man she had just dragged through the house.

"Don't look at me like that," she warned. "He's only staying a few days." Crouching to stroke the cat, Kendall was nearly bowled over by her faithful mutt. Patting him absently, she stifled a yawn. "I've had a hellacious day. I'm taking a shower and going to bed. I don't want to hear any fighting down here, got it?"

⌇∾⌇

Lord, he was tired. Football practice had been brutal. Harry felt as though he'd been run down by a locomotive instead of a linebacker. Hearing voices murmur downstairs, he smiled. Aunt Mona was busy in the kitchen, cooking all his favorites for the Thanksgiving break.

"Harrison? You still awake?"

He scrunched his nose in confusion. "Mona? Is that you?"

"Yeah, Sugar. Let's get you out of those clothes so you can sleep, okay?"

He felt her hands at his throat and twisted his head so she could unbutton his shirt. Her fingers were cool when they slipped the shirt from his shoulders. He groaned with the effort it required to move, frowning when his aunt gasped.

"Whass wrong?" He blinked, but there were two of her . . . and neither looked like Mona Traynor. She didn't smell like his aunt, either. She smelled like the cheerleader he'd been hitting on all season.

"Lord, you've got so many gashes." She dabbed at his chest and he felt a sting of heat. Harry didn't remember getting scratched at the game.

"Deborah? Is that you?"

"Nope. Not Deborah, either. You sure get around, Traynor."

"Deborah's sooo pretty. W-who are you?"

"I'm your worst nightmare, Sugar. Remember me?" He frowned when she chuckled. Was he having a nightmare?

"I'm Ken, remember?"

She began washing his chest and shoulders. When she finished with the front, she tugged him forward to rest against her chest. The warm hollow of her throat beckoned him closer, her soft, sweet scent tantalizing his nose. If she smelled this good, she probably tasted even better. Harry heard her gasp when his lips wandered over a sensitive spot. Her skin was unbelievably soft.

"W-what are you doing?"

"You taste good."

"I– um . . . well thanks, I guess."

He sighed appreciatively when she began to wash his back. "You smell nice, too." The sensation of the warm, wet washcloth felt impossibly good against his skin. His eyes fluttered open when warm water sluiced over his head and her fingers scrubbed gently over his scalp. "That feels incr– increable." Harry grinned, despite a twinge of pain. "Is that a word?"

Frowning when he remembered her name, he blinked, but there were three of her when he opened his eyes. She was dressed in a flowing white gown, her feet bare. Her long hair was dark and wet against her back, her kaleidoscope eyes a mysterious golden color.

"Ken's a boy's name." She patted him dry and pushed him gently back against the pillows. He sighed with pleasure, floating on a cushiony cloud with a golden-eyed angel tending his every need.

"Can't put one over on you, Harry."

Her soft, husky laughter skimmed his nerves, leaving a warm tingle behind. When she drifted away he experienced a jab of disappointment. Then he felt her hands on his foot and heard the soft clunk when his shoe fell to the floor. When she unzipped his pants, he waited patiently.

"Oh, dang."

Cloud girl was pissed. Harry forced himself to concentrate. "What-?"

"I forgot about your ankle cast. I'll have to cut your pants off."

His thoughts drifted to making love on a cloud. With an angel. "Okay."

"Damn, these look expensive. Why couldn't you wear jeans to the site?"

"Who's Jean?"

A few minutes later– or maybe it was days—cool air rushed against his legs. Her touch was so gentle he had a hard time finding her. First on his left, she reappeared on his right, like a firefly adrift on a hot summer night. Reaching for her, he came away empty-handed.

"Angel? You still here?" Her hands paused on his calf where warm, soapy water trickled down his leg. When she swiped it with a towel, he sighed.

"That's as far as the sponge bath goes, Traynor. I'm afraid my delicate sensibilities can't handle much more of your chiseled bod. You must live at the gym."

When the cool, crisp sheets brushed against his skin, he groaned. A blanket followed before the lamp snapped off.

"Goodnight, Harrison."

"I live on Parker Street." The soft, musical laughter washed over him again. Harry felt her breath against his cheek and instinctively turned to find her.

"Don't leave." The fear was instinctive. If this was a dream, he didn't want it to end.

"Go to sleep, Harry" she whispered. Floating across the room, her soft footsteps faded in the night. It finally dawned on him he hadn't seen any wings.

∽

He was naked. In a woman's bed. With the worst hangover of his life. Harry turned to the opposite pillow, relieved to discover it empty. A quick check under the sheet confirmed he still had briefs.

One-night stands weren't usually his style. Neither was drinking too much. So, where the hell was he? Shifting on the pillow, he groaned. *Holy hell.* Pain crashed in on him, his head clanging as though caught between two cymbals. And he remembered the fall.

"This is Ken's house."

Sitting up slowly, he wished he hadn't. Clenching his teeth prevented a moan of sheer agony from breaking free. Drawing a sharp-edged breath, Harry released it gradually, waiting for the shockwaves to subside. His body had become a symphony of throbbing pain that began with his skull and rippled over him, ending at his feet. Staring at the lump under the floral comforter, he remembered he'd broken his ankle. The other lump on the bed moved when he shifted. It made a sound mimicking disdain and stretched.

"Who the hell are you?"

The cat yawned, then stared at him. With one eye. The other eye appeared scrunched shut. She– and it could only be a she, Harry surmised, lost interest in him, leaping gracefully from the bed. Crossing the room, she disappeared, weaving through patches of filtered sunlight in the shadowed hallway beyond the door.

Holding his breath, he swung his legs over the side of the bed. His cane was hooked on the bedside table. Drawing a ragged breath, he made a grab for it. Damned if it didn't hurt to breathe. His ribs were as battered as the rest of him. Leaning heavily on the cane, he hobbled to the adjoining bathroom, each step more painful than the previous one.

Ten minutes later, he dragged himself back to the bed, his heart tripping from the effort. The simple task had exhausted him. After mopping perspiration from his forehead, he collapsed against the pillows. He'd barely had the strength to brush his teeth with the new toothbrush she'd left by the sink.

"Are you decent?"

Kendall Adams. *Please, God . . . no.* Harry groaned at the sound of her voice. He was trapped in a nightmare of pain. Why the hell couldn't it be with someone nurturing? With a woman who was– like a woman? Someone who didn't start an argument with every sentence? Someone whose voice didn't scrape over him like nails on a chalkboard.

She poked her head around the doorframe. "How're you feeling?"

"My head is about to detach from my body and after ten minutes of exertion, I'm ready for bed again." He frowned when she approached with a tray.

"You shouldn't get out of bed without help."

"I didn't think you'd be terribly interested in assisting me in the bathroom."

"The doctor said-"

"I don't give a damn," he interrupted. "Despite your attempt to kill me yesterday, I'm still able to manage my bodily functions." He had only the slightest twinge of conscience when Kendall's cheeks bloomed pink with embarrassment. But, damned if her eyes didn't nail him to the wall. Like a mirror to her thoughts, they widened with shock before the sparking, gold flecks dimmed, extinguished by the guilt she so readily assumed. Her anguish lanced through him. As quickly as he'd spoken the frustration-laden words, Harry wished he could retract them.

"I didn't mean that." Gazing at the ceiling, he sighed. "There isn't a spot on me that doesn't hurt. But I shouldn't take it out on you."

"You've been through hell. I'm sure the pain is terrible." Shrugging off his bad temper, Ken set the tray on the nightstand.

"I'm not the greatest morning person either." Harry was relieved when she laughed, the sparkle returning to unusual topaz eyes. Just like that, he'd been forgiven.

"That's not much comfort, Traynor."

"Why not?"

"You already slept through the morning. You've been out fourteen hours." She flicked a glance at her watch. "It's lunchtime."

It was his turn to show surprise. How could he have slept away half a day? Hazy memories floated before his eyes. "Did you feed me applesauce?"

"And some broth," she confirmed. "I was worried you'd get sick from all those meds on an empty stomach."

Sniffing the food appreciatively, Harry's stomach rumbled in response. "I may be ready for real food."

"Let's get you propped up and we'll go to work."

The mattress shifted when she sat down next to him and again when the cat bounded back up on the bed.

"Wink, you troll. Your food's downstairs."

"You call her Wink?"

She smiled. "Doesn't she look like she's winking at you?"

"How'd she lose her eye?" Before he realized it, Ken spooned beef stew into his mouth. He chewed. He swallowed. Chewed again. Until the bowl was nearly empty. Then sipped gratefully from the iced tea she raised to his lips, nearly draining the glass.

"I'm not sure. I found her at the shelter." Breaking a piece of bread, she popped it in his mouth. "She looked like she needed me, so I brought her home."

He digested the morsel of information along with an incredibly buttery roll. "You don't seem like the type to pick up strays."

"They sure seem to find me." She gave him an appraising glance. "Let me guess . . . you had me pegged for a trailer park, fridge on the porch and an old Chevy rusting in the yard, right?" Laughing at her own joke, she picked up the stew again, intent on feeding him another spoonful. A strange contentment washed over him when she chuckled. Why was the sound so familiar?

"Did you make this?"

"I make a big pot of something every few days. Then I don't have to cook every night. I grow the vegetables out back."

"And the bread? It's really good."

"When I have trouble sleeping, I bake." Kendall paused, cocking her head to acknowledge a sound on the stairs that reminded him of a bouncing ball. Thump . . . thump.

"What's that noise?" Harry raised his gaze to hers, surprised by how her eyes seemed to glow in the dimly lit room.

Ken picked up a section of orange and popped it in his mouth. "That's Lurch. He's been going crazy downstairs wondering what he's missing. Sounds like he's decided to pay a visit."

He chewed thoughtfully, his gaze following Ken when she turned toward the door. Her hair wasn't limp and straggly like he remembered. It was long and wavy. Really long. She had it pulled back in a ponytail, but several chocolate strands escaped, curling into her collar. Her slender throat appeared lost in the too-large work shirt.

"C'mon, Lurch. You're almost here." Turning back, she caught him staring, but Ken seemed oblivious to his perusal. "You ready for another piece?" Not waiting for his reply, she shoved another orange slice between his teeth. The sweet, tart juice trickled down his throat.

The head of a shaggy white dog appeared around the doorframe, much like Ken had poked hers around it earlier. The rest of him followed soon after.

"Ken– you have a three-legged dog."

"A woman from the shelter found him wandering. He'd been hit by a car."

Harry smiled when he guessed the rest of the story. "And you figured he needed you?"

"He's a wonderful dog. You barely notice he's missing a leg."

"Isn't it cruel to call him Lurch?"

Her winged eyebrows scrunched into a frown. "I got his name from the Addams family. Get it? Adams and Addams?" Leaning down, she ruffled his fur. "And Lurch likes it, don't you, sweetie?"

Harry slumped against the pillows, sleepy, sated and feeling the slightest bit better. "What's next? A canary singing show tunes?"

"I didn't realize you had a sense of humor buried under that stuffed shirt, Traynor." Rising from the bed, she set his tray on the bureau. She flicked a glance at what appeared to be a surprisingly delicate wrist. "Time for another pill. I've worn you out. And I need to head back to the site."

"Saturday afternoon?" He studied her while she refilled his glass with icy water before accepting the pill she handed him.

"There's a lot of daylight left. You'll be okay for awhile?"

"I'll be asleep before you hit the driveway." Kendall hesitated before tucking the sheets around his waist, her gaze carefully averted, her cheeks flushed with color. "Maybe tomorrow we can review your contract."

Her head shot up, eyes suspicious. "Do you ever relax?"

Harry ignored her question, skirting the issue. He was *not* a workaholic. He was capable of fun. Just because he stayed connected- "Where's my phone?" Her blank stare confirmed his suspicions. It was probably buried in the rubble of the construction site.

"It wasn't in your briefcase?"

He shook his head. "It was in my shirt pocket, so it probably got crushed."

"I'll check when I get back. Won't take but a couple minutes to scoot down there and look around."

He shuddered at the thought of anyone 'scooting' into the bowels of hell. "Don't bother. I'll pick up a new one when I get home." Ken's expression was determined as she edged away from the bed. Clearly, she wasn't crazy about others telling her what to do.

"So— no chance on the contract? It wouldn't take any time at all."

"Your brain needs a rest. No thinking." She finally met his gaze, he noted, once she was safely across the room. "Before you leave, we'll review everything. I want to straighten this mess out just as much as you."

As awful as he felt, Harry doubted he'd be able to do much of anything tomorrow. Still, there was always the possibility he'd be up and around. "If I promise not to exhaust myself, can I use your phone later?"

Nodding, Kendall slipped out the door. He smiled when her muttering voice floated back up the stairs. Something about him being too damned stupid to know he was seriously injured. He felt a prick of shame over his mean-spirited comment earlier. Maybe Ken wasn't so bad after all. She'd taken him in, nursed him, fed him a great meal.

Of course, that was after nearly killing him yesterday. Harry frowned at the sudden memory of a woman in white. Had Ken . . . bathed him? Nah. Not if she was embarrassed simply by glancing at his chest. He was careful not to shake his head. The pain in his skull had subsided to a dull monotonous pounding that became more bearable as the pill took effect.

Downstairs, Ken sang while rinsing his dishes. She certainly wasn't anything like he'd imagined— not that he'd spent much time dwelling on Kendall Adams. She wasn't the type of woman guys spent time thinking about. She was cute, he admitted, now that he'd gotten a closer look at her, and her eyes were pretty. But she was too petite– too opinionated. Too everything. And that smoky voice . . . She sounded ornery without even trying.

Certainly, she wasn't *his* type. An image of Deborah floated across his mind. Now, there was a woman men noticed. Tall, cool and beautiful. She was quiet and soothing on the nerves. There was never a hair out of place on her sophisticated, ash blonde head. She looked phenomenal in a suit or out of one. Together, they'd made a stunning couple.

Ever since his cousin Jake had tied the knot, Harry had mulled the idea of marriage. He wasn't getting any younger. And thoughts of starting a family seemed to crop up more frequently. With Jenna's two kids, Jake had a ready-made family, but the smoldering looks that passed between them indicated his cousin would be adding a few more. It was simply a matter of time.

His eyes drooping, Harry remembered he'd wanted to discuss his departure with Ken. He needed to get back to Stafford– to the pile of work he'd left on his desk. If he could convince Ken that Deborah would look after him, she'd probably take him home. She didn't have to know Deb was out of town. He could manage until Wednesday. By then, Jeff would return. And Mona. Hell, his aunt would take care of him for sure.

Sighing with drug-induced satisfaction, he settled back against the pillows. After four months, Deb's hints about their relationship had grown less subtle. Until Jake's wedding day, he'd been thinking along the same lines . . . Until he'd witnessed Jake's expression when he gazed at his wife– and Harry discovered a lump in his throat. The way they stared at each other had been almost painful to watch. Their smiles so confident– as though they'd unearthed a rare treasure.

Trying to imagine Deb looking at him that way had failed. He'd only ever witnessed that expression on a victorious day in court. She played to win, a quality Harry greatly admired. Deb Lawrence wasn't the warm, fuzzy type, but then, neither was he. They were compatible in so many ways. They respected each other. Many marriages were built on far less.

But Harry couldn't forget Jake's happiness– had been unable to shake the twinge of envy. He'd been forced to admit maybe he wanted more than compatibility. If it wasn't Deborah, he'd find the right woman– one who would fit the blueprint he'd sketched for his life. But unlike Jake, he'd operate from a basis of logic. Acting on some lovesick assumption would only cloud the issue.

His stomach pleasantly full, Harry gave in to his sleepiness. The thought of limping around his townhouse, living off canned soup held little appeal after Kendall's great meal. There was no hope of food in the Deborah scenario. He'd learned early in their relationship that Deb didn't cook. For anyone.

What the heck? Another day or two with Ken surely wouldn't kill him.

CHAPTER 3

The beast awoke at ten that night. Kendall glanced overhead, following the creaking floorboards when Harrison hobbled to the bathroom. Her forehead creasing with worry, she wondered whether she'd awakened him. After her day at the jobsite had gone horribly awry, she'd been pounding out her frustration on the piano keys. It was that, or wringing her stepbrother's neck. Unfortunately, she hadn't found a justifiable reason for murdering Lance– at least not one that would satisfy the authorities. Lance was never at work long enough to kill anyway. And if she didn't resolve the money issue with Specialty, there wouldn't be any work left.

Adams and Rey was nearly broke.

Two more pieces of equipment had broken down today. Jimmy had called with the bad news. Parts for the lift would cost fifteen thousand. And the damn thing was only three years old. This, after losing two skidloaders in the last month to theft. Kendall couldn't bear the thought of filing another insurance claim. Soon, her carrier would bail on her as well.

"I'm cursed. There's no other explanation."

She'd argued with Lance again. His answer to every problem was selling the company. Her daddy had taken leave of his senses, handing over a chunk of A & R to his new stepson. *Her* company– her blood and sweat– to that weasel bastard. All Lance cared about was the money.

Kendall wondered whether her father realized the hurt he'd inflicted– or if he cared. She'd sacrificed the last decade to A & R. In the darkest hours of the night, when her mind wouldn't let her rest, she could admit the gnawing certainty that Ken, Sr. knew *exactly* what he'd done to his daughter. The only mystery was why.

Lifting her fingers from the ivory keys, she stretched her neck in a futile attempt to unlock the kinks of stress. Her piano therapy would have to wait.

Harrison had slept the better part of two days. He had to be starving. After fixing a tray, she trudged upstairs, reluctant to discover what his mood would be like tonight. She knew Traynor didn't like her much. Normally, she didn't much care what people thought, but having Harrison Traynor under her roof left her edgy and out of sorts. She still hadn't recovered from the previous evening. Touching his fabulous body had been difficult enough. Then, he'd nibbled on her neck and her insides had melted like wax.

Ken didn't want to like him. Heck, she'd *liked* Harrison for years– though he'd never known she existed. But that had been a school girl crush. He'd rescued her on a cold, spring night . . . offering a lift to a pitiful, bedraggled girl in the rain. Harry probably didn't even remember that night. While she had been unable to forget it.

This however, was business. Traynor owed her money– and wasn't about to pony up. Harry was so damned attractive it would be easy to forget he was ruining her life. She needed to stay focused. Though she still owed him a favor for that night in the rain, it didn't mean she'd let him bankrupt her.

Approaching the bedroom, she froze, hand clutching the knob as butterflies swooped in the pit of her stomach. She hadn't experienced that sick, panicky feeling in a long time . . . of being trapped in a crowd of popular kids– knowing she was moments away from a taunting reminder of her place in the social order– the motherless, friendless, geeky loner.

Lurch hopped painstakingly up the steps, hating to miss any excitement. Kendall was grateful for his company. She couldn't afford to forget who she was– and what Harrison represented. Just like high school . . . he was one of the 'cool kids'. He would take what he wanted, then leave her high and dry. His slurred words the previous night returned to haunt her. She didn't have to meet Deborah to imagine Traynor's girlfriend. Ken was no *Deborah*.

"Harrison? Can I come in?" Chewing her lip, she waited for him to get situated.

"Aren't you going to ask if I'm decent?"

Her face heated at the amusement in his voice. Traynor probably felt trapped– with a lowly, second-class hick. A flicker of anger smoldered through her. High school was eons ago. Who cared what he thought? She wasn't seventeen anymore. And this wasn't the damn prom. She had nothing to be embarrassed about. She was the well-educated owner of her own business, damn it. And she was doing *him* a favor, whether he appreciated it or not.

"Ken? Are you out there?"

Pasting on a smile, she opened the door. "Ready for dinner?"

"Did I hear a piano?" Harry's expression was puzzled, as though it were unimaginable someone like her could play an instrument.

"Sorry if I disturbed you."

"No– it was amazing. When did you learn to play?"

"Just something I picked up," she dismissed breezily. *That and two college degrees, Superstud.* "Are you hungry?"

"I can't remember if I thanked you earlier, Ken. I really appreciate everything you've done."

"It was the least I could do after nearly killing you." Swallowing the lump of resentment, she ignored the stab of guilt following his kind words. Her business problems weren't Traynor's fault– at least not all of them. "How's your head?" Forcing her smile back in place, she tried to relax.

His expression was curious. "Headache's a little better."

Catching a glimpse of his muscled shoulders, her stupid heart began pounding in reaction.

"Are you okay? You look a little stressed."

"I'm fine," she insisted, wary that her frustration was a little too evident. "Let's concentrate on you." She set the tray on the nightstand with an angry thump. Why the hell he being so observant all of a sudden? He was easier to handle when he was dopey– slurring his words and calling her 'angel'.

When Harry appeared confused by her tension, she experienced a sudden rush of shame. "Traynor– I'm sorry. Please forgive me. I-I've had a terrible day."

"Is there something I can do? I'd leave, but you won't let me."

"It's not you."

Shifting, he pushed up with his good arm. "I can feel your stress way over here. What's wrong?"

Resolutely, Kendall pulled the table closer to the bed. "It's nothing. Forget about it." She attempted a smile. "I didn't think you'd want stew again, so I made an omelet. I grow the herbs out-"

"I'm not eating anything," he interrupted, "until you tell me what's wrong."

His green eyes bored through her until she squirmed uncomfortably. "Stop staring at me like I'm something under a microscope." Stabbing the omelet, she raised the fork to his mouth.

"You're shaking. C'mon Ken . . . what happened today?"

Biting her lip, she glanced away, desperately blinking back tears she knew were moments from flooding her eyes. "Please Harrison? I can't talk about it."

Startling her, he grabbed her hand with his good one. "Look, I can't make you stay. I can barely get out of bed. But sometimes it's easier to talk with a stranger than with a friend."

Expelling a breath, she forced herself back under control. "I don't know, Traynor. I'm used to working out my own problems."

He shrugged. "Maybe talking will help." He patted the pillow next to him. "Why don't you try?"

She eyed him warily, her tears temporarily under control. "I'll talk while you eat. But, don't look at me, okay? If I cry, I don't want you to see."

His expression amused, he pretended to consider her request. "I'll do my best to *not* comfort you."

"You first." She nodded toward his tray and he took a bite of the omelet before pointing the fork at her.

"Okay . . . my turn." Sneaking a quick peek, Harrison ignored her and continued eating. "As you've surmised, Adams and Rey is experiencing a cash crunch. With Specialty holding up our payment-" She shot him a hasty glance. "It's not just your job we've got issues on. It's two other digs, also."

"Kenny, let's look at those files tonight," he urged. "I want this settled between us. The *only* payment we're holding is last month. We've paid everything you're owed."

"I'm not blaming you, Traynor. I'm just trying to explain what's happening."

"Has it always been like this? The cash flow problem?"

"Hell, no." Ken bolted up. "I've been running the business for three years. And I've never had more problems than in the last six months. Out of the blue, two pieces of equipment broke down today. It'll cost twenty grand to fix them." She shook her head in disbelief. "I was just downstairs thinking it was a patch of bad luck. First the thefts, then you falling in that hole. Now this."

"What thefts?"

"It's a long story." Ken shifted to face him, sitting cross-legged on the covers. "No matter what I do, somehow it gets undone."

"What do you mean?"

"Like the fencing, for instance. I supervised the installation. I know it was solid. I'm always paranoid someone could fall."

"Accidents happen." Shrugging, he took another bite.

"No way." She remained unconvinced. "That system should've held up through a hurricane."

"How can you know for sure?" True to his word, Harry kept his gaze trained on the bread he attempted to butter with one hand.

"Let me." Taking the knife, she swiped the thick slice before handing it back. "I know because I'm a damn engineer, that's why."

"You have an engineering degree?"

She sent him a withering glance. He probably assumed she'd left high school and hopped on the back of a shovel. "Double major. Engineering and music."

She read the astonishment in his eyes. "How'd you have any fun with a major like engineering?"

"My daddy wasn't paying for fun." She smiled. "Look who's talking? The wild man who took accounting?"

"Touché." Harrison stabbed his fruit salad. "Go back to the money thing. When did you start having problems?"

"Six months? I know how to dig a giant hole in the ground, but I'm not super careful with the books," she admitted. "I'm tight with money, that's why I know there's something wrong. I don't spend a dime more than necessary. And I work with my estimator, so I know how much profit we should have if things go right."

"If you don't understand what you're looking at, how do you know when costs are escalating?"

"This will sound strange, but– I just know. I can . . . sense when things are getting tight."

Harrison shook his head in exasperation. "I've got to see your records. Do you keep cost reports?"

"I'm not stupid." She glared at him. "I keep a set of files at the job and one in the office. I thought we were updating weekly."

"Who's 'we'?"

"My secretary, Claire handles all that." Ken pressed her fingers to her eyes. "She works for me and Lance."

Harrison chewed thoughtfully on a banana slice. "Who's Lance? What's his role?"

Her mouth twisted in a grim smile. "My stepbrother. He's in charge of making my life miserable."

∞

"Did I miss something?" Harry set his napkin on the tray. Kendall was a damn good cook. "How does Lance make life miserable?"

"Let me back up." Sighing, she twisted her head from side to side as though she were in pain. "When Dad moved to Florida three years ago he took up with some woman and married her. Lance is his new stepson . . . and my new business partner."

No mistaking the resentment in her voice. Harry sensed it masked an even deeper sense of betrayal. She'd spent her life working for him. She'd obviously proven herself. Why would he hand over access to a complete stranger?

"Is he an equal partner?"

"Twenty percent. Just enough to make him move up here and demand a huge salary for doing nothing." Dropping her head, she massaged the back of her neck. "Just enough so he's always into everything– rearranging the office . . . the project records. My job's hard enough without having to go behind him fixing the havoc he wreaks."

"What's wrong with your neck?" he interrupted.

"It makes me want to kill him." Her eyes fluttered open. "Huh?"

"Does your neck hurt?"

She smiled and Harry sensed some of her tension ease. "All the time since Lance showed up."

"Why did your father-"

"That's the million dollar question, Traynor." Pain flashed in her eyes before she slid from the bed. "Guess he didn't trust me enough."

Harry fought the sudden impulse to reach for her when she rounded the bed to collect his dishes.

"I'll take these downstairs. It's time for another pill. I've kept you up long enough."

"I'm tired of sleeping," he said with a flash of irritation. "That's all I've done for two days. I want my briefcase. My head feels pretty good. We can review your files-"

Edging closer to the door, Ken shook her head. "The doctor said four days. It's barely been two-"

"Forget the doctor. I feel better."

Offering an impish smile, she stepped into the hallway. "No dice, Traynor. But thanks for listening. I feel a tiny bit better."

Kendall's steps faded as she retreated downstairs. He heard water running and pans clanging as she cleaned up. Just as he'd started making progress, she clammed up. Surprised, Harry realized he was disappointed. He'd enjoyed talking with her.

More than ever, he was determined to get a look at her books. When a snuffly sigh rose from the floor, he glanced over the side of the bed. Lurch remained sprawled on the rug. Cocking his head toward the door, the dog made an exasperated sound before flopping back on the carpet. Smiling, Harry swung his legs over the side. "I know how you feel."

Kendall heard him thumping around in the bathroom as she dried pans and returned them to the cabinet. Wink's ears twitched and she lifted her head, searching for the sound.

"What is he doing up there?" Wincing when she heard something clatter to the floor, she hustled to the stairs.

"Harrison?" Racing into the bedroom, she approached the bathroom door with trepidation. "Traynor? You all right?"

When he jerked it open, Harrison was nearly naked except for twin casts, startlingly white against the tanned skin of his left arm and right ankle. The loosely knotted towel he'd tied around his waist– with only one working hand, began a slow descent to lean hips she couldn't tear her gaze from. Dangerously loose.

"I've been in the same clothes for two days, now."

"Technically, you haven't been in *any* clothes the past two days," she reminded.

"I'm tired of lounging around in my underwear."

Kendall raised her gaze to the ceiling. "It won't kill you to wait one more-"

"I'm taking a shower," he interrupted. "Are you helping or not?" Her expression of horror incited a chuckle. "I didn't think so. You'd better trot out there and hide." He pointed a casted hand to the bedroom. "I'm in dire need of soap and water."

"But- I gave you a bath last night." His eyes suddenly fascinated, Ken retreated a step.

"I thought I imagined it." Harrison hobbled closer. "Well, this should be a breeze. You can help."

"Harrison- I can't help you shower." Heat crawling into her face, she took another step back. "It was dark last night. I sponged you off. I didn't-"

"See anything?" He smirked.

"No, dammit. Now, get back in bed," she ordered. "One more day and you'll be able to stand up by yourself without me worrying about you passing out."

"This is your fault," he pointed out. "We could've reviewed contracts." Turning, he hobbled back to the shower. "I have about twenty minutes of energy left. I'm devoting it to getting clean."

"You're not supposed to get your casts wet." Kendall fumed, listening for him to fall. Stepping into the shower, Harry stared at her.

"I'm dropping my towel."

She couldn't shake the image of him, slick with soap when he lost his balance and toppled over. He'd hit his head for sure and she'd end up back in the emergency room.

"Dammit, hold on." Okay- so he had a body that would likely keep her awake the rest of the night. It wasn't as though she would've slept much anyway. "I'm here," she announced, eyes scrunched shut as she inched toward the shower. "Just like you expected."

"I never assumed it was a lock." Harry's voice floated from behind the opaque curtain. Opening one eye, Kendall was relieved to discover she could only see the shadowy outline of his body.

"Stick your casted leg out here," she instructed. "Why don't you sit on the bench and I'll get the hand-held shower down for you. That way you won't fall."

"I knew you'd be full of ideas once you put your mind to it."

"We should bag up your hand so the cast doesn't get wet." She waited for him to sit before turning to leave. "Hang on while I run downstairs."

Kendall was out of breath by the time she hurtled back upstairs. She couldn't help noticing his underwear on the floor near the door where he'd dropped them. The appallingly vivid image of Traynor's naked body overtook her brain in a flash of heat. Mercy, she couldn't start thinking about him that way.

"Are you decent?" She winced at the croaky sound of her voice and inched closer to the shower.

"I always thought I was a decent person, but after meeting you, I'm forced to reconsider." Harrison paused. "I hate admitting this, but I'm pretty self-centered compared to you."

Despite her aggravation, she smiled. "Give me your hand." When it appeared from behind the curtain, she tugged the baggie down over long, tapered fingers. "Why do you say that?"

"I don't think I'd go out of my way for someone the way you have for me. I'm pretty sure I wouldn't have helped you."

She twisted the baggie around the top of his cast. "You would have left me there? In the bottom of the crater?"

"I'm not that bad," he hastened to explain. "I'd have taken you to the hospital. And I would've driven you home. But-" There was a long pause behind the curtain. "I'm sort of embarrassed to admit I would've avoided the hassle of taking care of a stranger." Ken startled when his face suddenly appeared, his green eyes thoughtful. "I'd think of all the work I could be doing or I'd wonder 'when will this person finally leave'." A frown creased his perfect forehead.

"I think that qualifies as a normal reaction."

"But not what's right." Harry wiggled his fingers to get her attention. When she raised her gaze, he smiled. "Can I have my hand back?"

"Oh— sorry." She jolted from her trance. "I'll get the shower handle down for you." She reached in through the front of the curtain, careful not to make contact when she held it out for him to grasp. "Tell me when your hair is wet and I'll wash it for you."

"I've learned a lot about you in one day."

Her interest piqued, she glanced at the shadow behind the curtain. "Okay, I'll bite. What do you think you know about me?"

"Well, I haven't seen the rest of your home, but I know it's Victorian because your bedroom is in the turret. It's probably pretty old because you've done some plaster work and painting. And that stained glass window on the landing appears to be original."

"It was built in 1918. How'd you know about the window?" she asked, suddenly suspicious. "Are you getting up when you're not supposed to?"

"Not yet, but I probably will tomorrow, so you'd better lock up your sexy underwear. I plan to snoop through the drawers."

"You'll have your work cut out trying to find them." Kendall chuckled. If she didn't know better, she would have sworn Harry could see her through the curtain.

"Is that a challenge?"

Surprised laughter bubbled free. Three days earlier, she couldn't have imagined a flirty conversation with the uptight, conservative guy she'd believed him to be. But Traynor was incredibly different from how he appeared. "Sexy underwear doesn't coordinate with my work boots. Anywhere else you'll be snooping? I should probably dust first."

"I disagree. Thongs go with just about any shoes." His voice was amused. "I'll probably check out the other rooms up here. Not sure I can handle stairs yet."

"How'd you know about the stained glass?"

"I can see the reflected light in the hallway from the bed. And despite my incoherent state the other night, before I collapsed on your porch I remember glancing up and seeing it. The window was lit up."

"Maybe you should be a detective instead of an accountant." She knew exactly when the water connected with his body because she could hear it sluice off his hard, muscled frame. Despite iron-clad intentions, her imagination was working overtime conjuring a mental picture. Breath hitching in her throat, she shifted from one foot to the other. "How's it going in there?"

"I always wanted to do something more exciting."

"Like what?"

There was a long pause before Harry responded. "I guess what I meant was meaningful. Accounting can be challenging. Sometimes there's an interesting mystery to solve, but not very often." He sounded disappointed.

"I'm sure once you get to be the size of Specialty, it's more than just accounting, right?"

"Well, sure. I have a staff for the day-to-day stuff. I focus more on investing and risk oversight." He sighed audibly. "I'll be ready for you in a minute."

"So, what else have you figured out about me?" Her cheeks burning, Kendall immediately regretted her words. What was she thinking– flirting with him? She wasn't in his league. Not only was he on a higher social plane, but he was also the man who would likely put her out of business.

"You're a sucker for injured animals and wayward men," he volunteered. "You're a great cook."

His pause seemed to go on forever. Humiliation washed over her. Why had she positioned herself to be embarrassed? Hadn't she experienced enough to last a lifetime? *And* she'd put him on the spot. Harrison didn't know anything about her. His interest was strictly polite.

"What I don't understand is how you manage to do it all," he finally said. "You run a business. You work in exhausting conditions for– what? Twelve hours a day? And it seems like you make time for a garden and baking and hobbies. I don't have any of that. I don't even have a pet."

Ken stared at the shower curtain, willing her panicky heartbeat to slow. "It's not difficult to adopt a pet, Traynor. Shelters are loaded with them. It's the commitment you're afraid of."

"Why do you say that?"

"Pets aren't like . . . plants. If you had a dog, you'd have to walk him. Feed him. Maybe chat occasionally." She was grateful he couldn't see her for this strange conversation.

"I don't have any plants, either." Despite his anxious tone, the image of impeccable, stunning, hunk-of-the-month Traynor upset over houseplants made her chuckle.

"I just realized my life might be shallow and meaningless and you're laughing?"

"I don't think pets and plants qualify as a full life. Besides, you're not exactly out of time to change your situation."

"Maybe."

She stifled the urge to laugh. "Did you rinse your hair? You're probably starting to prune up."

"I'm ready if you are."

Crossing her fingers, she released a deep breath to quash her nerves. "Okay, I'm coming in."

She kept her focus on the shampoo bottle, supremely conscious of the seriously naked man sitting before her. Keeping her eyes averted, she sought the relative safety of his shoulder. Though broad, his skin was pale– a man who didn't get outside much. Nervous, her gaze slid to his bicep– large, defined. Okay– so his workouts were limited to the gym. Hair on his chest trailed lower, but Ken was too embarrassed to sneak another peek.

"Your face always get that color or is it hot in here?"

Hearing laughter in his voice, she knew her cheeks were stained pink. Though she hadn't found the courage to meet his gaze yet, she guessed he was grinning over her nervousness. Shampoo in hand, she glanced cautiously in his direction. "How're you doing? Are you dizzy?"

He *was* grinning. "Are you? You look a little flushed, Ken."

When she scowled, his smile widened, revealing two amazing dimples. "Shut up. And close your eyes or I might smear shampoo in them just for kicks."

Obeying, his smile remained. She squirted shampoo into his hair and massaged his scalp, slowing when she neared the bruised spot. "Is that still tender?"

"It feels great. I think I'll require a shampoo every night."

"I meant the bump, Harrison."

"Oh, *that*. It still hurts."

Her snort must have been audible because his shoulders began shaking. "I'm going to rinse your hair. Can you tilt your head back without getting dizzy?"

He complied, eyes still closed, his perfect face completely relaxed. Kendall took advantage of the opportunity to enjoy staring at him without his laser-beam scrutiny following her every move. *Greek statue, my ass*. Traynor was seriously hot. A rangy, athletic body– Jeez, she really shouldn't have peeked. Her mouth suddenly dry, she resisted the urge to fan herself, afraid he'd jerk his eyes open and find her drooling. He was probably even sexier than usual with a two-day growth of beard staining his face. Forcing her gaze upward, her fingers lingered in his hair, though she'd rinsed out all the soap. What Harry didn't know–

"Okay, you're officially clean. Let's get a towel around you so you can hobble back to bed." Heart pounding, she took a step back, her limbs less sure of themselves than before. Dammit, she seriously shouldn't have looked.

Harry's eyes fluttered open, glancing around in confusion. "Are we done?"

Shutting off the water, she returned the shampoo to the shelf. "Are you lightheaded?"

"I feel . . . tired. Is it hot in here?"

"Let's get you out of there." Snatching a towel from the stack, she threw it over his lap. Wrapping her arms around his waist, she tugged him to his feet and scrambled for his cane. Though she'd hooked it on the towel bar, she had to grope behind her to find it. "Hang on, Harrison. Don't– fall." When he staggered toward her, she stumbled back into the wall.

Harry caught himself at the last minute, throwing his good hand out to lean against the wall in the tiny bathroom. Kendall waited, squashed between his large frame and the wall at her back.

"Take a deep breath," she instructed, focusing what little composure remained. "You're just overheated. As soon as we get around the corner to the bedroom, the air will be cooler."

"Right." Resting his forehead on his arm, he leaned into her, pressing her against the wall. She remained still, barely breathing– praying he wouldn't pass out. Finally, his gaze seemed to refocus and his green eyes locked with hers. "Did I hurt you?"

"I'm fine." As fine as she could be, pressed against his solid, fabulous-smelling, seriously naked body. "Ready for your cane?"

"Yeah." Taking it from her, he slowly pushed off the wall. She held his arm while he steadied himself, then reached for his towel, carefully averting her gaze from his incredible backside. The mirror made that task impossible. Ken fanned herself, grimacing when she caught a glimpse of her overheated face. As soon as Traynor was in bed, she'd need a long shower, too. A cold one.

CHAPTER 4

Limping back to bed, Harry collapsed with relief, breathing hard with the effort. Resisting the frustrated urge to fling his cane to the floor, he hung it carefully on the bedside table. Clearly, he wouldn't get far without it.

What the hell had just happened? One minute he was teasing Kendall and the next he was fighting to stay upright. He'd nearly blacked out in her bathroom.

Poor Ken had certainly received an anatomy lesson tonight. She was so damn skittish . . . as though she'd somehow managed to reach thirty without ever talking to a man– never mind sleeping with one. Yet, she worked in a male-dominated industry. She ordered her crews around every day. But with him, she seemed to blush every time they talked. Although . . . the naked part probably hadn't helped much.

He watched her shadow move around the bathroom. She still hadn't surfaced yet. Hell, she was probably in there laughing. And if he wasn't feeling foolish enough, he now had even less clothing than he'd gone in with. "Hell." Swinging his legs into bed, Harry jerked the covers over him.

"Ken? I didn't crush you, did I?"

"I'll be right out," she called. "Just mopping up the water."

Kendall emerged a minute later, concern still visible in warm, amber eyes. "Do you feel any better? You gave me quite a scare." She fanned her face. "I shouldn't have run the water so hot."

"Three days ago I could run five miles. Now, I can't walk ten feet without you holding my hand." Harry winced at the bitter sound of his voice. He had no right to complain– and even less right to take it out on her.

"Yet," she suggested. "The doctor said it would be several days before your head feels better. And the rest of you will heal . . . it just takes time." Inching closer to the bed, she switched on the lamp.

"I'm not the most patient guy," he admitted. When he glanced at her, he did a double-take. Ken had pinned her hair up– probably due to the heat. Twisted carelessly, the riot of mahogany waves was secure, except for a few wayward strands. Absently, she tucked those behind her ear as she searched for his pill bottle. Unable to stop staring, Harry swallowed, his mouth suddenly dry. In the glow of the lamplight, her cheeks were flushed pink with exertion, her golden eyes warm with concern. Her mouth- When his gaze traveled to the shadowed gap in her blouse, he jerked back. *Jesus.*

"Look how much you've improved in two days," she reminded, oblivious to his sudden realization as she handed him a pill.

Bewildered by his erratic thoughts, he shoved them aside. "Do I have to sleep with this?" Groping for a safe topic, Harry held up his hand, still encased in the plastic bag, waiting for her inevitable chuckle. He'd decided in the shower he liked the rich, smoky sound of Kendall's laugh. Her voice conjured images of an aged, sweet Glenlivet. A shadowy jazz club. Hot, bed-wrecking sex- *Wait– what the fuck?*

"I think it's safe now." He startled when she tugged the bag from his fingers. "You should get some sleep. You've had enough excitement for one night."

"You're right." Grateful when she snapped off the light, a jumble of illogical thoughts cluttered his brain. *It must be the concussion.* He released a ragged sigh over the sensible explanation. She was nearly to the door when she turned.

"G'night, Harrison. Call if you need anything."

"Ken?" He waited until she'd taken a step back. "Although it may appear I don't have any secrets left, I'm a little uncomfortable with the idea of becoming your love slave. Any chance I can have some clothes tomorrow?"

She raised a hand to her mouth, her eyes sparking with humor as she remembered his naked state. Her expression made Harry forgot his awkwardness.

"Sorry, Traynor. I forgot."

"You *forgot* I was naked." He smiled. "I'm not sure my ego can take much more of this."

As expected, her cheeks bloomed with color. "I didn't say I forgot what I saw."

He chuckled when her eyes widened, as though she'd revealed something she hadn't intended. "Maybe the love-slave thing is the excitement I'm missing."

Winged brows drew down in a frown. "I'll check the spare room. My dad sometimes leaves stuff behind when he visits."

Relaxed in a way he couldn't explain, Harry listened to her footsteps fade down the hall. With something close to amazement, he acknowledged Kendall was pretty. Why hadn't he seen it before? Freckled from the sun, her nose was damned cute. Full, red lips that were nearly always curved in a smile. Even her voice had changed. He'd noticed in the shower. Behind the curtain, the husky, sensual tone was not what he'd remembered. The discovery raised more questions than it answered. How would she sound when she moaned? Instead of nails on a chalkboard, the smoky rasp had scorched along his nerve endings– leaving certain things obvious in his naked state. It was a good thing she'd been too shy to look.

"Here we are."

Kendall drifted back into the room, her slender body framed in the light from the hall. Her face in shadows, she had several items of clothing draped over one arm.

"I'm not sure about the fit, but these should help you feel less . . . exposed. I'm washing a load of clothes tonight, so you'll have clean underwear when you wake up."

"As long as they aren't female, they'll be fine." Setting the pile on the foot of the bed, she turned for the door.

"Goodnight, Kendall."

"Night, Harrison. See you in the morning."

His last thought before drifting into a peaceful, drugging sleep was a memory of a soothing angel in white. Calling to her, he hoped she would visit again. Soon she appeared, drifting through the mist. Remembering the serenity of her smile, he wanted to see her face again. When she finally drew closer, his eyes widened with surprise. The angel's face belonged to Ken.

Unable to sleep, Kendall closed her eyes, concentrating on the instrument, not on notes or composition, but the feel of the flute in her hands. The melody was haunting and wistful, as though searching for something out of reach. Whatever she yearned for was unattainable in a way even she was uncertain why.

Time drifted away as she gave herself over to the sensation of peace, the flowing echo of her instrument vibrating from her fingertips straight into her soul. She loved when this happened, when every worry, every puzzle, every problem trickled from her mind like rain and washed away with the music. Wink purring melodically at her feet, she played forever, until the notes slid away and she returned to the shadowed room. Releasing a sigh of sheer pleasure, she finally opened her eyes.

"That was incredible."

Ken didn't startle, didn't feel surprised. Although she hadn't heard Harrison slip into the spare bedroom, she'd known he was near. The clarity of his presence had been overwhelming. And a little disturbing.

She didn't want to like him too much . . . didn't want her mind conjuring stupid fantasies of a man like Traynor. Kendall knew her limitations. And he was so far beyond what was attainable it was laughable. That thought brought a quirky smile to her lips as she returned to earth. Perhaps her music was the mournful wail for all things impossible– in this case, the out-of-reach Harrison Traynor.

"What are you doing up? Are you hungry?" He'd slipped on a tee shirt and a pair of her father's shorts. But Harrison didn't look anything like her daddy. The faded cotton stretched tight across his chest, sculpting to muscular shoulders. Swallowing, she wondered how he'd managed to squeeze into it.

He pushed off the doorframe. "That arrangement– I don't think I've ever heard it before."

"I made it up."

"Y-you wrote that?"

She shrugged off his astonishment, inwardly cursing the tiny flicker of joy sparking in her heart.

"But you didn't look at any music. Your eyes were closed."

"I don't like writing it down. I just play and the melody comes." Playing from sheets of music took the fun out of it.

"You could play professionally." He took a step closer. "How long have you played the flute?"

"I started in high school." Suddenly grateful for the darkness cloaking them, Ken wondered how long he'd been listening.

"I have season tickets to the symphony."

"Me, too," she admitted, annoyed that the first thought in her head was whether she could muster the courage to suggest attending together.

"I always wished I could play an instrument. Piano and flute," he mused. "What else do you play?"

"I- um . . . play the cello a little." And any other instrument she could get her hands on. When Harrison took a cautious step toward her, her senses flared with warning. Ken didn't like the shivery feel on her spine, or how wonderful his sleep-husky voice sounded when it floated through the shadows, praising her. There was intimacy here in the dark, one they didn't share in the light of day, one they could never hope to share.

"You have one here?"

"Have one?" Instead of fantasizing about Harrison, she should be paying attention.

"A cello?" At her nod, he smiled. "Can I hear you play?"

In the dim light, she couldn't tell whether he was serious. "I don't usually play in front of people."

"It's just me, Ken."

"I-I'll think about it." Her heart tripped nervously at the thought of playing for him. She'd never been comfortable with an audience– but alone in a room, she was fine. "Why don't you play?"

"My parents gave me lessons in grade school, but after seven years, Bucky insisted I sounded the same as when I started. He made me stop."

"Bucky?"

"My dad– his name was Buchanan. We called him Bucky."

"To his face?"

Harrison smiled. "Very intuitive of you. He wasn't crazy about the nickname."

"I'm sure you couldn't have been that bad after seven years."

"Wanna bet?" He raised a brow in challenge. "Easy to say when you're gifted."

"What'd you play?" Her mind refused the words of praise, but her stupid heart wrapped around them, holding them close.

"Saxophone."

"Sax is pretty difficult." Kendall surprised even herself when she gave him a slow, appraising perusal. "You don't strike me as someone who'd have much stamina for it."

His mouth lifted in a smirk. "I've never heard that complaint before."

She refused to be drawn in. "Seriously Traynor, it's pretty difficult. I'm sure you would've been great at one of the other horns. They handle easier in your mouth."

"Are we still talking about the same thing?" His smile told her he was enjoying himself.

Ken dissolved in laughter. Never any good at flirting, she doubted her skills had improved with age.

Smiling, he edged a step closer. "I don't know whether to take that as a compliment."

"Trust me, you need good pipes and great lips to handle-" Heat crept into her cheeks. The expression in his eyes was one of barely contained amusement. "Never mind," she stammered. "I'm sorry I woke you. I didn't think the sound would carry." Distracted, she set the flute on the table and would have turned on the lamp but hesitated. She wasn't sure what message would be written on her face.

"I was awake anyway. The sound floated down the hall." Harrison leaned heavily on his cane, shifting from bad leg to good. "I heard you last night, too. The music was so soothing, I figured I must be dreaming."

The reverence in his tone had panic throbbing through her. "You should get back to bed."

"Another minute won't hurt. Why do you play so late at night? Can't sleep?"

"It relaxes me." She needed sleep to handle all the problems daylight brought, but the problems of daylight made her too edgy to sleep.

"Sometimes I have trouble. Not lately, though." He stifled a yawn and bent to pat Lurch's head. "Your bed is very comfortable."

Her dog hadn't left his side since Harrison had arrived, a show of solidarity for a fallen brother. She tried not to care that her loyal friend had abandoned her for Traynor.

"I can't believe you hobbled all the way down the hall."

"I told you I was going to snoop through your stuff," he reminded. "I'm
just a little early."

"You should be resting," she admonished. "I'm not taking you home until someone can look after you."

"I'm battered, Ken, not broken." He scowled, his stance that of an edgy warrior.

She brushed past him through the doorway. "I'm not insulting you. Three days ago you were half dead."

He released a sigh of frustration. "I didn't mean to jump you. My whole life, all I heard was the pretty boy stuff," he explained, his voice irritated. "My father never missed the opportunity to remind me I wasn't good enough at football. So, I tried out for soccer. But making that team wasn't good enough, either. I was supposed to be the best. No matter what I did, I couldn't shake his image of who I was supposed to be."

Stunned, she was unsure how to respond. Reluctant to break a spell the night had woven over them, Ken's first reaction was compassion. She knew what it was like trying to please someone and failing. But Harry wasn't a man who would appreciate sympathy.

"I'm sure it was a real hardship having cheerleaders hang all over you."

His smile flashed white in the dark. "Okay. So there were a couple perks." Following her into the hall, his smile faded. "I guess I'm just as hard-headed as him." At her questioning glance, he sighed. "Instead of construction, I chose finance for my career. Until the day he died, all I ever heard were wimpy accountant jokes."

"I'm sure he was proud of you. He just didn't know how to show it." Kendall sensed his focused gaze cutting through the shadows. "At least you tried. I gave up trying to please my dad . . . and he's still alive."

"Why-"

Blurting out secrets hadn't been in the plans. Time to change the subject. "Are you saying that under the Superman exterior you're really Clark Kent?"

Harry didn't smile. "I'm just a guy doing his job. I don't do things halfway." Hobbling through the archway, his steps were slow and clearly painful. Kendall waited, careful not to approach with an offer of assistance. When he caught up to her, she slipped under his available arm, casually borrowing some of his weight. Together they methodically moved down the hall. When they reached her room, he was out of breath.

"I can't change who I am." Harry spoke with a weary sarcasm that came from years of self-defense. Years of teasing, jealous comments over something he couldn't control. His appearance. His very nature. Kendall couldn't help but be drawn to it– to what she had experienced.

She chuckled at his grumpy comment. "If it makes you feel better, you don't look quite as perfect as you did Friday. I like your bed head better."

Limping closer to the bed, he sank into it with relief. "Thanks, Ken."

As he struggled to remove the too-tight shirt from around the bulky cast encasing his wrist, she stepped forward and gently tugged it over his head. Harry fell back against the pillows, clearly spent from the exertion.

She waited, uncertain why she lingered. They'd traded one dark room for another, yet this bedroom somehow seemed less threatening. She resisted the urge to fluff the pillows behind his head– and the stronger one to run her fingers through his hair.

"Can I get you anything? A glass of water?"

"Water sounds good." His voice slurred with sleepiness. He barely lifted his head when Lurch scampered to the bedroom door, growling low in his throat.

"What's up with him?"

"A watchdog he's not," she muttered. Ken headed to the door. "What's the matter, Sweetie?" When she stooped to scratch behind his ears, Lurch shook her off and stumbled into the hallway. The staccato barking began a moment later.

"Maybe he hears something."

She waited with him on the landing, stroking his rigid body and straining to hear the noise bothering him. But like every other night, the only sound was the familiar song of the crickets. As quickly as he'd gone on alert, Lurch strolled back to the bedroom. Once he'd flopped on the rug by Traynor's feet, she picked up the water pitcher. Harrison's even breathing told her he'd already fallen asleep.

Waiting in the bathroom until the water ran cold, Kendall snapped out of her strange reverie. She couldn't afford to forget what Harrison represented. He was the man forcing her company into bankruptcy. His injuries were a result of her company's carelessness. They would be used against her, she was certain. Traynor had a job to do– protect Specialty Construction from potential liability.

She *was* that liability.

∽

Harrison was awake and broodingly alert when she arrived on his doorstep with juice and toast a few hours later. Unlike him, Kendall was groggy and punch drunk from lack of sleep. "Hope I didn't keep you waiting." She tried to inject some cheer into her voice. As soon as she had a minute, she would down a handful of aspirin for the headache starting behind her eyes.

"What's wrong? You look terrible this morning."

"I tried wearing a bag over my head, but I spilled your juice on the way upstairs." Frustration flared as she stalked to the bed. She jerked his make-shift tray table over the bedspread, averting her eyes from his seriously chiseled chest.

"No need to be cranky about it."

"This is how I look with two hours sleep." She set the tray down forcefully, wincing when orange juice sloshed over the side of the glass. "You only have to tolerate me a few more days."

"Chill out, Ken. I meant that you look exhausted– not hideous."

On her best day– one with eight hours sleep, perfect hair conditions, all the bills paid and absolutely no worries– Kendall Adams could look halfway decent. She was presentable in a way that didn't smack of 'beautiful', but in the right light could pass for 'cute'. There were only a handful of those days– clustered around the year-end holidays, when it was too late to make her self-imposed budget and too early to worry about failing in the new year.

"Oh." The silence lengthened. "Sorry." Scooping up the toast that had skidded off his plate, Ken avoided the scrutiny she knew she'd find in his eyes after her tirade.

"I'll get your coffee before my shower. Then I'll move you downstairs before I run over to the site for a few hours."

"Don't worry about me. I can get downstairs. Take care of yourself and go."

Her back to him, Ken raised her gaze to the ceiling. Too late, she glanced in the mirror and realized he'd caught her expression. Lord, would she ever learn to be more careful? She spun around to face him. "Look Traynor, no offense to your manhood, but you're gonna need help. I don't want you taking another header–especially not down *my* stairs. The insurance company doesn't like me much."

"I'm completely capable-"

"Will you *please* not argue? Just this once?"

Harrison stared at her, any trace of warmth gone from his eyes. Regretting her words, Kendall acknowledged the obvious. *This* is what she did to men. She provoked the hell out of them. But she hadn't meant to lash out. Swallowing her pride, she yielded to gnawing guilt.

"Please, Harrison. I don't like leaving you alone. The doctor said you've got to be really careful. I promised to watch over you and instead, I'm always leaving you. I'll feel much better if you let me help you get comfortable."

"Alright," he conceded reluctantly. "Let's stop talking about it. Go take your shower."

It would have been perfect. In his mind, Harry envisioned himself firmly planted on her couch with Lurch by his side, the remote in one hand and a mug of freshly brewed coffee in the other. His expression would be just smug enough to indicate disdain for Ken's ridiculous concerns. Unfortunately, Harry's mind wasn't working clearly. For the first time, he wondered whether the blow to his head was more of a concern than he realized.

He'd made it to the landing where he leaned heavily on the banister. He was sweating profusely and his damn leg was killing

him. He'd also managed to wrench his good shoulder when his
allegedly good leg buckled and he'd dove for the railing to keep
from plunging to the first floor. Lurch wasn't helping, teetering on
the landing with him, yipping excitedly while bouncing underfoot
on his three legs.

How had it all gone south? The moment he'd heard the shower
start, his feet hit the floor. Now, he had to get downstairs before
Kendall appeared with another of her withering I-told-you-so
looks. Tipping his head back, Harry winced when she tried to
reach a high note in the shower, oblivious to the fact that her
musical ability clearly didn't extend to her slender throat.

He groaned at the fleeting image of her in the shower and
resolutely shoved it from his mind. All night he'd tried to erase the
mental picture of her. The only word Harry could think of to
describe the way he'd felt was mesmerized. Standing in the dark
watching her, awed by the sheer wonder of her talent and by the
ethereal loveliness of the woman herself. He swallowed around the
sudden dry patch in his throat.

She'd been serene and mysterious in the moonlit room. Long,
flowing hair trailing down her back, her body limber and graceful
in the thin, cotton gown. When she'd opened her eyes– when she'd
finally returned from the beautiful place she'd visited, Kendall had
turned to him. And smiled.

And his heart stuttered.

Almost afraid to breathe for fear of breaking the spell she'd cast
over him, even now, Harry wasn't certain whether it was the
woman or the haunting music that had mystified him. Later, after
the house had gone silent, he'd debated whether he'd conjured her
in a dream. Or if she'd merely been a side effect from all the pain
medication. For how could a person be so completely different
from an original impression? The question still stumped him.
Because there was no way the fragile, luminous beauty he saw in
Kendall was locked inside the prickly shell of Ken Adams.

This morning he'd waited, eagerly– to see her again. To search
her face in the light of day and find the intangible woman he'd
discovered in the moonlight. Instead, she'd stomped into the room
and glared at him, her fathomless, golden eyes shadowed with
fatigue instead of mystery, her face strained with worry, instead of
the joy he'd witnessed during the night. Her creamy skin flushed

with anger. The no-nonsense, tough as nails Ken Adams had returned.

Harry was startled from his reverie by the unmistakable sound of the water shutting off and a moment later, by the loud thumping of his cane, crashing end over end down the long flight of stairs. This was followed by a series of ear-splitting barks from a now spastic Lurch.

"Shit. I'm in trouble."

Harry didn't have time to turn before the bathroom door jerked open upstairs and Ken flew through it. She careened around the corner, skidding to make the sharp turn for the stairs. Before he could warn her, she'd plunged down toward the landing. Amber eyes widened with shock, acknowledging his presence in the split-second before she crashed into him and sent him sailing into the wall.

CHAPTER 5

Harry went down in a heap, tripped by Lurch, who howled in protest when he inadvertently stepped on one of the dog's good legs. When Kendall tumbled down on top of him, he didn't have time to brace himself. Instead, he received a faceful of wet hair. The fleeting thought that she smelled amazing was lost a moment later when the rest of her body smashed into him with the power of a defensive tackle.

The force propelled him to the corner of the landing. In a last ditch effort to contain the damage, he tried to protect Ken from hurting herself. Catching her in his good arm, Harry took her with him when he slammed into the elaborate Victorian chair-rail and slumped to the floor.

They groaned in unison on impact– her with him– him with the wall. Waiting for the stars to clear from his vision, Harry realized the expression actually had merit. When he finally came to his senses, he jerked forward, wincing as pain shot through his back. His good arm was trapped between the wall and the woman on top of him.

"Ken? Kenny– are you alright?" He tried to touch her with his casted arm, but the angle was too awkward for his fingers to reach her. When she didn't respond, panic flared through him, his pain forgotten. Dammit, had he hurt her?

Lurch reappeared at his side, creating a commotion of bouncing and licking that Harry could have done without. His heart ricocheting in his chest, his headache returned with the ferocity of a sledge hammer.

"Sit, Lurch. Sit, damn it." He shifted on the landing, twisting Kendall's prone body until she was sprawled across his lap.

Confirming the gentle rise and fall of her chest through the soft cotton bathrobe, he sighed with relief when she groaned.

"Kendall, honey– wake up." Sweat dampened his forehead at the possibility he'd injured her. How could he have been so stupid? Dammit, he could have hobbled downstairs after she left. But he'd wanted to prove her wrong. "Ken– please?"

Harry's hands shook when they traveled over her soft legs, still damp from the shower. From what he could tell, there were no broken bones. She hadn't bothered to dry off before bolting from the bathroom. Hell, she'd probably guessed he would try something stupid.

Another wave of guilt crashed over him. She was tiny– nearly a foot shorter than him, and so damned fragile. She'd never appeared small when she was on her feet and snapping at him. He glanced up the stairs to the second floor. There were only five stairs up and about twenty going down. How would he haul her back upstairs on one leg? His cane had landed clear across the foyer downstairs. If he could manage to get to his feet, he'd carry her up to the bed and call for an ambulance.

Scooping her up, Harry slid his casted arm under her legs and hoisted her against him with his good arm around her back. The flimsy cotton robe stretched taut across her breasts. *Perfect, naked breasts.* Christ, he couldn't think about that right now.

He had to focus. How could he safely get to his feet without dropping her?

"Okay, Lurch. Help me out, pal and stay out of the way."

"If you've finished groping me, would you mind telling me what the hell you were doin' out of bed?"

Harry froze. Her glacial eyes fixed on him, a scowl planted on her irritated face. "How? When did you. . . I mean, were you–"

"Get your hands off me."

He complied, relief pouring through him when she scrambled away. She scooted up one stair and sat down with an unmistakable wince. His relief turned swiftly to guilt. "Are you hurt? You were knocked out-"

"I'm fine," she interrupted.

"What the hell were you thinking, rounding the corner like that? If I hadn't been here to break your fall you would've tumbled down the stairs."

"If you'd stayed in bed, I wouldn't have been running downstairs to find you. I heard all the noise and thought it was you clunking down, ass over teakettle."

Harry dragged himself back on the landing and leaned against the wall. Lurch flopped down beside him, his tail wagging with excitement. "Well, this certainly didn't go according to plan."

"I'll say." With a groan, she leaned forward, elbows resting on her thighs. "You got any more bright ideas, Traynor? Because I think you should know I'm not accustomed to this much activity before seven in the morning."

"I'm sorry. I thought I could make it downstairs. I'm tired of being such a burden. I've stayed in bed for three days. I can't stand the thought of another." His sigh was exasperated. "I was making progress but I tripped on Lurch and my good leg buckled and the rest is history."

"I didn't hurt you, did I?" Anxious eyes revealed embarrassment.

Wearily, Harry rubbed the back of his neck, feeling heat rising in his face. "Nothing's broken. I've probably added a couple bruises, but this time it was my pride that took a beating." He met her uneasy glance and smiled. "You're quite a tackle."

"It comes from chasing down contractors for money."

Like him. Harry winced, not missing the meaning behind her statement. "Did I hurt you?"

"Nah. It'd take a bigger man than you to take me out." Her expression smoothed out as she finally smiled. "Although you felt more like the man of steel than Clark Kent when I rammed into you." Rising to her feet, she teetered on the step before regaining her balance. Hobbling over to him, she slipped under his shoulder. "Now . . . are we going up or down?"

"Any chance we can go down? If I have to spend another day in bed, I'll go nuts."

"What if you get tired?"

"I promise I'll rest on the couch." When her arm slipped around his waist, Harry was shocked by the answering singe of awareness that jolted through his system.

Great. Now that he'd discovered her perfect body, his own would be unable to forget it. "What about you? You're limping." Though determined to push the revelation from his mind, she smelled incredible. The fresh, clean scent clinging to her skin was making his head swim.

She pondered his question as she wrestled him down several stairs. "You landed on my foot. It hurt for a minute, but it's already fading."

"What about your head? I thought you fainted." Gripping the banister, he tried to shift some of his weight from her. "You scared the life out of me."

Halfway down the stairs, they stopped, both panting to catch their breath. Her gaze ran the length of him before she finally smiled. "Haven't you had a woman throw herself at you before?"

"Seriously, Ken. I think you passed out."

"Whatever. . . I'm fine," she dismissed.

She slid under his arm again, tucking her body against his as they descended again. His body responded in kind. *Jesus, he was getting hard.* Her warm curves plastered against him sent his imagination into overdrive. How was he supposed to forget the perfect breasts her plain Jane bathrobe had revealed? *Do not look down.* The order from his brain was futile.

Dammit, he looked. Big mistake.

Her robe gradually slipped open as they struggled with each step. His heart tripped in response to the view, his blood quickening with each glimpse of long, slender legs. He quickly shifted his gaze to the steps. Ken's feet were small and bare. Her toes, he discovered, were painted a surprisingly feminine shade of violet.

His senses on overload, Harry hesitated on the next step and she staggered to a halt.

"You need to rest?" Her voice was husky from exertion.

"Uh– no. I'm fine." Stunned by a ferocious urge to capture one of her small feet in his hands and massage the aches away, he fisted his hand. *What the hell was wrong with him?* He could not afford to be attracted to Kendall. If she knew what he was thinking, she'd drop-kick him down the rest of the stairs. They were both out of breath when they reached the first floor.

"I need another shower." She flipped a strand of wet hair back over her shoulder. "You still hungry, Traynor?"

Hell, yes. But not for food. "I could eat." When Ken discovered the problem with her robe, Harry glanced away, pretending to focus on the airy openness of her kitchen. Her eyes appraised him as she quickly retied the sash, her cheeks staining pink with awareness. No way in hell would he risk embarrassing her with a joke– not now.

"I-I'll run upstairs and change before I cook breakfast." She beat a hasty retreat up the stairs while he hobbled to the farm table and pulled out a chair. Lurch plopped down at his feet.

Harry was starving, all right. But he seriously doubted breakfast would cure his hunger. How could he fantasize about a woman who was the antithesis of everything he wanted?

He could not pursue her. He didn't *want* to pursue her, he corrected. He wanted someone like Deborah– except with sparks. She'd been right for him in every way. Except . . . he'd felt only fondness.

Kendall Adams had to remain strictly business. Ken was a business *nightmare*. Her issues could threaten the outcome of the project. If A & R defaulted, she could take Specialty down with her. His heartbeat slowed to a reassuring thump. He had a job to do. One that would likely result in her shutting down. He couldn't allow a stupid, ill-timed attraction sway him. Nor could he allow his gratitude interfere with the decision he would make.

One thing had become startlingly clear. If he hung around Ken much longer, his decision would become impossible. She was too easy to get used to.

He glanced around the sunny kitchen. Herbs spilled from pots on the windowsills, filling his senses with the earthy aroma of rosemary and basil. Her kitchen smelled alive. The buttery, yellow walls were a warm cheerful shade that would brighten even a gloomy day. His gaze rested on an old buffet. The scuffed wood had been lovingly repainted, a field of daisies dancing around the cabinet's base. The surface was cluttered with photographs and a collection of chipped pottery in a rainbow of colors.

Glancing away from the happy noise of her lively kitchen, he wondered where she'd stashed his briefcase, ignoring the guilt stabbing his chest for thinking about what lay ahead. His head pounded in a symphony of crashing cymbals that had more to do with dread than his latest tumble.

Today they would review her files. Headache or not, he would clear up the billing confusion– likely in a matter of minutes. Harry knew on whose side the chips would fall. Specialty's accounting team didn't make mistakes.

In a heartbeat, Kendall would go from tolerating her battered houseguest to hating him. Sometime today he'd have to find a ride home. He couldn't continue to stay here knowing his actions would devastate her business— and her life. He'd catch a ride home to hobble around his empty house, leaving Ken to pick up the pieces. And he'd try not to think about what he'd done to her.

Jerking the trailer door open an hour later, Kendall trudged inside. Despite two showers, her shirt clung to her back in the stifling humidity.

"Mornin', Claire. Has the mail come?"

"Morning, Kenny. No checks— if that's what you mean. I've called the stragglers, but you know how that goes."

"If anything comes in, drive it over to the bank as soon as possible."

"Gotcha. You've had two calls this morning from that equipment rental place." Her secretary rounded the desk with a fistful of messages. "And another creepy hang-up."

"It's summer, Claire. The kids have nothing better to do."

"Well . . . it's starting to freak me out. It's bad enough at the office. Now they're callin' out here, too?"

Wincing, Kendall headed to her office. It was the supplier calls that made her sweat. The financial noose was tightening. She wouldn't be able to hold out much longer. The discussion she dreaded more than anything would happen today.

Despite her resolution not to think about him, her thoughts returned to Harrison. The battle over their contract still loomed. It would be better to get the pain over. She didn't want her financial troubles spilling over on anyone else. Specialty would have to pull her contract and find someone to finish the job. Short of a miracle, nothing would save A & R now. It wasn't fair to keep Traynor waiting.

Harrison had been quiet over breakfast, leaving her wondering whether he'd hurt himself worse than he'd let on. In true Ken Adams style, she'd pretty much knocked him off his feet on the landing that morning. She still couldn't believe she'd seen stars after colliding with his chest. Talk about a swoon.

When she'd awakened to discover his hands running over her, she'd thought her heart would catapult from her chest. His Hotness was touching *her*– the social geek– the anti-prom queen. Sure, he'd only been checking for broken bones. But every fantasy she'd allowed herself to have about Harrison Traynor always started and ended with those sturdy, capable hands.

Then she'd discovered her robe flapping open. Shaking her head, she blushed all over again. Without doubt, she was the biggest fool in the county.

He'd asked her to bring home the files, in fact had been insistent they review the contract when she returned for lunch. Harry wanted to get it over with, too. After nearly killing him again this morning, Traynor probably couldn't get away from her fast enough. She had the sinking feeling their talk wouldn't go well.

"So, look who's finally decided to show up. And you wonder why we have financial problems."

Ken glanced at her watch. With the eventful morning, she was indeed late. Raising her gaze to the sneering eyes of her stepbrother, her stomach tightened with both anger and dread. "This from the guy who works three days a week."

"Unlike you, I have other business interests besides this dump." Pushing into her office, he flopped into the chair across from her desk. "You give any thought to what I said?"

"What's to think about?" She forced her gaze to the window, avoiding the serial-killer eyes buried in a bloated, fleshy face.

"Look, Sis. This place is headin' into the toilet. We both know it. Let's save our asses and get outta Dodge before you're left holding the bag."

"You own twenty percent of this mess."

"Yeah. I'll be sure to stick around for that." He began chortling.

Kendall's face heated. Without doubt, Lance would walk– free and clear.

"Look, idiot– I can't sell without you and vice versa. Unless one of us gets hit by a bus . . . we're stuck together." He examined his grubby nails before returning his attention to her.

"That's not a bad idea," she muttered.

"Yeah, I thought so, too."

"I'm not selling, Lance. So if you're not going down with the ship, I suggest you run home and see what other assets you can bleed out of my father before he realizes what a scumbag you are."

The chair tipped over when he stood. No longer laughing, Lance's eyes flashed fury. He lunged around the desk. "Don't mess with me, bitch or I'll make you sorry."

"You're threatening me?" Kendall held her ground, praying he couldn't see her heart pounding through her shirt. Instead, she took a step closer, running her gaze over him as though he were a pile of garbage. "Because I don't take kindly to threats."

When he raised his fisted hand, her eyes widened. Dang– she might actually be in trouble.

"Kenny. . . I need you to-" When Jimmy entered her office, Lance lowered his arm. Shooting a glance to her burly foreman, she shook her head. Jimmy had probably been eavesdropping outside her office door. If it were possible to dislike Lance more than she, what Jimmy felt was pure loathing.

"I believe we're through here," she dismissed, her voice icy.

"Not by a long shot, hon." Rounding the desk, he shoved Jimmy out of the way, muttering as he stalked out.

"Thanks, Pop." She sank down in the chair, her limbs shaking. "I owe you."

"Why don't you let me beat the tar outta him, Kenny? We've been savin' a corner of the parking deck just for him. The concrete guys hate him, too."

Kendall smiled, her heart sinking. "As much as I'd enjoy that, it won't solve our problems." She scanned the bustle of construction activity from her window and turned to question him. "Everything going okay?"

"Yeah. When you get a minute, hike over to the east quadrant. There's somethin' I wanna show you."

"Give me twenty minutes."

Her foreman left, shutting the door softly. Ken tried to remember the last time she'd enjoyed coming to work. She'd grown up with the knowledge she would run the company one day. For three years, she'd enjoyed the challenge of making the business her own. Until Lance arrived. Since then, each new day drained her spirits a little more.

She kneaded the base of her skull where the familiar pounding had already begun. Half the guys on her crew had been there since high school. They'd never worked anywhere else. Where would her employees go when she shut down? The staff at Adams & Rey were like family– accustomed to her easy style. Her loyalty. Many of them wouldn't be hirable at another firm. In a tight labor market, no one would want her motley crew.

Hot tears clogged her throat. She was out of options. The realization hit her like a blow. Worse, she was out of time. Woodenly, she walked to the door and flipped the lock. Drawing the blinds on the window, she returned to her battered chair and sank down to a chorus of squeaks. Then she laid her head on the blotter and cried.

Hearing a vehicle approach, Harry hobbled to the window. Kendall hopped down from the truck, tossing her hard hat on the passenger seat. His interest piqued, he watched her peel off a dusty work shirt and toss it on the hood.

"Jeez." His brain registered the skimpy tank top Ken wore underneath. The simple cotton fabric clung to breasts he knew approached perfection. Her hair was woven into a braid that trailed down her back. Standing near the truck with her eyes closed, long, slender arms stretched to the heavens, Harry was again struck by her subtle beauty. She radiated strength and softness at the same time. All that energy bound up in an explosive firecracker.

His gaze followed the graceful flutter of her hands until they reached her neck, absently kneading the spot that seemed to house her stress. He experienced a stab of guilt, acknowledging he would soon add to her turmoil.

When Kendall turned, he stumbled from the window, hastily conjuring thoughts of Deborah. Willowy and graceful, a lawyer on the fast-track, she worked hard to be witty and well-read. All assets in the blueprint he'd mapped of his future. Along with the perfect wife were two children, preferably a boy and girl. He'd been an only child– and he wouldn't have wished it on anyone. Since meeting Lurch and Wink, Harry had added a pet to his plan– dog or cat, but certainly not both.

So why was his heart hammering like a teenager's over an obstinate, backhoe-driving flutist? Until now, his vision of the perfect woman had been reedy and gentile, with alabaster skin and a mysterious smile. Kendall's sun-kissed face was not the one sketched on his plan. Her supple body wasn't the one he envisioned holding at night. She had freckles, for God's sake.

Whistling as she trudged up the steps, Harry smiled despite his rising panic. She was just so damn sweet. His smile dissolved when he thought of the approaching conversation. Though his decision was strictly about the numbers, his stomach wrenched at the thought of hurting her. The end result was *he'd* be the one putting her out of business.

He'd hobbled back to the dining room by the time the front door opened. "I'm in the kitchen."

"I figured you'd be sleeping." Dropping a disorganized pile of folders on the farm table, she flopped into a chair. "Wanna take a look?"

"Why don't we eat," he suggested. "I made lunch. It's in the refrigerator."

Her expression revealed surprise. "You shouldn't be on your feet."

The sharp pain in his ankle acknowledged the truth of her statement. But he was tired of sleeping. Tired of her waiting on him– especially now. When he knew what he'd be forced to do. Hobbling to the counter, he rested his leg, relieving some of the weight.

"Now, this I've got to see," she murmured.

"It's not much," he qualified. "Not like what you make."

Kendall's smile seemed to light her whole face, her pleasure at the small surprise evident in her eyes. "I'll help you carry it to the table."

Harry pulled out a tray of sandwiches and the vegetables he'd discovered after hobbling through her garden. He'd spent the last hour slicing up a bounty of treasures she'd somehow managed to plant and nurture while running her construction business.

His knee buckling caught him by surprise. Kendall's eyes widened when the platter shifted and she lunged forward to catch it before it toppled to the tile floor. In one fluid motion, she turned, slid the tray to the counter and turned back to catch him as he stumbled.

"You did too much." Her voice was muffled against his chest as she absorbed his forward motion.

Pain nearly as bad as the first night shot through his ankle, forcing him to lean heavily on her. *Could he be any more useless?* "I think– you may be right."

"Let's get you to the table. Then I'll get your pill and you can take it with lunch."

Perfect. The woman whose life he was about to destroy comes to the rescue again. "But the files-"

Ken glanced up and smiled. "They'll still be there when you wake up."

Three-legged hobbling to the table, she gently pushed him into a chair. Flustered and frustrated, he was out of breath again. When the hell would his strength return? Her refreshingly honest eyes level with his, she lowered him to the chair. Steeped in regret, Harry avoided her sympathetic gaze. Her face only inches from his, he realized he was still clutching her waist.

"You okay?" She brushed his forehead with her fingertips. "You're a little warm."

Her touch jolted through him. "I– I'm fine," he choked out. Or would be, once she backed up a few steps. Her whiskey-soaked voice slid over his senses, firing visions of her . . . them. A darkened room. The scent of warm skin, sunblock and flowers was suddenly clogging his brain, making him dizzy. He was so damn aware of her he could barely breathe.

"Are you sure?"

Today, her eyes appeared hazel, ringed by an amazing shimmer of gold around the pupil. Her expression was one of confusion. The cute freckles Harry swore he didn't like, fanned out over her cheekbones. His gaze dropped to her bottom lip, fascinated by the way she'd captured it nervously between even, white teeth.

"Kenny." Releasing her waist, he reached up to trace the contours of her face. His erratic heartbeat accelerated when she startled. Her pupils flared with desire and an emotion he would have described as utter bewilderment.

"Harrison– I'll . . . um . . . you know– get the tray-"

Before she could escape, he leaned in to capture her mouth. Helpless to stop himself, Harry brushed his lips against hers. Absorbing the shudder that swept through her, he tugged on the full bottom lip that had tortured him all night. She opened to him on a murmur of surprise. Heat surged through his veins as he took the kiss deeper. Stroking her warm, sweet mouth, he groaned when her tongue tentatively met his. Driven by a desperate need for more, he pulled her into his lap.

And was floored.

Kendall was warmth and sunlight. She was laughter and teasing passion, rolled up in a walloping kick of arousal that left him wanting so much more. He'd never tasted anything sweeter or more perfect, never wanted anything as much as he wanted to kiss her again.

"H-harry." Her soft, sensual whisper quickened his already galloping heart. He wanted . . . more. In the space of a heartbeat, his mouth covered hers again. Arched against him, Kendall wrapped her arms around his neck. Her tongue dancing against his, Harry went slowly crazy. Tentative at first, she became as ensnared in the sweet sensation as he was.

The combination of innocence and reckless enthusiasm inflamed a raw need to experience more. How could one simple kiss be so incredible? Balanced in his lap, her lithe body pressed against his erection. Shocked by the raw intensity of his desire, Harry wanted to lower her to the kitchen floor and make love to her until Ken's smoky voice moaned his name. Until her beautiful topaz eyes glazed over with desire for him. Until he quenched the inferno torching him.

Instead, he drew back, dragging in a shaky breath while he fought the compelling urge to kiss her again. Stunned by the enormity of his action, regret lanced through him. He just wasn't sure whether it was over kissing her or stopping. His gaze remained riveted on Kendall while he dragged much needed air into his lungs. His brain refused the sputtering attempt to jump-start, too focused on the flustered beauty still clinging to him.

Her dreamy, amber eyes glittered with confusion and unspent passion, her sweet, sexy mouth bruised and trembling with reaction. She'd been awakened. To a desire Kendall kept hidden from the world– perhaps even from herself.

Mine. The wave of possessiveness caught Harry off guard when it rocketed through his chest. His brain was functioning again, because panic began seeping through the hazy cloud of pleasure.

What the hell had he done? That was no simple kiss. His body still throbbing with awareness, his chest hurt to breathe.

How had he allowed Ken to get to him? And where had his sense of responsibility gone? His goal was protecting Specialty– even if that meant ruining Kendall. He couldn't back down if he'd wanted to. Specialty wasn't his company to risk.

But if there was even a slim chance A & R could be saved, Harry owed her the diligence of his best effort. Instead of kissing her, he should be analyzing her cash flow. Instead of allowing her false hope, he should maintain a professional distance. Instead of wishing he could tear Kenny's clothes off and make love with her on the table, he should be focused on their mutual business problem.

His confusion must have shown in his eyes because Kendall's flared with panic and something akin to shame. Her hands froze on his shoulders before she launched away from him, still trembling.

"Kenny, wait-"

"I-I have to. . . get b-back to the site-" Golden eyes burning in her too pale face, her shock set in– vibrating out to encompass him. Making Harry feel even worse for what he'd done.

"Please, Ken . . . we need to talk. I-I had no right to do that."

"It was a mistake, okay?" she interrupted. "I know this doesn't change what you have to do."

"Why I'm here has nothing to do with kissing you." His voice tightened with anger. How could he have been so stupid? "You're so pretty . . . but- Hell, I just should've tried harder."

Though she attempted to hide it, her eyes betrayed confusion. "Don't-" She shook her head. "Please don't insult me."

The hurt in her voice fisted his stomach. He was struck by how vulnerable she was despite her pretending to be unaffected. Stripped of the tough layer of veneer, she was defenseless. "Kendall, you may think I'm a bastard by the time this is over . . . but I will never insult you." The magnitude of what he'd done tightened his chest. "When I say you're beautiful, I mean it."

He held the power to destroy her– in more ways than one. Ken wasn't fishing for compliments. She simply wasn't accustomed to hearing them. The bigger question was who had made her feel unattractive– to the point she hid her beauty under such a thorny disguise?

Harry had stumbled into dangerous territory. Anything he said held the potential to hurt her feelings. Yet, she'd been honest with him. She deserved honesty in return. "I know this isn't an acceptable excuse– and believe me, I'm not trying to make one for myself– but I can't get involved-"

"Because of Deborah," she interrupted. Kenny had drifted to the doorway, her arms wrapped protectively around her waist.

Startled, he met her troubled gaze. "How do you know about her?"

"You talk in your sleep," she said, retreating another step. "The first night– you thought I was her."

"We're not together anymore." He tugged a hand through his hair, wincing when he felt stitches. Now wasn't the time to discuss his former girlfriend. "Kenny, I shouldn't have kissed you . . . for several reasons. I respect you– and I like you." Distracted, he avoided the question in her eyes.

"Traynor, it's okay."

"I still have a job to do. My job is to protect Specialty– and that might mean-"

"Putting me out of business."

Kendall's eyes filled with tears she clearly fought, her expression one of futility. Her sorrow weighted in the pit of his stomach. But he couldn't lie. Her pain would be worse if he tried to soften the blow. Harry sensed she'd sooner lose everything than ask for help.

"My job," he corrected gently, "is to review your finances from every angle. I'm willing to help you if I can– but if I can't, I'll be forced to withdraw your contract and find someone else to finish the job."

Suppressing a shiver, she dashed the tears away with her forearm and nodded toward the table. "The files are there."

He stood awkwardly. "Kenny, I'll consider any feasible course of action that might help your company get back on its feet."

"I need to get back to the site. Sorry about lunch, but I'm not hungry anymore." She nodded toward the pile of folders, resignation in her eyes. "We'll talk tonight when I get home."

Her steps echoed through the foyer as she let herself out. Harry ignored the nearly overwhelming urge to hobble after her– to wipe away her tears and hold her until they both felt better. But he'd given in to two impulses today– and both had ended in disaster. Resolutely, he limped to the far end of the table where his briefcase lay open. His gaze flicked over the haphazard stack of files before he methodically withdrew a legal pad and his calculator from his precisely organized briefcase. Blocking out the image of her tear-drenched eyes, he opened the first folder and went to work.

CHAPTER 6

Kendall pulled over twice on the drive back to the construction site. First, to find the box of tissues and allow herself the good old-fashioned cry she no longer had the strength to hold back. The second time she stopped her battered pickup, she swallowed several aspirin and searched for sunglasses. The rearview mirror confirmed her red-rimmed eyes. She could count on one hand the number of times she'd cried in the past decade. Today, she'd already bawled twice.

She was unsure which event upset her more. Acknowledging she was one step closer to losing her business. Or kissing Harrison Traynor. The first was all but inevitable. But the second had been a fantasy come true. Kissing Harry had been like a winning lottery ticket; a perfect hair day; a five pound weight loss and ice cream for dinner all at once. Kissing Harry had been downright incredible. Shivering, she remembered his mouth on hers– his warm, insistent, sensual lips moving over hers. Equally amazing was the moment *before* he'd kissed her. If such a thing were possible, Kendall wanted to relive the magic of *that* moment– when the expression in his beautiful eyes had been desperation.

For her.

In the timeless moment he'd kissed her, she'd known only wonder. And knee-buckling heat. And need. So much damn need. She'd never felt such a burning ache before . . . never experienced such regret over stopping. She'd never kissed a man and completely forgotten where she was. The expression in his eyes had taken her breath– made her willing to throw caution to the wind and do it again if he asked.

But the flash of regret in his eyes had pierced her soul. Ken didn't know which was worse. Imagining what a fling with Harrison would be like– or realizing the opportunity would never present itself again. Yet, she couldn't fault him for being honorable. Even in the heat of passion, he'd considered the consequences.

No, she couldn't be angry with Harry for being a gentleman. There were too few left. The only reason she could find for hating him was introducing her to something so wild and sweet and addictive, knowing she would never get the opportunity again.

Blowing her nose a final time, Kendall skidded back out on the rutted road. Sunglasses securely in place, she wished she'd been more vigilant. Wished in vain she hadn't lowered her guard to Harrison Traynor. And prayed she would summon the strength to raise her shields to him once more.

∽∾

Once at the site, she stopped by the trailer to check her messages. Scanning the note from Jimmy, she stuffed it into her pocket before waving to Claire and bolting from the trailer. Striding across the site, she spotted him talking with the crew chief. Woody would need to hear what she was about to confess to Jimmy.

Fingers to her lips, Kendall whistled. The shrill sound carried over the cacophony of construction activity. Her foreman turned his head in recognition. The bulldozer belched once before dropping the load of dirt it carried.

Several minutes later Jimmy huffed into talking range. "What's up, boss?"

"This message– what were the police doing out here?"

His eyes sparked at the incident she knew he'd already forgotten. Kendall recognized the harried expression– carried it herself most of the time. At some point during the hectic buzz of each day, issues arose suddenly, decisions were made quickly and little incidents got lost in the controlled chaos of the site.

"Oh, yeah. I forgot." Raising a flannel covered arm to his forehead, he mopped perspiration. "Cops showed up right after you left for lunch. Bonehead wasn't here either, so I said you'd call them back."

No need to clarify Jimmy was referring to Lance. "What did they want?"

"They wanna know more about the equipment thefts."

Her nose wrinkled in confusion. "Again? We filed a police report last month." Insurance companies wouldn't pay without it.

"Said they were lookin' into the possibility it's a big operation."

Ken smiled in acknowledgment as Woody approached. Her gaze took in his hulking presence, noting the difference between the two men. Where Jimmy was short and stocky, Woody was enormous. Together, they reminded her of junkyard dogs. Hardworking, loyal men whose menacing appearance was merely a bonus. As a woman running a construction operation, the motley pair had come in handy more than once. Lance kept a healthy distance from them– only bullying her when he knew they weren't around. Not that she was afraid of her stepbrother-

"A stolen equipment ring– here?" She shook her head doubtfully. "The police must be having a slow day."

"Well, you know Miz Adams . . . me an' Jimmy were thinking it might be true. Remember those tracks we showed you out in the east quadrant?"

Tilting her head back, Ken shaded her eyes to meet his gaze. "Tire tracks don't mean much on a construction site, Wood."

"Yeah, but we're not workin' over there yet," he argued. Turning his hulking frame to the east, he pointed a meaty finger. "Out there you wouldn't worry about fallin' in a hole. It's only two hundred yards to the access road. If you were fixin' to steal stuff, I reckon you could be outta here in a couple minutes."

Jimmy chuckled. Woody had obviously given a great deal of thought to his theory.

"C'mon, Jimmy," he argued. "You said the same thing."

"It's possible," her foreman agreed. "But we've got bigger fish to fry. Kenny's concerned with the dig . . . not the possibility we got backhoe bandits out here."

"Backhoe bandits? You boys think that up?"

"Catchy, ain't it?" Jimmy's leathery face creased, his blue eyes squinting against the sun.

Kendall laughed and for a moment, the weight of worry lifted from her chest. This was how it used to be. Before Lance. Before the money troubles. Working hard and laughing with her crew.

She'd let the strain get to her– allowed worries to consume her. But the added tension wouldn't help solve her problems.

No matter what happened to her business, Ken had a choice to make the best of it. In her desperation, she'd forgotten she still had options. Whether A & R remained open for business, *she* would survive. She'd simply have to make certain her crew survived as well.

"I'll call the officer back." Squaring her shoulders, she spun around to face Jimmy. "Can you lower me into the parking garage for a couple minutes?"

"What the hell d'ya want down there?"

Kendall met his questioning gaze. "Two things. I need to find Traynor's cell phone."

"He's rich. Let him buy another."

"Jimmy, we're lucky they haven't thrown us off the job," she pointed out. "Besides that– we nearly killed the man. The least I can do-"

"It's a damn mess down there. You ain't gonna find shit-"

"I'm *also* checking the safety fencing from the underside," she interrupted coolly, ending his tirade. "I want to know why it collapsed so quickly."

"This guy is gonna put you out of business. Don't be goin' sweet on him," Jimmy warned. "Traynor's here for one thing– but if he can have some of that while he waits, he'll take it."

"Have you lost your mind?" Kendall cursed the mortified heat flooding her cheeks as her foreman gave her an appraising look.

"All I'm sayin' is– it's gonna hurt bad enough to shut this place down, Sugar. I don't want to see you hurtin' more because of Traynor."

"That's Boss Sugar to you."

"I mean it, Kenny," he persisted. "You're not used to players like him. He'll take advantage of you."

"Pop– you're so wrong on this." She gave him an affectionate squeeze. "Nothing I've got would interest a man like him."

"That's hogwash."

"I *know* why Traynor's here. Hell, I can't fault him for protecting his company. I'd do the same," she reasoned. "But I can't abandon him. He had nowhere else to go. The least I can do is put him up for a few days."

"You shouldn't be goin' down in that hole for a damn cell phone."

Kendall held his stony glare. "Will you help me or should I ask Woody?"

"Five minutes," Jimmy conceded. "Before I haul your ass out. The soil test results aren't back. It might not be safe."

"There was no cave-in," she argued. "Something happened to that fence and I need to-"

"You're more stubborn than your daddy." Throwing his hardhat to the ground, he dragged thick fingers through his salt and pepper crewcut. "Wait here," he growled before stalking off to the equipment trailer.

❧

"Five minutes," Jimmy reminded as he latched a hook to the rope he held in his gloved fist. "If you're gonna keep swingin' like a monkey, we need new equipment. Two of your ropes were frayed. I had to dig around to find a good one."

Kendall frowned. "I bought new ropes last month. You threw away perfectly good-"

He snorted in disgust. "I know crappy equipment when I see it. One of 'em was hanging by a thread."

She managed a distracted nod, her mind on more pressing problems. "Remind me when I come back up. I'll only be a minute or two on the bottom," she explained. "Then I want you to pull me up slowly." She checked the flashlight, satisfied she'd be able to see in the gloom at the bottom of the pit. "I want to swing under the fencing and check my anchors."

"Just remember, this gear is for climbers– not trapeze artists. It ain't gonna hold while you flip around down there."

Before edging over the lip of the crater Kendall saluted, acknowledging her friend's serious expression with an answering grin. "Yes, sir."

It took only seconds to glide to the rocky foundation, kicking off the walls and free-falling most of the way down. She loved the freedom of soaring through space, loved even more, the security of the burly man on the other end of the ropes. Jimmy would never let her fall.

When her feet touched, she walked to the spot where Harrison had landed. The cell phone had to be nearby. Clicking on the flashlight, she tasted dirt as she followed the glowing orb through the dusty haze.

"Got it," she muttered. A brief perusal confirmed the phone was miraculously intact, despite a cracked screen. Tucking it in her pocket, she tugged on the rope. Jimmy's stop watch was still running. He'd yank her out when the time was up– whether she'd completed her inspection or not.

As Jimmy pulled her closer to the top, she examined the fencing, checking the anchor bolts for damage. All appeared to be holding as designed. The same held true when she swung under the fencing and careened to the back wall. Here, the bolts held tight. Why had it given way in just one section?

Bringing her fingers to her lips, she whistled shrilly, waiting for Jimmy's shadow to appear. "I'm gonna hang for a minute. I want to test it."

"Be quick about it."

Chuckling over his resigned tone, Kendall slackened her hold on the rope before raising her hands to the fencing above. "Here goes."

Her gloved fingers caught the fencing and wrapped around it reflexively as she dangled over the gloomy pit. Despite knowing she was attached to a safety rope, fear sliced through her. The fleeting image of Harrison's body hurtling through the darkness made her wince. He was lucky to be alive.

Swallowing her panic, she clung to the mesh, testing its endurance. Should the fencing collapse now, she wouldn't have time to swing clear. That thought had her scrambling for the side.

Arms aching, Kendall tugged on the ropes and felt them tauten in response. Though loathe to admit such a weakness, she was grateful when Jimmy's face loomed up to greet her.

⚬∾⚬

At six, Harry heard her truck pull in, tires crunching on the gravel drive. He'd spent the afternoon crunching the numbers. And analyzing the kiss. Mentally, he was prepared on both fronts. The numbers would speak for themselves. There could be little opposition to fact-based logic. But the kiss– had been nothing short of illogical. Defying explanation. Exhausted by reviewing it from every angle, he'd decided to write the kiss off to momentary lunacy.

Leaving the window, he hobbled to the door. The problem with writing it off was the challenge of forgetting it. One stupid kiss and his knees had buckled– even on his good leg. And her taste– an addictive, spicy heat had haunted him all afternoon. Reviewing Kendall's financials while envisioning her in his lap hadn't made the analysis easier. How the hell was he supposed to forget the incredible softness of her lips? And the sweet, sexy sound she'd made. . .

Harry's pulse rocketed at the memory. When the porch steps creaked under her soft tread, he mentally prepared himself for the sight of her. Hot, dusty and tired. That's what she'd be. Not soft. Not sexy. Not edible. Dragging in a breath for confidence, he waited for her to appear.

"How was your afternoon?"

"Okay, I guess. You get through the files?" Worry flashed in her eyes before she doused it, wrestling her emotions into a carefully neutral expression. A neat tactic that was hard to learn. Somewhere along the way, Kendall had developed an impenetrable coat of armor.

"We can review them now, if you'd like." Harry trailed her through the foyer as she methodically placed her keys on the counter and emptied her pockets.

"I have your cell," she replied absently.

Harry repressed a shudder. Christ, he still couldn't think about that fall. "You went back down there? I told you to forget it."

A flash of resentment sparked her beautiful eyes. "*I* decide what happens on my dig. Not Jimmy. Not you." Dropping into a seat at the table, her gaze challenged. "Let's get this over with. I need a shower."

Jimmy was the foreman, he remembered. Obviously, he too, had grilled her over climbing down that damn hole. Judging by her scowl, he'd succeeded in ticking her off in the process. Now Harry would finish her off with another round of bad news.

Limping to the table, he slid the folder under her restless fingers before he tugged a chair around to sit beside her. "Here are your figures," he pointed out. "And these are mine. I verified the checks with my office this afternoon. They've all cleared."

"Then why-"

"You're missing a payment– the record of a payment," he corrected. Dragging his finger down the printout from her files, he tapped the page. "Right here. This payment of three hundred seventy-eight thousand. As far as I can tell, our payment wasn't applied to this project."

Confused golden eyes raised to his and Harry's stomach dropped. He swallowed awkwardly around the dryness suddenly constricting his throat.

"Then where is it? How could I misplace nearly four hundred thousand dollars?"

"My first guess is your secretary misapplied the payment, but I'd need to see your ledger to determine that. The money's probably been credited to another project."

She shook her head. "If that were true, I'd *have* enough money. It would just be in the wrong place." Her voice edgy, she drummed restless fingers on the table. "You're sure?"

"I've got the clear dates from our bank."

"But it's not *in* my bank." Her voice dropped to a whisper. "Where did the money go?"

Harry shifted uncomfortably. Reading the despair etched on her face, a swift burst of anger swept through him. Why did it have to be him hurting her this way? When everything in him wanted to help? Bewilderment warred with frustration in her expressive eyes. Tears clouding her voice, the words he dreaded trembled from her lips.

"God, Harrison, what will I do?"

He resisted the urge to capture her hand. Touching her wasn't a smart idea. Not with her eyes swimming with tears. Not with him lacking willpower. "I'd like to see the records in your office. Not just these files– I want to see your accounting system."

"What good will that do?" Her fingers danced nervously over the reports before her, yet Harry knew her eyes weren't seeing numbers.

"We can see where the money's been misapplied." Pride prevented Ken from meeting his gaze. Her lips trembled when she pressed them together, fighting for control. "How about tomorrow?" Her soft sigh of defeat made him gentle his voice. The silence lengthened, wrapping around him as she wrestled with the setback. "You could drop me at your office on the way to the site."

"I'll go with you," she decided. "I've wasted enough of your time with my problem. Maybe you'll find a miracle and we can end this tomorrow."

Finally meeting his gaze, Kenny's eyes mirrored pain to their very depths. He recognized she'd already conceded defeat– without ever asking for help. His memory flashed back several years. A long ago night in the rain. The tortured expression of the girl who'd been abandoned in the cold. Miles from home, she'd been trudging through a torrential storm when he stopped, her prom gown spattered with mud. He'd been unable to forget the expression on her face. Instead of relief that someone had finally stopped, her eyes had been drenched in shame.

Like Kendall, the girl hadn't wanted his help– hadn't wanted a witness to her humiliation. His chest tightened with regret. Similar to the slender, young girl with the wounded eyes, Kenny would associate him with all the pain to come.

"I can stick around another day or so– help you clean up the ledger once we find the mistake," Harry offered, knowing it would be rebuffed.

"Thanks, but I'll handle it." She offered him a half-hearted smile. "At least you'll finally get home."

"Yeah. That's great." Trying to muster enthusiasm, he felt only the sting of failure.

Rising from the table, she rested a hand on his shoulder before turning for the stairs. "You didn't create the problem, Harry."

All he could offer were his financial skills and she'd made it clear she didn't want them. The helpless frustration he'd felt that night in the rain returned to haunt him. *Shut out again*. Her shoulders rigid, Kendall trudged up the stairs and Harry felt more defeated than he had in years.

✑

The numb, haunted gloom of failure eased after a warm, scented bath. It wasn't often Kendall indulged in small luxuries, but surviving a day that would have broken most people, she'd earned the right to relax. It wasn't every day a woman lost her business. After months of struggle, endless nights of worry, she could finally acknowledge the obvious. A stinging failure on her watch. Though emotionally drained, a sense of calm slipped over her as she knotted the belt on her bathrobe. Over the next several months, there would be time for tears and recriminations, for fear and frustration. But tonight, she didn't have the stamina. After dropping his bombshell earlier, Harrison had insisted on making dinner. For once she hadn't argued.

For tonight, she would pretend everything was fine. That her business was okay. Her financial worries didn't exist. And she'd convince herself she wasn't falling for the strong, enigmatic, out-of-reach man in her kitchen.

"What are you cooking?" Shoving her wayward thoughts aside, Kendall sniffed the air appreciatively, her stomach growling over crispy, smoked bacon after the long forgotten lunch.

"Due to my limited culinary abilities, we're having breakfast for dinner." Harry shot her an appraising glance over his shoulder. "I hope that's okay? I make a decent pancake."

Ken knew those gorgeous eyes assessed more than her interest in dinner. She'd witnessed the flare of panic in them when he'd relayed the bad news earlier, wondering whether she would crumble to pieces before him.

"Sounds great. I'm starving." Somehow, his compassion made the news of her imminent demise more difficult. She wanted to rail against him– against *someone.* If he'd represented an evil conglomerate. If only he'd been cold and nasty, she could have unleashed her anger on him. But Traynor was so damn nice. His sincerity made her failure seem worse. He made her wish they were friends– that she could overcome her discomfort and accept his help. Harrison was a man made for leaning on. Rock steady. Reliable. If that weren't bad enough, he made her yearn for things she could never have– things she had no business imagining in the first place.

"Can I help?" Observing his economical movement as he whipped up the simple meal, she remembered the lunch tray he'd prepared earlier. "You're not as helpless in the kitchen as you claim."

"I have approximately a five meal repertoire." Carefully flipping strips of bacon, he turned the flame down. "Grilled cheese, cans of soup, burgers . . ." He glanced over his shoulder. "Does toast count?"

"Not technically a food group." She smiled. "The tray you made for lunch looked delicious."

He shrugged. "You did the hard part. Your garden is amazing."

"I guess I never outgrew my love for playing in the dirt," she admitted. "I can cook because my dad insisted I learn. But I never enjoyed it until I lived alone."

"Isn't is supposed to be the opposite? Enjoying cooking for a crowd but not for yourself?" He flipped a pancake and the griddle sizzled in response.

"After my mom left us, Dad assumed cooking was *my* job." She withdrew two plates from the cabinet and slid them to the counter. "I resented that he never asked. He just demanded."

"How old were you when your mom left?"

"Fourteen." Sensing him studying her, Ken turned away. The unasked question hung between them. *Why* had her mother left? She sensed his hesitation, could almost hear wheels turning in his brain— wondering how to respond.

"My mom died when I was seventeen," he offered. "Living with Bucky was never easy, but it got rougher after Mom passed. At least I was grown. I can only imagine it was worse for a kid."

Kendall froze, silverware clutched in her hand. She hadn't expected that kind of insight from him. "I'm sorry, Harrison. Had she been sick?"

His demeanor changed in a heartbeat. When his beautiful eyes went flat and cold she suppressed a shiver. "She was an alcoholic. Forty-seven when she drank herself to death."

"That must have been awful."

"A long time ago." Harry's voice grew distant. "Probably worse for a young girl." Speaking of his mother probably made him remember things he didn't want to recall. Another similarity they shared. Memories of her father made her angry. How her childhood *should* have been. All the things he *could* have done to make life easier for a devastated, lonely girl. But he'd chosen to withhold. He'd built a new life for himself— a new family that didn't include her— and she'd finally done the same.

"My mother was a decent person," Ken offered, aware of the sudden intensity radiating from Harry. "But she let my father bully her. She never defended herself . . . or me." Setting the silverware on the counter, her stomach tightened— a reflex ingrained decades earlier. "She didn't care enough to fight for what was important."

"That's a decent person?"

"She was lazy," she admitted. "Complaining was easier than being responsible for her actions."

"Something we have in common," he admitted. "Mom blamed us for her drinking. My father worked too much. I was too noisy. Too messy. Too much . . . work." Harry's stunning face was sober, his eyes reflective. "By twelve, I was cooking, doing all the laundry. The housework and the yard . . ." He shook his head. "And Bucky still expected perfection in every other area. School. Sports. Everything."

"Maybe it was his way of trying to maintain a front." The words left her mouth before she knew to stop them.

"What do you mean?"

"Like– if I hold it all together . . . then nothing's really wrong." Her cheeks heated as a truth spilled from her lips. How she'd pretended for so many years not to be bothered by her fractured family. How she'd hidden the truth from the few friends she had. Friends who had 'normal' families. Kids with parents who cared where they were at night– for reasons other than the list of chores that needed doing.

Harry's eyes flared with an emotion she didn't recognize. Holding her breath, she prayed he wouldn't pursue the uncomfortable path she'd accidentally stumbled upon. "Where'd your mom go?"

"I don't know." Relief coursed through her as he eased away from her revelation. "Leaving my dad was the first brave thing she ever did. Once she did, she never looked back."

"Brave isn't how I'd describe someone abandoning her daughter." Anger thickened his voice. "When life gets tough, you just run away?"

Resting her fingers on his arm, she felt rigid muscles contract. "I don't hold it against her anymore. If running was the only way to save herself-"

"Leaving a young girl behind to fend for herself." His glance pinned hers. "Would you do that?"

The air between them shifted. Kendall felt hot and cold at the same time. "No." Her voice suddenly hoarse, she swallowed. Unsure why it felt like a revelation, she experienced a surge of adrenaline. "I could never do that."

Still staring at her, he flipped the last two pancakes on the mounting stack. "Don't make excuses for her."

"I'm a lot stronger than she was. I wouldn't stay in a bad marriage."

"You think you'll beat the odds?" Amusement tinged his voice.

"Damn straight I will . . . assuming I find someone crazy enough." Rising to the challenge, she continued. "The secret is being prepared to go it alone."

"Your recipe for a successful marriage is . . . *not* marrying?"

"Go ahead and laugh, but I'm a firm believer in fate."

"You'd trust fate on a til-death-do-you-part decision?" Harry raised an eyebrow.

"I'm not talking knight on a white horse fate," she explained.

"How many kinds are there?" A dimple winked in his cheek.

"If I'm *fated*," she emphasized, "to meet the man of my dreams, it'll just happen." Ken shrugged off his disbelief. "And if I'm meant to be alone . . . I'll still be happy. The wrong man won't make my life better."

"I agree with that part– but lots of solid marriages are based on far less than the 'person of your dreams' philosophy," Harry argued.

"That's where your bad odds come in," she pointed out. "People who settle for 'good enough' eventually end up searching for 'better'."

He smiled. "I'm out of arguments."

"Even with the mystical man of my dreams, it will *still* take work to maintain balance. But I believe my odds will be better because fate brought us together."

"What if you're not paying attention when fate calls? What if you miss the signs?" Transferring bacon to a serving plate, he glanced at her. "Do you get a second chance?"

She smiled over his puzzled expression. "You accountants like definitive answers. Credits and debits have to balance. Everything's black or white?"

"Having a plan is practical," he admitted. "If you don't know where you're going, how do you ever know you're there?"

"With the right person, it doesn't *matter* where you end up." His expression of mock horror made her chuckle. "All I know is it's hard work. Merging two lives, two sets of expectations and opinions . . . Anyone who says otherwise is a moron."

He switched off the stove. "You're a fighter."

Meeting him, Kendall retrieved the platter. "I'm tough," she corrected. "In this business I wouldn't survive."

"Does anything scare you?"

"Eating your cooking," she teased as they sat down. Still smiling, she took a bite of fluffy pancake. "Mmm . . . maybe not. Beyond the usual bump-in-the-night stuff?"

"Everyone's afraid of those."

"I think . . . failure. I'm most afraid of letting people down." Adding a drizzle of syrup, she took another bite and sighed. "These are wonderful."

"Thanks. I practically lived on them as a kid." Sipping his juice, Harry set it on the table. "Mom was usually passed out by dinner."

He'd had it worse. She envisioned the serious, disciplined boy he'd been forced to become. Harry probably never had the chance to run wild, without a care in the world. With the knowledge he was nurtured and protected by parents who loved him. His world had been defined by his mother's illness and his father's rigid attempts to control it. No wonder he'd chosen accounting. Numbers were solid and orderly in a world of chaos. Safety had won over passion. She wondered whether he'd ever questioned his choices.

"This fear of failure . . . what does that mean to you right now?"

The intensity of his worried stare forced heat into her face. Defiantly, she met his scrutiny. "It means I'll survive. My life won't be over if I lose my business." Her eyes suddenly swimming, she glanced away. *No crying.* Not tonight. Not in front of this man.

"My first obligation is to my employees. Some have worked for my family for thirty years," she explained. "I'll protect my crew— pay my debts. Then pick myself up and start over."

"All by yourself?"

"I don't know any other way." A sad smile tugged her mouth.

"My offer still stands . . . even if you don't want it."

Could she accept his help? Heart thudding, she avoided his gaze. It was so tempting. Someone to lean on– occasionally. Confide in. *Trust.* "I'll . . . consider it."

His smile quirked, sending streamers of curious energy through her system. "Wow. That's major progress."

Heart sinking, she picked up the syrup. She'd begun to suspect she *could* trust him. Recognizing dangerous territory, she shifted the subject. "What are you afraid of? I spilled so now it's your turn."

"Is that how it works?" His eyes heated with amusement. "Okay. The thing I'm most afraid of is– heights."

Kendall clapped a hand to her mouth, mortified at the implication of his calm statement. The fall into her pit. . . had to have been a nightmare for him. Yet he'd never lost his sense of humor– even when he'd lain broken and bleeding at the bottom.

"Oh, Harry-"

"Hey, I survived. I can handle high places. . . I just don't go looking for them." He reached across the table to pry her clenched fingers open. "I have a picture in my wallet to remind me."

"Remind you?"

"Occasionally, fear has to be confronted," he explained. "Two winters ago, I went skiing with the guys. In Utah . . . some resort they dragged me to."

The photo she'd seen– and judged. Gorgeous, happy Harrison on a mountaintop. "How'd you do it?"

"I blocked my eyes on the lift ride up." He searched her face for reaction. "And then I skied down slow, like a ninety year old woman."

"That's amazing." She smiled over his confession. "You should be proud of yourself."

"Full disclosure: As soon as I hit the bottom, I hurled in a trashcan." When she cracked up, he joined in. "That slope felt ten miles long."

"You should be proud of yourself."

"Remember that next time you go swinging into your crater. I'll be the one cheering you on . . . from a football field away."

❧

Harrison insisted on cleaning up the kitchen after dinner. Kendall knew his leg bothered him, had seen him wince every time he put pressure on his foot. She knew by the fine lines of tension around his eyes that his head ached as well. But she'd grown to understand he wouldn't appreciate her coddling him. Like the other important issues they weren't discussing this evening, she pretended not to notice.

Instead, she swiftly cleared the table, stacking dishes on the counter near the sink. Then she casually withdrew and let him get to work. He didn't see her slip out onto the deck a few minutes later, flute case in hand. The need to play had her hands itching with impatience, but the night was too peaceful, the sunset too spectacular to spend an evening sitting behind the piano.

The first soft notes were tentative as Ken waited to see where the music would take her. Closing her eyes to the beauty of the night, she let the sound wash over her, let the notes seep under her skin and into her blood. Only by pouring herself into the pulsing, living flow of music would she gain any peace.

In a dim corner of her mind, a smoldering ash of hope flickered. That Harrison would join her. Without seeing him, she knew he'd paused in the kitchen to listen. Her vision of him was vivid, her connection startlingly strong. Ken didn't want to feel the link between them, but knew instinctively it was not something she could choose to ignore.

She would play for him tonight. Indeed, she already was. The notes were soulful, the haunting melody a mournful cry for something intangible. Tonight, she experienced no self-conscious fear of him watching her. Tonight she would share a part of herself that few people ever saw. Her vulnerability. Ken wanted to reach out to him, letting the lyrical beauty of the music reveal her wishes. Tonight, her instrument acted as an extension of her soul, conveying hope. Uncertainty. The desire she knew in her heart she'd never be brave enough to confess. The need she knew only Harrison could assuage. For tomorrow, he would be gone.

∽∾

Harry set the pan on the counter, careful it didn't slip through suddenly nervous fingers. The flute's haunting sadness tightened his chest. Kendall spoke to him in a way he'd never experienced. And he no longer knew how to react. How could he be so in sync with a woman he barely knew? Drawing a ragged breath, he leaned against the counter. He was so damn aware of her– every expression that crossed her face, the fleeting joy in her smile, the whisper of sadness in her eyes.

This desire for her was completely unplanned. The magnetic pull he felt every time they were together was not something he'd factored into the equation. And the escalating compulsion to touch her was a force that would grow rapidly unchecked if he didn't put a stop to it.

While Kendall had taken her bath, Harry had checked email. Avoiding the erotic images his overworked imagination drew for him, he'd listened to messages, forcing a much-needed dose of reality to his situation. Messages from the boring, predictable life he'd placed on hold. Relieved to hear Mona's voice, he learned she'd planned a family dinner two days later to welcome Jake and Jenna home from their honeymoon.

Since the moment he'd tumbled over that precipice, Harry hadn't been himself. Despite his injuries, he felt lighter, easier, less serious. And the unfamiliar feeling was unsettling.

Tomorrow, when he finished at Ken's office, she'd drive him home. He could hobble around for a day or two until everyone returned. More than ever, Harry wanted the familiarity of a noisy gathering with his cousins– needed the reassurance his life hadn't changed. *And wouldn't.* The impulsive desire to invite Kenny along? He would simply ignore it. Living with her was becoming too comfortable. The sooner he wrapped up this assignment, the better.

Because no matter how hard he fought it, the nagging voice in his head grew steadily louder– tempting him to forget the complications and live in the moment. To take what he knew he could convince her to give.

Kendall was unlike any woman he'd ever spent time with. She was so damn strong-willed, so purposeful– he'd instinctively been drawn to her. But Harry's innate sense of right and wrong prevented him from taking the fantasy too far. He never acted carelessly. He'd never *not* been in control with a woman. Nor would that change. He'd witnessed firsthand the damage that resulted from loving someone. He'd *lived* the sickening weakness. Until the day she died, Buchanan had worshipped his mother Sarah. Blind to her faults– to her appalling lack of control, to the embarrassment she'd become. Bucky forgave everything. Her drinking– her sorry excuses for abandoning him and their son. Hell– Bucky *made* excuses. All in the name of love. No one else had mattered to his father. Certainly not his son.

Harry wanted no part of it. Love could only ruin him, subjecting him to the whims of a woman who would likely prove unreliable.

Love could only destroy the balanced life he'd forged for himself. Since Jake's wedding, he'd been deluding himself that he might be missing something. That maybe he should hold out for someone he could love.

Dude, you don't need it. He could settle for affection– from a woman who wouldn't make unreasonable demands– who wouldn't require the emotional stuff he could never provide. Maybe something could be worked out with Deborah, after all. They didn't have love, but in four months, they'd developed a strong friendship.

Or had they? Harry's messages revealed she'd called exactly once– responding to his call from the hospital– when he'd been desperate for *anyone* to rescue him. So he wouldn't have to rely on Kendall. Deb's response had been lukewarm. *Too bad you're hurt. Hope you're feeling better.* She hadn't sounded worried. Despite knowing he'd been injured, she hadn't felt the urge to follow up. The knowledge unsettled him. One call in five days?

The woman who'd hinted of marriage hadn't volunteered to return from her business trip. Yet Ken had come to the rescue of a man she barely knew. A man she knew to be her enemy.

Annoyed with himself for being disappointed, Harry threw the dish towel on the counter. He had responsibilities. He had a satisfying life– worlds away from the stubborn, trouble-prone woman on the deck. The woman who had somehow managed to slip under his skin. Drawn by the magnetic pull of Kenny's music, he edged closer to the patio door.

He wasn't being fair, he admitted. Blaming Deborah for their mutual lack of consideration was an easy excuse. How often had he thought of *her* over the past week? And when Deb *had* crossed his mind, he'd done nothing but compare. She'd been a diversion from thinking about Kendall.

Harry thrived on his calm, predictable existence. He liked knowing what came next. If he didn't explore the possibility of change– he wouldn't be compelled to acknowledge something missing. He wouldn't be forced to confirm the gnawing doubt that maybe he was too eager to settle for something average– when a little risk might yield something great.

Watching Kendall through the window, his body responded to her graceful movement. His fingers tightened reflexively on the door handle while he absorbed the bewitching lament of the instrument that had become one with her tapered hands. Her peaceful beauty enchanted him. His blood throbbed with new awareness, while his brain clung desperately to the known– to the familiar.

The need to be near her was strong. And alarming. He resisted the urge to jerk open the door, to startle the golden light in her eyes and unlock the secrets she kept hidden in the darkest corners of her soul. Why should he be the only one suffering? The only one in turmoil? Why should he-

The flash of insight rocketed through Harry, catching him off guard. Kendall *was* in turmoil.

She played for him.

More frightening than the answering drumbeat of desire strumming through him, was the awakening of a wild restlessness Harry had never known. Panic jagged down his spine at the mere thought of the chaos it would cause. The messiness of the unplanned– the unexpected. He needed certainty in his life. He craved it. Wanting Kendall had disaster written all over it. Loosening his grip on the handle, he backed away, fear of the unknown squeezing the breath from his chest.

He had to stop this craziness– had to get away from her before he did something stupid– before the damage he inflicted was to more than just her livelihood.

The answer was space– distance. Where Harry could clear his head. Return to the business of his life. Away from Ken, he'd stop thinking about her. The crazy doubts running through his head would cease. Life would return to normal.

But . . . would normal ever be good enough anymore?

CHAPTER 7

Harrison was quiet as Kendall drove them to her office. Breakfast had been awkward as well. Shelving her disappointment, she kept her gaze on the narrow road. He'd disappeared the previous night, not bothering to say goodnight. She'd known the attraction was only one-sided. Had known in her heart he couldn't possibly be interested in someone like her. Obviously, the camaraderie she'd thought they'd developed had been solely on her part as well. Traynor had a job to do– and today he would finish.

"We're almost there," she said in an effort to break the silence. "It shouldn't take long to run the reports. Then I'll drive you back to Stafford and get you settled at your place."

"We have plenty of time." He kept his gaze to the window, studiously avoiding eye contact.

"I'll have someone deliver your car." Pulling into the driveway, Ken frowned when she spotted another truck. "That's odd."

"Who's here?" He leaned forward in his seat.

"My stepbrother. But– he rarely shows up for work before noon." Pocketing the keys, she sighed, annoyed that she'd have to contend with Lance this early. The last thing she needed was a verbal sparring match– especially with Traynor as witness. It would only confirm her troubles were worse than simply financial.

"Did you ever get along?"

"I was willing to try," she admitted. "Since I was stuck with him." Keys jostling, she took the steps two at a time. "But despite his knowing nothing about construction, Lance's attitude from the beginning was that he was in charge."

The office was quiet and still. The reception area smelled stale, as though the windows hadn't been opened in days. These days

Claire was spending all her time at their largest project. Kendall wondered what else wasn't getting done in the office. "Funny– he's not here. This place needs some air."

"Why did your father give him part of the company?" Harry slipped in the question he'd been dying to ask.

"My father is fond of games." Kendall met his surprised gaze. "No matter how I distance myself, he likes to remind me I can't go far."

"I thought you said the company was yours."

"He still holds a stake. Just enough to keep his foot in the door." Harrison shook his head. "I don't get it-"

"Your father wasn't a control freak, Traynor," she interrupted. "Senior didn't want me to be too successful. So he planted a few time bombs in the contract. The last one went off six months ago."

"When Lance arrived."

"My lawyer tried to line out the clauses. But his terms were non-negotiable. It was Ken's way or no deal." She followed his gaze around the small reception area, wondering at his thoughts. A& R wasn't fancy– certainly nothing like what he was accustomed to.

"How long can he keep interfering?"

"Lance was the last of the damage. My father can't hurt me anymore."

⁂

The hurt in her voice confirmed Harry's doubt over her statement. The old man sounded like a bastard. How had Kendall survived unscathed? No wonder she was a fighter. Her small, determined body was protected by a tough veneer– coating layers of pain and betrayal. Yet she still managed to find happiness– on her terms. He thought of her music . . . her pets. . . her garden. Kenny allowed entry into her solitary life only to those who would never hurt her. Who would love her. Unconditionally.

Suddenly uncomfortable, he swallowed around the restriction in his throat. "I guess we should get started."

Drifting around the scuffed receptionist desk, Ken nodded for him to follow her down the narrow hallway. "I hate the thought of losing, but I'll be glad when this chapter is finished," she admitted. "At least when I start over, it'll be on my terms."

"You don't know it's over," he reminded. "This could be a simple coding error. If we clear up the missing check you're still in business."

Tossing her keys on a desk in the cramped office, she shrugged out of her jacket. "I'm starting to think shutting down might be best. I get rid of Lance and my father."

She waved him to her desk. "You can sit here. I'll borrow Lance's office next door to catch up on some paperwork."

Harry set his briefcase on her crowded desk, resisting the urge to straighten the clutter into organized piles. He was pretty sure Kendall wouldn't appreciate it.

A few hours later Harry printed the last of the reports he wanted to study. *For now.* Something was wrong at A&R. Adrenaline and certainty surged through him. The problem was not knowing exactly what he was searching for. He'd been working steadily for nearly three hours. Though Kendall had finished long ago, she hadn't disturbed him. He'd sensed her growing impatience through the thin wall separating them.

For him, the thrill of the hunt had just begun. Harry would've been content to pore over her records for the rest of the day. Kendall's numbers didn't add up and he wanted to know why. But the day was steadily evaporating and Ken probably wanted to be rid of him so she could get back to her own life.

Downloading her ledgers onto a flash drive, he squeezed as much financial information as he could absorb from her computer. Whether Kendall ever broke down and asked for his help, he would provide it anyway. The least he could do was make some sense out of the jumbled confusion of her records.

Hearing the scrape of the front door, he snapped his briefcase shut. "Ken? I'm ready if you are."

She poked her head around the corner. "Let's go." Acknowledging the noise in the reception area, she sighed. "Damn, that's probably Lance. I'd hoped to avoid him."

"I'll be right out." Harry checked the flash drive one last time before he snapped off the computer. He'd pulled enough information to get started, but knew that a meticulous analysis would require a second visit.

Frustration was evident in Kenny's raised voice when Harry rounded the desk a minute later. He remembered to scoop up her keys and grab her jacket before he snapped off the light. The man in the reception area was loud, his tone clearly hostile.

". . . I don't like you messin' with stuff in here when I'm not around."

"Unfortunately, the rest of the world operates on a full-time schedule."

"Look, smartass . . . you ain't doing anything without my knowin' it. You hear? That's my money you're screwin' with."

Harry's blood pressure spiked over her stepbrother's antagonistic tone. Rounding the corner, he discovered the burly man's grubby hand on Kendall's wrist. Annoyance flashed over to fury when her cry of pain caught him straight in the gut.

"Get your hands off her." Harry dropped his briefcase with controlled violence, anger throbbing through him.

Releasing her, Lance took a menacing step toward him. Kendall fell back against the desk before catching her balance.

"Who's the gimp?"

The squat, little bully was smart enough to shout the belligerent question at Kendall, unwilling to shift his gaze from him. *Wise move, asshole.*

"Touch her again and I'll break your hand."

Lance chuckled, giving him the once-over. "I'd like to see you try."

Hot, volcanic fury surged through him as he hobbled closer to her stepbrother. The relief that flashed in Kendall's eyes did nothing to assuage him. The glint of tears only served to inflame him. How long had she dealt with Lance's ugly temper? And why hadn't she said anything?

"Why don't we find out?" Harry taunted, knowing full well he shouldn't egg the bastard on, but the urge to beat Lance senseless proved too great to resist.

Hurtling in front of him to block his next step, Kendall's warm body thrust back against his as she tried to halt his progress.

"Lance. . . this is Harrison Traynor– as in Specialty Construction? The mall we're building?" Her voice held barely controlled anger. "The mall we need to finish digging if we're gonna get paid?"

Lance struggled to contort his mouth into a smile of civility. Harry watched him fail miserably in the process. "I can't say it's nice to meet you."

"You'd get aggravated too, dealin' with her." Lance's tone shifted, becoming oily and ingratiating. "If you'd like to sit down and discuss the progress, I'd be happy to review the schedule with you."

Kendall's snort of disbelief nearly made him smile. Her prickly armor back in place, she'd obviously recovered. Lance was smart enough not to extend his hand in greeting. Given the opportunity, Harry would rather break it.

"I think Miss Adams has filled me in on all I need to know."

"Did you tell him we intend to sell? As soon as we finish your dig, that is," Lance added hastily.

"Specialty is our client, Lance. He cares about the project– that's all."

"Specialty's a big player. I bet he'd know of interested buyers, wouldn't ya, Traynor?"

"Once you complete this project, I'd be happy to assist you– if that's what Miss Adams wants."

"She don't know what she wants. But she will– real soon." Lance's chuckle grated over his nerves. Suddenly, Harry couldn't wait to get outside . . . to breathe fresh air and dispel the tension that had arrived with her step-brother.

"Kendall, are you ready?" Her grateful expression only served to infuriate him when she nodded and moved past her stepbrother. The damned deck was stacked against her. Was anyone on her side?

∽✺∾

"Did he hurt you?"

"Dammit, Traynor." Kendall skidded to a stop in the parking lot. "What were you thinking– picking a fight with him? You can barely stand up."

"Thanks for the vote of confidence." Harry chuckled at her outrage. "Should I have let him break your arm while I stood there? That's quite a brother. You should check your coffee for rat poison."

"My food taster quit last week." Absently massaging her bruised arm, Kendall absorbed a shiver of apprehension. What if

Traynor hadn't been there? Lance was out of control. Jimmy had prevented him from hitting her at the site. Like it or not, she'd have to start taking precautions. She hated feeling vulnerable, but if Lance chose to, he could make her life miserable. Just the thought of him near her home. Her pets. . .

"How long has he harassed you?"

Her cheeks heating with embarrassment, she averted her eyes when he climbed into the truck. "I can handle him."

"How about a restraining order?"

The hostility brimming in his voice made her smile. How long had it been since someone had defended her? "I can see why Deborah hangs on to you. Under that steely reserve, you're just a big, strong teddy bear."

He turned to stare at her, emerald eyes flashing anger. "I'm serious."

Without ever realizing it, Harrison could damage her spirit more than Lance could accomplish in a lifetime. Because Harry made her feel hopeful. He made her wish for foolish things. He made her vulnerable in a way Lance never could.

Kendall turned the engine over, smiling as it revved to life. "Just be glad you get to head back home today, Harry." *And leave her in the rearview mirror*. "You'll be safely back to your comfort zone."

"Just because I'm back in Stafford doesn't mean I won't help you. It's in both our interests to get to the bottom of your cash flow issue."

As she shifted the truck into reverse, a dim corner of her subconscious recognized something wasn't right. Where was Lance's truck? Frowning, she checked the rearview mirror. If he was still upstairs in the office, why wasn't his truck parked near hers? And where had he been earlier?

When she parked it again, Harry turned to her. "Forget something?"

"It's probably nothing." He'd already begun the laborious task of climbing down from his seat. "Stay here. I'll just be a minute."

His response was a scowl. "If you think I'm leaving you alone with that psychopath, you're mistaken. Now, tell me what the problem is."

Exasperated, Ken blew a strand of hair out of her eyes. "I was just wondering where his truck is. It was here before and *he* wasn't. Now, *he's* here and the truck's gone."

"You're right. That doesn't make sense." He hobbled around the hood of her dusty Chevy. His progress slow and methodical, he stopped a few feet away and waited.

"You need to get off that ankle."

Harry leaned on his cane. "As soon as we're done here."

"I am capable of handling that idiot."

He started across the lot. "C'mon, let's go back upstairs and check it out."

"You are so stubborn." Kendall strode past him, launching up the stairs.

"Don't even think about opening that door before I get there."

She turned back to glare at him and heard him whistling. "The orthopedist is going to have my head on a platter next week. You've done nothing the doctor ordered."

"I'll talk my way out of it."

"What about your party tomorrow? You'll show up limping and your family will hate me."

"Mona will hover over me and I'll milk it because she loves me," he added with a wicked grin.

"If I were her, I'd kick your butt." Traynor was baiting her, pure and simple. But she was in no mood for him to turn whimsical. Where had Mr. Conservative gone– the sexy stuffed shirt who would put her out of business? The beautiful eyed enigma who'd kissed her senseless, then couldn't look her in the face?

Harrison paused several steps below her, a chuckle escaping his lips. "Ken Adams, dominatrix. I guess it could work-"

"Please-" She snorted in response.

"Do you smell something?"

Kendall whipped around at his tone. Harry was serious this time. She sniffed the air tentatively. "Something's burning. That moron probably flicked his cigarette into the wastebasket again."

Fumbling with her keys, she dropped them once before managing to unlock the door. As usual, it stuck. She was just getting ready to give it a swift kick when she fell back on the stoop. Landing on her butt, she looked up to find Harrison's broad back blocking her from entering the door.

"What the heck are you're doing?"

Palms flat against the door, he swept down the panel. "Making sure we don't meet up with a fireball when I open this. Stand clear," he ordered.

"Why would Lance set the building on fire? You heard him . . . he wants to sell the business, not burn it."

Traynor offered her a brief glance over his shoulder before he turned the knob and pushed against the door. "If I were as desperate to sell as he seems to be, I'd probably be reckless enough to settle for the insurance money."

She shook her head. "You've watched too many movies. Besides, he's still inside. Do you think he'd actually set the place on fire and then wait it out?"

"You just pointed out his truck is gone."

"The only way he could've left without us seeing him . . . would be to jump off the stoop and cross the front lawn. But then how'd he get his truck?"

"Maybe someone got it for him. Maybe someone was waiting out front."

Dusting off her rear end, Ken rose to her feet. "You're so suspicious-"

A moment later they were both doubled over and coughing in the thick, black smoke roiling from the reception area. Sweat poured into her eyes as heat of the blaze seemed to envelop them.

"I'll see if the bastard's still in here." Harry covered his mouth with his good hand. "You stay here," he ordered.

"What? Harrison-? No! Where are you?" The popping sound of wood crackling hurt her ears. The air thick with the acrid fume of burning fabric, the fire would soon be an inferno. Seconds later, she heard the tinkling of broken glass when the windows exploded.

"Harry!" Shielding her eyes from the intense heat, she took another step forward, feeling her way through suffocating smoke. *Where was Traynor?* He'd been right beside her a minute ago. Her heart lurched when she thought of him, lost in the swirling black smoke.

"Harrison? Where are you?" He'd disappeared in the dark, pulsing heat. How would she ever find him? Kendall took another step and stumbled into a desk. "Harry!"

Taking shallow breaths, her lungs burned with the desperate need for clean air to breathe. Dropping to the floor, she covered her mouth with one hand and continued searching, her hand sweeping out in the hope of bumping into him. Seized with panic, she tried to shake off the dizziness that wanted to engulf her. It seemed only moments had passed before her ears began buzzing. In her confusion, the blackness swirled, smothering her with a heaviness she couldn't combat.

With a muffled cry of agony, Kendall realized she was lost.

"Here. I'm over here." She felt a jerk on her arm as he yanked her back toward the open doorway. The rush of fresh air felt like heaven against her overheated skin. Scooping her into his arms, Harry took the stairs two at a time, not stopping until he'd dragged her halfway across the front lawn. After depositing her on the grass, he staggered to the ground. Rasping in great gulps of clean, fresh air, Kendall coughed for several minutes before raising her head to stare at him. Harry's beautiful eyes were red-rimmed and bloodshot from the billowing clouds of smoke they'd endured. He was covered from head to toe in sooty, gray ash. She could only assume she looked even worse.

"You okay?"

She tried to answer but discovered her scorched vocal cords refused to cooperate. After another fit of coughing, she simply nodded in agreement.

"Just sit tight. Someone'll be along to help us," he rasped.

"Where's your cane?" Ken choked out the strangled words around the stabbing soreness in her throat. Talking was still not a good idea. She cocked her head in response to the faraway wail of sirens.

"In there." He gestured toward the building.

"God– your ankle–" He'd put all of his weight and most of hers on his broken ankle when he dragged her from the fire. "Your cast is a mess. They'll probably have to re-set it."

Nodding, Harry's gaze remained on the burning structure a hundred yards behind her. The building seemed to be a living creature, throbbing with the intense heat of the blaze. Nothing would remain standing. Her place of business would be a total loss.

"Lance?"

"Long gone. I checked both offices." He glared at her. "What the hell were you thinking? I told you not to move."

His voice still raspy from smoke, Harry sounded furious with her again. She'd been responsible for nearly killing the man, not once, but twice. "I thought you were lost."

"Kenny, I nearly had heart failure when I couldn't find you."

"Same here."

"Do you ever follow directions?"

If the string of bad luck she'd been experiencing before today hadn't already sealed the fate on her business, the fire would do the trick. Most of A&R's expensive equipment had been stolen over the last several months. The few remaining assets she had left were the inventory of heavy equipment parked on various job sites and the pieces she had stored in the garage. Thankfully, her garage was out of reach of the flames that continued to engulf her office. But equipment alone wouldn't save her.

She was finished.

Together, they watched the roof collapse as fire trucks roared up the street, too late to save her building. . . her dream– too late to do anything but hose down the smoldering pile of rubble that remained. Three years earlier she'd been charged with the responsibility of carrying out her father's legacy. And just three short years later, she'd failed. Miserably.

Three decades of history had just gone up in smoke.

Tears burned in the back of Ken's eyes, and she was helpless to stop their spill down her soot-blackened cheeks. The brilliant colors of her flaming building softened and muted, a horrific watercolor of flickering orange shadows through the sheen of drenching tears. The rough plaster of Harry's cast scraped her fingers when his hand found hers.

"Don't cry, Ken."

His words released the floodgates. Clasping her hand, he hauled her back against him as she wept.

Harrison held her patiently, his heart thumping reassuringly against her ear, his good arm slung around her shoulders. She sniffed and hiccupped in shuddering breaths. "I guess you're gonna be really late getting back today."

"Stop calling yourself that," Harrison ordered for the second time as he stepped into her bedroom. The morning ripe with promise had been beaten and burned into submission, melting effortlessly into mid-afternoon. "You're not a jinx, Ken. This fire has nothing to do with bad luck. I'm betting on arson."

Toweling her hair, she paused mid-scrub to shoot him an incredulous glance in the mirror. "Knowing that idiot, it was probably a cigarette butt."

"We'll see what the arson investigator has to say," he shot back, his voice still raspy from the smoke he'd inhaled. His eyes still burning, he still felt a thousand percent better since he'd showered. He'd coughed so much he would have sworn he'd sacrificed a lung, but compared to the thought of burning up in that inferno, Harry felt fantastic.

It was the image of Kendall lost in that building that he couldn't seem to shake. What if he'd allowed her to enter it alone? His stomach knotted at the thought of how close they'd come. Leaving her to search the back offices had been a nearly fatal mistake. When he'd crawled back to the reception area, she'd been gone. In that moment of blinding panic, he knew with certainty they would die. Because there was no way he could have left without her. His heartbeat accelerated at the truth of his acknowledgment.

It had been nothing short of a miracle he'd stumbled into her. A miracle he'd stayed conscious long enough to drag her out. A shudder rippled through him as he stared at her reflection in the mirror. Another minute and they both would've-

"I'll be done in five minutes. Then we can finally head back into town." She flicked a glance at her watch.

"Why don't I just stay another night? The fire marshal wants to see us tomorrow anyway." He hated the thought of leaving her. Not after what she'd endured today. "Or . . . come with me."

They'd watched the fire burn for nearly an hour, then been examined by the paramedics who had re-set his ankle. As he'd stepped from the ambulance, they were met by the police, who questioned them repeatedly. Kendall had been on automatic pilot, answering questions while fighting back tears.

"Harrison, take my advice– save yourself." She tossed her towel on the bed, filling the air with the scent of her shampoo. "Go home

. . . get some rest and when you wake up tomorrow, just pretend you never met me."

"You're not *that* bad."

Flouncing back in the chair, she tucked one shapely leg under the other before picking up her brush. "I'm a walking disaster." She waved him away when he would have argued. "I'll escort you safely back to your old life . . . and then I'm done."

"I can't leave you– not after what's happened."

Resigned golden eyes met his. "What more can happen?"

"Don't tempt fate," he warned.

"I just want to fall into bed. Get drunk and fall into bed," she corrected. "When I wake up tomorrow, I might have the strength to handle all this." Reading his disbelief, she sighed. "I'm fine."

"Damn it, you're not fine. It's okay to cry." She was so stubborn. Hearing the tremble in her voice, Harry knew she was fighting tears. He couldn't understand why she didn't simply give in. What was so wrong with being human?

"I've cried more in the past week than I have my whole life. And where has it gotten me?"

"I'm not leaving you alone today. If you won't go with me, I'll just stay here with you." Glaring at her, he tugged on the neck of the too-tight shirt he'd been relegated to wear. Stafford, and his closet full of well-fitting clothes was still tantalizingly out of reach.

"Please, Harrison. I've– had it. Okay?"

Finally. He detected the tiniest crack in her impenetrable armor. She was coming undone.

Glaring at his reflection in the mirror, Kendall wrestled a comb through her wet hair. Even with the five foot clearance he'd given himself, her scent wafted out to torture him. She smelled delicious. Free of makeup, and with her incredibly soft skin scrubbed clean of soot, Kendall Adams was a stubborn, curvy, sexy-as-hell woman he wanted to know better.

"Come with me," he suggested. "Stay at my place tonight. Take your mind off things. We'll meet the fire marshal tomorrow and then we'll stop by my cousin's party."

She set the comb down with a thump. "Take my mind off things? I'm bankrupt. My business just burned to the ground. I've got a lunatic stepbrother who wants to push me under a bus. Pets who need to be fed and walked," she ticked off. "I'm not up to meeting all your relatives at some stupid garden party where I'll feel completely awkward."

"It's not a garden party. It's a welcome home for my cousin Jake and his new wife."

"Perfect. It's too . . . happy. I'll only ruin it."

"You'd like them. I want them to meet you. The Traynors always like to meet the subcontractors we're out to ruin."

His joking comment received only a wan smile. Harry couldn't leave her like this. He'd gotten used to her take-no-prisoners attitude. Defeat didn't suit Kendall at all. Worried by the prospect of losing the argument, he persisted. "It's just a barbecue."

"I've had enough barbecuing for one day."

Advancing into her line of vision, Harry picked up the comb she'd thrown on the vanity. Taking another step closer, he carefully went to work on the tangle, ignoring the way his heart began to race. Her breath hitched in surprise. Hell, he'd shocked himself, too.

"I don't like you being alone out here. Lance is dangerous."

"How often do I have to tell you I can take care-" Ken jerked up from the chair, forgetting he was still holding the comb that was now imbedded in her long, thick hair. Instead of pushing him away, which was surely her intent, she stumbled into him. Harry released the comb and heard it clatter to the floor as he caught her, balancing them on his good leg. As her maddening scent enveloped him, he tightened his hold on her shoulders. So silky. So soft. Her skin was like satin under his fingers.

"I can handle Lance," Kendall continued, as she righted herself and tried to pull away.

"I'll be the judge of that." Knowing his words would receive an immediate reaction, she didn't disappoint. Annoyance swept over her features.

"That's not how this is gonna work, Traynor." She swatted at his hands as though brushing away a pesky fly. "You can let me go now."

"No. . . I don't think I can." Harry absorbed the ripple of surprise as he tugged her closer. Transfixed by magnetic, amber eyes, he watched annoyance morph to confusion as his words registered. Her eyes were his window to the truth. It was the only place, he realized, where Kendall couldn't hide her thoughts.

Hours earlier, he'd stayed by her side as she'd dealt with the aftermath of the fire. Covered in soot, her voice as smoky as her clothing, she'd held herself together through sheer will. Amazed by her strength, he' been unable to shake a nearly overwhelming urge to comfort her. To fold her against him and kiss her. Even now, nervously chewing her bottom lip with even, white teeth, Harry *needed* to taste them. He was tired of fighting it. This inexplicable desire he had for her soft, pink lips. To nibble them. To watch the flecks of gold heat her gaze as she gave in. And when she opened to him on a gasp, he wanted to swallow the soft, sweet breath that would hitch in her throat– a sound that had haunted him the past two days. He remembered the fresh, sweet taste of her, the burst of warmth he'd felt and he wanted to experience that heat again. He wanted more. More kissing, more touching, more Kendall.

More than anything in the world.

Kendall stopped fighting him. That last moment, when Harry could have come to his senses, when he hesitated, drinking in her flushed, beautiful face, he felt her resistance melt. Replaced by eagerness. A heady rush of exhilaration tore through him when she reached up to entwine slender arms around his neck.

"Kenny-" Her mouth yielded to his crushing need, opening to him on a moan of both hope and defeat. She could no sooner resist him than he could her. Harry swept past her defenses before she could think of changing her mind, before *he* could think of changing his. Pulling her against him, he nearly groaned at the collision. Her soft, pliant body snug against him as his suddenly trembling hands traced the contour of her delicate spine. Pausing to touch and stroke every inch of gorgeous skin before finally cupping her perfect rear end, he tugged her even closer. How could he have thought her too small? She was the perfect size. Everything about her was absolutely perfect.

For him.

Kenny's eyes fluttered open at the sensation of his hands on her body, the golden irises glittering in the softly lit bedroom. "We shouldn't do . . . this."

Her sentence ended on a gasp when his mouth left her lips to trace the scented column of her throat. The soft fluttering pulse he found there was irresistible. She stretched reflexively, allowing him access to her sensitized skin. "Oh, God– but I want to."

"You're right. We shouldn't do this," he murmured against her throat. Raising his gaze to hers, he smiled over her confusion. Stroking her shoulders, he lingered, playing with the narrow straps of her tank top. Trailing his hands down the silky length of her arms, he delighted when she shivered with awareness. Her nipples straining against the faded cotton of her shirt, he felt the answering punch of awareness in the pit of his stomach.

"We'll stop when we come to our senses," he agreed before giving in to the magnetic pull of her soft, bruised lips. Lowering his mouth to hers, he hesitated only a heartbeat away from her. "God, Kenny. I hope that isn't soon."

Kendall was smiling when Harrison kissed her again. She wanted to burrow into his well-sculpted chest and never leave. His skin was warm and firm under her fingertips. He was so sturdy, so confident– his body so incredibly beautiful under his clothes. She wanted to feel all of it . . . before Harry changed his mind. Thick, ropey muscles contracted under her touch when she stroked his back. She shivered, awed by the wanton thrill of power she seemed to possess over the beautiful, kind man. How was she possibly capable of doing that to him?

Before he regained his senses, she wanted to know everything. His incredible mouth on her skin, the strength of his body lying next to her, on top of her, inside her. She'd dreamed of her teenaged hero for more than a decade, but her raging fantasies were for the man he'd become. Harrison had rescued her from the fire in his quiet, confident way– held her hand and made the ordeal more bearable, simply by being there– just as he'd rescued her all those years ago.

She should feel guilt. It was wrong to use him for pleasure– for comfort. It was wrong because he belonged to someone else. She should feel shame that he was using her, too. Because once the moment was over . . . *they* would be over. But today, Ken couldn't feel anything. Today, too much had gone wrong. Too many circumstances were beyond her control. She was numb to everything . . . except sensation. She would have a lifetime to feel empty. To mourn the loss of her business. To pick up the pieces. But she had only today to experience the pleasure he would give her.

Tugging his shirt free of the faded shorts, Kendall paused to run her hands down his sculpted backside. "Clothes are absolutely wasted on you, Traynor. Your bod is meant to be shown off."

Dropping his head to her shoulder, he shook with laughter. "Are we back to the love slave thing?"

The expression in his beautiful, green eyes stole her breath, brimming with amusement and passion. She nodded. "Today, you're all mine." Just for today, she wouldn't think beyond the moment. She would do something wild and rash and completely out of character . . . Today, she would act with reckless abandon– a different person than she'd been a week earlier.

Harrison stared at her as though he couldn't wait to touch her– as though she were desirable. His eyes said she was beautiful. For one brief moment, Ken would believe him. Tomorrow would be soon enough to curse her weakness.

"I think you should take this off." Her voice urgent, the anticipation of his perfect hands on her body was almost too much to bear. She wanted his strong, capable fingers on her skin, stroking her, touching her the way she'd imagined in her wildest fantasies.

⸎

Hell, yes. Unable to stop touching her, Harry rained kisses down her face. When Ken's fingers clawed at his shirt, he moved swiftly to the neck of the too-tight shirt. Jerking it over his head, he hesitated, stunned as he stared into her face. Kendall's smile nearly undid him. It was so pure and honest. So eager and expectant. Lightheaded, he experienced a fleeting sense of wonder– as though this experience would somehow be different from any before. Though unlikely, he planned to enjoy the hell out of it. For a single night, Kendall would be his. But even now, with need throbbing through him for the flushed beauty in his arms, a corner of his brain was weighing his actions.

Though it was growing difficult to hang onto a coherent thought, Harry paused as the worry nudged him. "Ken, are you sure?" His words, groaned against her mouth– her irresistible, kiss-swollen lips caused a rippled of tension. Jesus– he didn't want to stop. But later– when he was home in the comfortable familiarity of his everyday life, Ken would be here . . . alone. He didn't want her to remember this night and feel remorse. They'd become friends. He liked her too much to risk chancing a misunderstanding.

"Kenny– sweet, you have to be sure." Despite her tough, no-nonsense attitude, she was innocent. And too soft-hearted. A sinking sense of desperation pulled at his chest. *Please don't say no.*

"I've never been more sure of anything." She pulled his mouth down for another hungry kiss. "This is what I want . . . what we both want."

Releasing the breath he hadn't realized he was holding, he steadied himself, drawing back to watch her as Kendall slowly drew her shirt over her head. She was so beautiful, her golden skin soft and glowing. Lush waves of mahogany hair trailed over her shoulders, the curling ends brushing against perfect breasts. Her innocent beauty so honest. How could he have been so blind not to realize it? How could any man not see how extraordinary she was?

Cupping her full breasts, she leaned into him with a shudder. "Kenny . . . God, you're . . . perfect." His voice a painful rasp, his senses were drowning in her warm, scented flesh. Her dusky nipples pebbling under his fingers, he bent to taste one. Nipping it with his teeth, she rewarded him with a soft, breathy moan. Sagging against him, her hands grew frantic as she sought the waistband of his shorts.

"Harry– please."

"Easy, love. We have all night." His cock hard and aching, he questioned the accuracy of that statement. It was entirely possible he might explode from the exquisite sensation of her in his mouth. But it was her hoarse cry of wonder that had Harry completely enthralled. Kendall quivered in his arms, her breath coming in short, wondrous gasps as she drew his head closer. He loved the sensation of her frantic fingers tugging through his hair while her sun-streaked curls brushed against him, teasing his skin where she touched him. When her fingers moved to his zipper, Harry shuddered. A moment later he nearly lost his balance when a warm, capable hand wrapped around him.

"Mercy, Harrison. Let's get you to bed before I forget myself and knock you to the floor."

The floor would work. "Kenny . . . God, yes. Touch me." Jerking against her stroking fingers, he wanted to take her there . . .

standing up. Against the wall. On the damn floor. *Hell . . . anywhere.* Hot and hard, throbbing with the effort to hold back, he groaned, his voice as hoarse and rusty as hers. "If you keep that up, we won't make it that far."

"Let's go."

Harry hobbled with her the ten feet to the bed, skin to skin, her hand molded to his butt as she assisted him. When she gently pushed him back against the mattress, he watched, speechless as she stripped off the rest of her clothes and joined him.

"God, Ken . . . you're beautiful. Your skin is soft and gold. You're like a goddess." Her chuckle bathed the room with the sexy sound of her throaty laughter, her eyes alight with amusement at the thought that she could be considered sexy. Harry reached out his casted hand, tracing the curve of her cheek and smiled what he was sure would qualify as a stupid grin.

"Maybe I should put you back on painkillers, Traynor. Those nights you thought I was an angel," she teased.

"How did I manage to catch you?"

"I've been right here . . . waiting for you. All these years," she confessed, her voice whisper soft. Harry had only a fleeting moment to wonder what she meant before Ken pulled his head down for a mind blowing kiss that left him breathless. Finally able to touch the long legs that had driven him to distraction, his hands trailed the curves of her gorgeous body. Keenly aware of her response, the smooth skin of her thighs contracted under his fingers, revealing the taut muscles hidden beneath the surface. Like the woman herself, she was a study in contrasts. Satin-coated steel. Kendall's quiet, magical beauty was locked away, out of sight and off-limits to all except those she trusted.

Him. Harry's hands shook with the revelation. Ken trusted him. It was an incredible gift–one he vowed not to fail. Ignited with happiness, he drank in her scent, her smile, her throaty sighs. Her beautiful body was an instrument that would sing in the right hands. Drawing a deep steadying breath, he prayed those hands were his.

"Kenny, love. Tell me what you like."

"Everything."

Staring into her eyes, he absorbed every shuddering breath. Each trusting glance, every honest, exuberant smile. Stroking between her legs, the heat against his hand made him shudder. "This?" Harry resisted the urge to sink into her, wanting instead to drive himself as crazy as he would make her.

"Yes," she groaned, her body jerking against his hand.

She was so hot. So ready for him. Dipping a finger into her heat, she writhed against him. His heart thundered in response. "How about this?"

"Everything. I like everything you do." Her words ended in a gasp as her body rose against his hand. "Harry, please . . . don't stop."

"I've thought about you for days." Stroking her again, he smiled when she nearly leapt from the bed. But his smile slipped as his control began to fray. Images of her legs wrapped around him. Of gorgeous, amber eyes glazing over as he made her come.

"Dammit Traynor, give it to me." Helpless to her passion, Kendall rose against his hand, urging him to take her.

"Soon, love." Driving himself a little mad, his fingers moved inside her slick opening, making him desperate with the need to be inside her. Kendall was hot and wet and ready for him. He shuddered at the thought of finally giving in to what would likely be one of the most memorable sexual experiences of his life. The next few minutes just might kill him. She opened to him, eyes dilated with passion, her lips rosy and bruised from his mouth.

"Now," she ordered. Reaching for him, his cock jerked against her hand as she guided him to her.

A wave of possessiveness streaked over him, fisting in his stomach as her body rose to greet his. Harry barely had time to tear open the condom before she hooked a warm, silky leg around him and he was lost. His entry was sure and swift. Embedded in her tight hot center, he groaned at the absolute wonder of it. He was home. And Kenny was with him all the way. His name spilled from her lips on a cry of delight before he captured her mouth for a hot, drugging kiss. His tongue was wild in her mouth, thrusting against hers as he sank into her again.

Harry was lost– in the pounding breakers of sensation–in the exquisite flood of heat and blinding satisfaction. He was lost in her.

"Harrison . . ." She arched against him, her frantic voice sending him over the edge. "Yes. Oh– Harry."

Too soon, Ken tightened around him, her release rocketing through him, forcing his own. "Kenny– my God." Words tumbled from his lips in a haze of pleasure nearly too intense to bear. His body took over for his brain, thrusting through waves of dizzying passion that threatened to drown him if they lasted even a moment longer. The tremors continued to wash over him even after he'd collapsed beside her, his arms too weak to draw her closer, too enervated to do anything but stroke her dewy skin.

And wonder what the hell sort of sensual dream he'd just experienced.

Kendall awoke to the exquisite sensation of Harry's hands stroking down her body. Eyes still shut, she tried to remain still as he worked his way down her body. Because when she awoke from the fantasy, he would likely be gone.

Or maybe not.

When his warm, wet mouth latched on to her nipple, she shuddered against him. "Harry-"

His breath fanned her breast when he chuckled. "I thought that might force you to open your eyes."

Heat coiled through her, her stomach fisting with need. "I didn't want . . . you to stop." Stretching against him, she was replete with sensual awareness. His body warm and heavy against hers, the weight of it both comforted and ignited her own. His heated gaze swept her from head to toe before his dark head drifted lower to trail over her stomach.

"So much beautiful skin. So little time."

His whispered words made her shiver, her muscles contracting with a will of their own. A pleasant strum of tension began building as his hot mouth moved lower. Her breath hitching in her throat, she startled when he nuzzled her thighs open. "H-harry . . ."

"You said you didn't want me to stop."

"I didn't mean-" She forgot to breathe when he parted her folds, his tongue stabbing into her with lazy precision. Her insides liquified on a vortex of pleasure. "Oh god."

His mouth, warm and insistent, pressed deeper, his tongue working her still quivering body into another spiraling peak. Kendall's sharp cry broke the stillness as she jerked upward, her body helpless against the spinning sensation catapulting her through the air.

"Give in to it, honey. You taste so sweet." His rasping voice muffled against her, his excitement evident in the increasingly frenzied movement. She fisted her hands in his hair as Harry continued the sensual assault, his mouth moving against her, faster now as she grew more frantic for release.

"Harry– please . . . God, don't stop." Excitement crashing over her, she was aware of every heated flick of his tongue. Of his shadowed cheeks grazing her thighs. As the world exploded in a sensation of heat and color, a moan tore from her throat, her body contracting on fists of pleasure.

Falling back against the pillows, Kendall tried to capture her wildly careening thoughts, the world still spinning as she fought to regain her balance. Harry collapsed against her chest, his breath coming in short rasps. Her body still pulsing with release, she clutched his head to her breast, desperate to feel the certainty of his weight pressing against her.

"That was amazing." Harry propped himself up on his good arm, the heat in his eyes burning her with intensity. "*You* were amazing," he corrected. Still thick and heavy, his erection taut against her stomach, he seemed content to stare at her as she slowly returned to earth.

Running her fingers through the beautiful, dark hair, she gentled her touch as she traced his stitches. "You look like a pirate with these." Pulling him down for a drugging kiss, she whispered against his lips. "Today must be a day for firsts."

He grinned. "The multiple orgasms or the pirate fantasy?"

"Both," she confessed. "I'm having crazy, hot sex with a gorgeous, heroic pirate." Shifting to her side, she moved against him, brushing against his erection. Her curls still damp from his mouth, she slid her leg between his. Her wetness brushing against him made him shudder.

"That's dangerous." He groaned as she slid against him.

Out of control and uncaring of the risk, she pushed him back against the pillows. Straddling him, Ken reached down to stroke him, marveling as the beautiful, emerald eyes heated. Holding her gaze, his breath huffed out on a groan when she cupped him.

"Kendall-"

A smile playing around her lips, she trailed her mouth down his stomach, leaving a path of wet kisses. His breathing grew more erratic, his voice hoarse as he pleaded with her. When she touched her tongue to the hot, hard length of him, Harry came off the bed.

"Baby . . . I won't be able to stop."

Undeterred, she planted a wet kiss to the throbbing tip, smiling as Harry shuddered in his battle for control. "Just another taste-"

His hands were shaking as they reached for her. "Kendall– please."

She sat back to stare at him. "Please . . . this?" Lowering her head, she slowly took him into her mouth. His big hands tearing at the sheets, he released a tortured breath.

"Yes! God . . . yes."

Using her tongue to work him into a frenzy, she felt his control erode. A moment later, Harry blindly reached for another condom. The moment she sheathed him, he surged into her. "We're going to do this slow." His voice strained, he held himself in check.

"I want-" Their bodies joined, Kendall sank down on him, stretching as he filled her. "So big-" Through a haze of sensation, she moaned her disjointed thoughts. Harry stilled inside her. Gazes locked as she pushed against him, she witnessed a flurry of emotions cross his face.

Wonder. Over the impossibly good sensation of her body clenching his. Lust. His gaze nearly melted her, his expression incredibly serious as he absorbed another wave of pleasure. And perhaps . . . . worry? But by then, she couldn't make herself care why. Though Harry was letting her lead, he was hot and throbbing inside of her. Her body flushed with heat on the first contraction.

"Look at me." His hoarse command broke through the sensual haze, his vivid green eyes glazed with passion. Helpless against the knowledge in his expression– that he could see over the walls she'd erected around her heart, she shuddered with a mind-blowing release that was more about the man she was with than the cataclysmic sex.

His groan suggested an end to his control. As her body clutched him, Harry thrust into her, filling her spirit with light and happiness. With hope. And with an arcing flash of love so intense Kendall wondered how it was possible he couldn't feel it, too. Lost to a storm of emotion, she left her worries behind.

Tomorrow would come soon enough.

CHAPTER 8

She couldn't seem to stop smiling. A fool, taken leave of her senses. After an afternoon making love with Harrison, they'd finally risen and showered together. Then made love again. Sharing a simple dinner on the deck, they'd sipped wine and stargazed. Holding hands and telling stories. Unwilling to break the spell, neither mentioned the fire they'd survived earlier in the day. Ignoring the ringing phone, they'd postponed reality for another day. Her business. The missing money. The dig. All of it had been suspended for a single night. Every fantasy she'd ever imagined had come true in a single night. Sharing them with the man of her dreams.

The next morning, Kendall stared at the stranger in the mirror and wondered who the luminous woman staring back could be. Her damn skin was glowing. Her hair flowing loose over her shoulders, the unrestrained curls brushed sensitized skin. Harrison's hands had been there less than an hour ago. And damned if she didn't want them there again. She tried to feel appalled by her behavior. And failed.

The entire map of her life had changed course in the space of a week. As she stared at the stranger in the mirror, Ken acknowledged she would never be the same. Tomorrow– when the fantasy ended and the ugly reality of her life returned– she would handle it differently. Not because her business was falling apart. And not as a result of the fire. She was different now– because of a man. Who'd fallen straight into the hole in her heart.

And filled it.

Traynor's crime was one of epic proportions. He'd made her realize what she'd been missing. Soon, he would leave. He would return to his organized, methodical life. And she would never be the same again. Instinctively, Ken had known what would happen if he touched her. Bottled up for so many years, in twenty-four hours she'd become a seething volcano of hormones. With a groan, Ken covered her eyes. What would she do with all this passion? What would she do without Harrison?

Hearing footsteps behind her, she met his gaze in the mirror. Harry's expression was one of lazy satisfaction as he hobbled up behind her to drop a kiss on her shoulder. After her stupid body finished reacting– shuddering helplessly at the brush of his lips on her skin, she scowled at his reflection.

"What?" An eyebrow raised skeptically over her annoyance. "You can't expect me to stop now– when I've already kissed every inch of this soft, beautiful skin." Resting his hands on her shoulders, he stroked them as he continued to scrutinize her in the mirror. "I can't seem to get enough of you."

The rough plaster cast grazed her skin, leaving it sensitized. The hypnotic expression in his eyes made her dizzy. Kendall gulped in a much needed hit of oxygen and closed her eyes to the message in his. "We can't– You. . . I'm taking you home. You need to get back-"

The sound of glass breaking in the foyer downstairs startled them. Harrison tightened convulsively, instinctively jerking her back against him. "Stay here," he ordered.

Ken nodded, her hand at her throat when he left, running through her bedroom as though demons nipped ferociously at his heels.

"Your cast-" Ignoring her plea, he thumped down the stairs where Lurch barked in the foyer. Her mind clicked swiftly into gear, panic becoming secondary as she jerked a shirt over her head. Hoisting on the only skirt she owned, she hopped halfway across the bedroom before she could get it zipped.

At the sound of crunching glass, she leaned over the banister. "Harrison– what's broken? Are you okay?"

"It's your window. Put on shoes," he called. "Only two panes, but the glass went everywhere."

Several minutes later, she surveyed the parlor with a frown. "Dammit. I'm sick of replacing windows."

Harry's head jerked. "This has happened before?"

Still angry, Ken sighed in exasperation. "It's not what you think. The neighborhood kids cut through my yard. It's a shortcut to the woods. Sometimes they kick up rocks. Once it was a baseball."

"This is a brick, Ken."

"Okay, so this time is different." Annoyance creeping into her voice, she released a shaky breath. *Not his fault.*

"You deserve a brick today." Harrison read the scrap of paper again before tucking it into his pocket. "Someone has a twisted sense of humor. When was the last time your windows were broken?"

She thought for a moment. The baseball had been at least a month earlier. The rock was ages ago. "I don't know who I've ticked off lately," she muttered. "I'll go find the broom."

"How about your delightful stepbrother?"

"I can't picture him skulking around winging rocks through my window."

Harrison's eyes narrowed in annoyance. "The only time I met him, he had your arm twisted behind your back, ready to break it. Fifteen minutes later, your whole damn building went up in flames. So please forgive me if I disagree with your perception of Barker as a harmless moron."

Flicking a glance at her watch, she frowned. "We need to get moving if you have any hope of making your party this afternoon."

"When are you going to start taking these threats seriously?"

"They're not threats, Harry. Let's clean this up and get moving." Kendall started across the room, intent on retrieving the broom from the kitchen.

"Fine. We'll swing by my cousin's place for an hour and then you can stay at my house tonight."

"Fine– wait. What?" Heart pounding, Ken jerked back around to face him. "*Stay* with you?"

"I think you should pack a few things and stay with me a couple days– until you get the report back on the cause of the fire."

Overwhelmed by the events of the previous twenty-four hours– by her own swirling confusion, Ken was careful not to lash out at him. "I think I'm better equipped to know what's best for me."

"Clearly you aren't," Harry argued. "Since you're hell-bent on ignoring the obvious."

"I have to be at the site by seven tomorrow morning," she reminded. "Unless you'd like to bankrupt me sooner than originally planned, I have a responsibility to salvage what little remains of my company." Hands on hips, she advanced on him, her nerves shattering like the glass under her feet. "I can't move to Stafford and become your groupie, Harrison-"

"Where the hell did you get-"

"Wait. That didn't come out right." Ken stopped him, her palms warming against his chest when he advanced. "What we shared was amazing. Hell, it was incredible, okay?" She risked a glance at him. "But that wasn't real. It was one beautiful, perfect night. We both know that."

"Kenny-"

She couldn't hear his fancy words right now . . . not when her defenses were weakened. "Just because you've written off A&R as a total loss doesn't mean I'm willing to throw in the towel yet."

Ken should have been warned– by the way Harry's beautiful lips compressed into a tight line– by the flames of anger igniting in gorgeous eyes. And if she'd missed those signs, then the tick in his left cheek was hard to miss.

"First of all, I haven't written off A&R. I haven't even had the chance to review the records I downloaded yesterday." Harrison took a step closer. "So, I'd appreciate you not jumping to conclusions about my intentions. Second– and I'm only saying this once, Kendall. . . so listen closely. I care about you. Whether you ever agree to see me again doesn't change the fact that I'm worried for your safety."

Speechless as his words registered, Ken groped for an appropriate response. Meanwhile, Harry continued to advance on her, his expression determined.

"I asked you to stay– no– I'm *insisting* you stay with me because this is more serious than you're willing to admit. And until the fire department rules out arson, you'd be safer staying with me than being out here all alone."

"Insisting?" Heart pounding a wild beat, Kendall seized on the anger flickering to life. "Let's get one thing straight, Traynor. You don't get to *insist* anything . . . except as it relates to that contract."

"Someone heaved a brick through your window and you're too stubborn to admit it's a threat. You could get hurt."

"I'm not leaving my h-home. My business is . . . gone. This place is all I have l-left." To her horror, Ken felt tears pricking in her eyes. "I won't leave Lurch. I won't leave Wink. They're all I've got." Though Harrison hid it quickly, she caught the flicker of stunned surprise over her confession.

"Great. Now you think I'm pathetic. And you know what? Maybe I am." Angry for revealing more than she intended, she swiped her eyes. "I won't be forced from my h-home. I'd rather stay and fight."

"Babe. . . you're not pathetic."

"I don't care-"

"Let me finish, would you?" Harry was gentle now, any trace of anger gone from his posture and voice. Somehow, the change made her feel even worse.

"I want you safe. If you think it'll be okay, then . . . come back here tonight. I won't try to stop you."

"You w-won't?" Dammit, what was wrong with her? First she was angry that Harrison cared enough to worry over her. And now, she was upset that he'd decided not to stop her.

"No." Closing the distance between them, he pulled her into his arms. The chaste kiss he dropped on her forehead left Kendall more confused than if he'd kissed the breath out of her. Why had he changed his mind? Was she that easy to write off? Or had he finally come to his senses and remembered Deborah? Perfect, willowy Deborah– waiting for him back home.

That thought was enough to firm her resolve. Pulling back abruptly, Ken turned on her heel for the kitchen. Better to get this over with, before she dissolved in a puddle of tears at his feet. "Let's clean this mess."

❦

Harry didn't want to hazard a guess what she was thinking now. Shooting a questioning glance in her direction, Ken kept her eyes focused on the road. She'd acquiesced when he insisted she turn on several lights. It would be dark before she arrived back home. Until he could arrange for someone to watch her house, he wanted it lit up like a roman candle.

His senses strummed with warning. Something was seriously wrong with Ken's business and whatever the problem was, it likely centered around Lance– the not-too-smart, but dangerously capable of violence stepbrother. Barker was probably bleeding the company dry. The question was how much? And were his actions actually illegal or just greedy? What worried Harry more was that Lance didn't have the intelligence to handle it by himself. If he *was* doing something illegal, it was unlikely he acted alone. If Lance had fallen in with real criminals– what would happen if Kenny got in the way?

Harry glanced at his watch. The party was well under way. He hoped his cousin Andrea and her husband Charlie would still be there when they arrived. A state trooper, Charlie could advise him on what to do about Barker.

With a little luck and with Jake and Jeff's approval, he would spend tomorrow getting caught up in the office before heading out to the site. If the only way he could help Kendall was to stick to her side, he intended to do just that. His cousins shouldn't have a problem with him monitoring their most critical project.

"I promise we'll keep it brief. I'll introduce you to everyone and then you can take me home, okay?"

"Whatever you want, Harrison."

"No argument? I could learn to like that," he teased. Before Ken could scowl, he snatched up her free hand and drew it to his mouth, smacking her fingers with a noisy kiss.

Instead of a frown, he discovered a reluctant smile when she glanced at him. Reading the stunned surprise in her eyes, he decided that acting completely out of character was beginning to grow on him. Her fingers still clutched in his hand, he reluctantly released them.

"Don't get used to me being agreeable. I'm no pushover."

Except in bed. There, he could do no wrong. There, he couldn't say the wrong thing. And Kendall loved everything he did. "I like that you don't back down when you think you're right." He smiled when she averted her eyes, a fiery blush climbing into her cheeks. "I'm starting to enjoy arguing with you. Those sexy eyes snap at me and your face gets that luscious shade of pink."

"Most men find me annoying."

She blushed when she was excited, too. Harry's stomach tightened as he remembered. Each time he'd whispered what he wanted to do with her, Kenny's response had been immediate and rewarding. Her beautiful, golden eyes had widened, dusky pupils dilating with his words. Her silky, tanned skin blushed a dewy apricot. And her breath would hitch in her throat with a soft, sexy gasp that made him hard just remembering the sound.

Jeez, what had happened to him? Harry wanted to pull over to the side of the road and take her in the bed of her truck. Something about Ken had him acting like a caveman. She was unlike any woman he'd ever known. And he was completely captivated.

Kendall was not gorgeous. In fact, the first word that came to mind was adorable. Yet, her skin, her eyes, her beautiful smile . . . added up to steal his breath away. When he added intelligence, a razor sharp tongue and a curvy body he would never forget– he was sunk.

He'd been delusional to think he could rekindle a relationship with Deborah. No matter what happened with Ken, whether she agreed to keep seeing him or not, Harry knew with absolute certainty there could never be anything with Deborah. And he wondered if there ever had been. Their relationship had been convenient. Until recently, that might have been enough for him.

Kenny wasn't convenient. Their business dealings made that notion ridiculous. Involvement would be messy. It would require effort to keep it going when A & R finally bit the dust. She would be resentful, hurt, angry. Mostly with him. Yet, that thought didn't scare him as it might have a week ago. Harry wanted to be there. He *wanted* to help her.

She wasn't part of his blueprint. She was a sweet, sexy diversion from his master plan. Great sex didn't equate to a great relationship. A strong foundation required common goals– similar values and beliefs. And when it came time to settle down, Harry would be more in control than he felt now. Kendall was too strong-willed and stubborn for her own good. His life thrived on order. There was a *reason* why he dealt in facts. Numbers didn't lie.

The fact was– on paper, Deborah still scored higher. On paper, Kendall Adams wasn't a close second. Yet as he stole another glance her way, he found her humming, a lopsided smile perched on her face, hair blowing in the summer breeze rushing past the open truck window, and his stupid heart began to pound.

For the first time in his life, Harry didn't care. About the numbers. About facts. About logic. Or his damn plan. He wasn't living his life on paper. As different as they were, they shared common ground. Ken was fiercely loyal. She was generous to a fault– giving of herself in a way he'd never known. She'd taken care of him when he'd needed help the most. Although different in circumstance, their childhoods had been similar in nature. Lonely. Alone.

They were good together– for as long as it lasted.

Kendall smiled, lowering her guard another notch. She'd mingled with the Traynors for nearly an hour and thus far hadn't made any mistakes. So far, it had been– fun. Harry's family was like the families she used to dream about. The summer Ken turned ten, she'd started riding her bike to the park. Spying on families spending time together, she'd longed to be one of them. To spend time with parents who loved each other– who loved their kids. Drinking in the sights and sounds, she watched them from the woods– sharing picnic lunches and playing on the swings. And laughing. Always laughing.

Ken smiled at the shrieks floating across the lawn. As a child, it had been painful to see the way her friends lived– to be invited in for glimpses– only to experience what she would never have at home. Now, she was content to watch from the sidelines. She could appreciate being part of the dynamic for a short while– before retreating to her peaceful, solitary world.

She'd been self-conscious when they arrived together– Harrison, the gorgeous, perfect successful CFO and plain old Kendall, the backhoe operator. How could she possibly measure up to the elusive Deborah? Yet despite her misgivings, she'd been welcomed by everyone.

Hand to her eyes to block the last shining moments of sunset, Ken surveyed her surroundings from a bench under an oak tree. Jake's home was a sprawling Colonial, brimming with kids and animals and toys. He'd inherited two children when he married Jenna, and according to the newest Traynor, Jake had taken his instant fatherhood in stride.

Jenna had been kind and welcoming . . . taking the time to introduce her to everyone at the party. The youngest Traynor, Jeff– remembered her from the days when she visited Specialty with her father. And there was Harrison.

He was different here . . . surrounded by his family. Discovering him in the center of a crowd of children, she smiled. Moments later, he was embroiled in a water fight instigated by Jeff. Wrestling the squirt gun away from Jenna's daughter, he fell to the ground, returning fire. In her wildest dreams she couldn't have imagined Harrison with a squirt gun in hand. Yet with his family, Harry seemed more like the man she'd come to know over the past few days. And less like the stuffed shirt she'd assumed him to be.

"Have you met everyone, Kendall?"

Her thoughts scattered when Harrison's aunt appeared at her side. "Yes, ma'am. I think I've got everyone." Crossing her fingers, she continued. "You're Mona, right? Jake and Jeff's mother?"

"And Andrea's, too, dear, but this isn't a test."

"Would you like to sit? I should warn you we're in firing range here." Ken tucked her head to her chest, prepared for the soaking that seemed inevitable.

"They wouldn't dare." To prove her point, Mona remained standing as the cacophony of shrieking, water-drenched children enveloped their safe haven. Raising her voice, she issued an ultimatum. "If I feel so much as a drop of water, no one gets dessert later."

"Cease fire, guys." Jeff barked the order to his troops. "What'd you make, ma?"

The only word Ken could find for Mona's smile was smug. "Brownies."

A chorus of groans met Jefferson's order to change targets. Harry caught her glance and smiled before the battle drifted down the hill to the rear of Jake's expansive yard.

Kendall waited for the noise to die down before she turned. "Those must be some incredible brownies, Mrs. Traynor."

"They're my secret weapon. It was the only way I was ever able to keep those boys in line."

She was surprised when Mona joined her on the bench to watch the younger children as they moved to the elaborate swing set. "It looks like Megan and Alex have already made friends with the whole neighborhood."

"I'm thrilled to have a few more grandchildren." Mona turned to her. "Did you meet Jenna?"

"Yes, she's been very kind. She introduced me to everyone." Her gaze followed Mona's across the lawn to the newly married couple. Almost on cue, Jake brought their clasped hands to his lips, kissing her knuckles. Her breath catching, Kendall watched him tug her closer, brushing his lips against hers. Even from her perch on the far side of the lawn, she could see the love in his eyes.

"They look so happy." Sighing with satisfaction, she smiled when Mona dabbed her eyes. "Are you okay?"

"How could I not be? My oldest son is finally happy."

Hope and sadness mingled in her chest. Jake was proof of the possibility of love– and how elusive it was. At thirty-one, she hadn't come close. Her thoughts troubled, she searched the sea of faces for Harrison. What if the man of your dreams was out of reach?

"What about you, Kendall? Have you found the right guy?" Mona nodded in Harrison's direction.

"Omigosh, no. No. We– we've only just met, Mrs. Traynor. I– my company . . . we're doing the sitework for the new mall. He . . . we– have to iron out some pretty serious business problems."

She shook her head. "Business tends to get in the way. Trust me on that."

Content to sit quietly as the breeze picked up, Kendall scooped her hair from her neck, enjoying the cooling gust before it drifted away. A tall man with a booming voice stepped out on the deck, a tiny woman by his side.

"Who's the man with the silver hair? I haven't met him."

Wincing at the sound of his voice, Mona looked as though she'd sipped bitter lemonade.

"Linc Traynor– my ex-husband. The empty-headed woman standing with him is Zoe– or Chloe . . . Unless, of course, it's someone new. These days, Linc changes women rather frequently. I can't keep track."

"Mr. Traynor would probably remember my father. I'll have to say hello before I leave." Risking a glance, Kendall was surprised by the twin spots of color blooming in Mona's pale cheekbones. Was it possible Mona was still angry with him? Had their divorce been acrimonious? Harry had mentioned she'd remarried.

"I should probably find your nephew." She wanted to make her escape before Mona started quizzing her again. "I have a long drive back and Harrison will want to get home after being away so long."

"Don't leave, dear. I'll be forced to walk over there and say hello. If we stay here and chat, perhaps they'll go back inside." The older woman's grip was like iron on her forearm. "Sit and tell me all about you and Harrison."

"I– there's really not much to tell." Tiring of her hesitation, Mona jerked on her arm and Kendall flopped back on the bench. "I guess I can stay another minute."

"I've heard you took care of Harry when he fell in that hole. Thank goodness he had you. I was halfway across the country visiting my sister." Finally releasing the death grip on her arm, Mona launched into a detailed discussion about her sister's recent fall. "I could barely help Marcie. How did you manage Harrison, dear? He's so big."

"Once I got him into my house, he's– been– sort of . . . trapped there ever since."

"And those clothes. . . I don't think I've ever seen Harrison in a polo shirt. Either he's in a suit or he wears those ratty running sweats he's so fond of."

"His suit was ruined in the fall. I had to cut away what was left of his pants to get around the cast-"

"You cut his pants off?"

Kendall realized her mistake the moment the words left her lips. Mona Traynor's mind, like her grip, was a steel trap. One little toe over the line and the trap door slammed shut. "I– we . . . borrowed some of my dad's clothes-"

"Your father lives with you, then?" Harry's aunt interrupted, a gleam in her eyes. She'd picked up her scent of fear and would hone in for the kill.

"Uh– no. He lives in Florida now." Damn, Kendall should have seen that coming. What if Deborah found out? If she'd been thinking clearly, she could have protected him.

"I like that shirt he's wearing today. It's completely out of character."

The woman had a one-track mind. "Well . . . after the fire yesterday . . . Harry had even less clothes."

"I'm so sorry, Kendall." She clutched her arm again. "Thank God you were both able to get out of the building."

"We were lucky. Harrison dragged us to safety. The whole building went up soon after."

"On one leg?" His aunt's hand fluttered to her heart. "He failed to mention that part. Do the investigators know anything yet? Harrison said it might be arson?"

Ken frowned. Traynor shouldn't be speculating. There was no official proof Lance started the fire. *Yet.* "The fire department hasn't confirmed anything."

Inching to the end of the bench, she searched the yard for Harrison. If she didn't make her getaway soon, who knew what information Mona would wrangle from her next. Thankfully, she spotted him. Soaking wet, he was talking with Andrea and her husband. As though sensing her interest, Harry turned, catching her staring. He waved, signaling he'd be over in a minute.

Who knew how much more damage she was capable of in sixty seconds? She should make her escape now– before Mona launched another conversational missile. "I think I'll get another glass of lemonade. Would you like some?"

"Wait." She stopped her. "You were explaining how you got Harry to wear normal clothes."

"My dad's stuff didn't really fit . . . and we didn't have time to stop by his place today." If his girlfriend learned any of this, Harry was done for. He'd never talk his way out of it. "We stopped at the mall on our way here to get him a shirt and shorts that would fit over his cast."

Willing herself to stop talking, Ken knew her face was on fire. Risking a glance at the older woman, she froze. Mona was smiling the brownie smile she'd used to control the water fight– soft, secret . . . smug. A smile of knowledge and power.

Mona knew. Maybe everything. Certainly that she'd slept with her nephew.

It was too horrible to contemplate. *Had she glimpsed the woman in the mirror?* The one who couldn't stop smiling? The stupid, happy woman who was hell-bent on ruining her life?

The woman who was in love with Harrison Traynor.

⁂

Something happened.

Clear across the yard, Harry read the panic in Kendall's eyes. And it made him move. Without excusing himself, he hobbled across the lawn to where Ken stood near his aunt. Bewildered, he glanced from one to the other. Mona was smiling as though the two women had shared a secret joke. But Kendall . . . looked about to cry. "Can I get you ladies anything? Kenny?"

"No, thank you. I- I'm . . . fine."

She was anything but fine. Her smoky voice scratched along his nerves and it took everything he had to not reach out and capture her hand. But the husky sound of unshed tears stopped him short.

"Harrison, I'm sorry to cut your evening short, but I need to head back."

"No problem. Give me a minute to say goodbye to everyone and we'll leave."

"I don't want to ruin the party." Glancing at his aunt, Ken edged further from the bench. "Maybe someone here could give you a ride?"

"I'd rather-"

"Kendall, dear," Mona interrupted smoothly, "I'm sure Harry would prefer leaving with you."

For possibly the first time in his life, he was grateful for her interference. "She's right. I'll be ready in two minutes."

"Fine. I- I'll meet you on the deck. I need to say hello to Mr. Traynor." Kendall smiled at his aunt. "Thank you for the invitation. I enjoyed meeting everyone and I had a wonderful time."

"You're welcome, dear. Harry will have to bring you to one of our barbecues out at the farm. Don't you agree, Harrison?"

"Kenny's a real animal lover, Mom. I think she'd love to see the horses."

"I . . . um . . . thank you. Maybe we can sometime." Kendall's reluctance couldn't have been more obvious. Her expressive eyes weren't cut out for lying.

"I'll wait for you on the deck."

Watching her dodge lawn chairs in her effort to get away from him, Harry chuckled. "She's crazy about me." Linking arms with the aunt who'd been more like a mother than his own, he watched her slip through the crowd.

"She's delightful, Harrison."

"I know."

Mona glanced up, her expression nearly hidden in the deepening twilight. "Possibly more interesting than the other one you've been seeing?"

"I- I'm . . . we're not seeing– I mean . . . she doesn't. . ."

"That's odd. I've never heard you stammer before."

Her amusement made him laugh. "Let me start over. Kendall is a very nice woman. She took me in after the fall. She's taken care of me all week– but, that's it. We still have a huge business problem to work out-"

"Harry, don't let Specialty ruin what could be a lovely relationship."

"This woman could be very dangerous to Specialty. If her company goes under, she could take Specialty down with her," he explained, his gaze on Kendall as she spoke with Linc on the deck. "Are you suggesting I throw that out the window because you find her delightful?"

"I'm suggesting you not lose sight of what's truly important in life." Frost tinged her tone.

A hug seemed to ease her scowl of frustration. "If it's meant to be . . . she'll still be there when this job is over." Kendall might be there– but would she want to speak to him? He couldn't change what was about to happen and he'd be damned before he'd act recklessly– not with Specialty at stake.

"Do you remember fishing in the creek with the boys when you were little?" Interrupting his jarring thoughts, Mona shielded her eyes from the last rays of twilight.

Harry raised an eyebrow at the swift change of subject. "What does that have to do with anything?"

"You'd spend hours splashing in the water . . . only to come home empty-handed because you never bothered to bait the hook."

"That was half the fun. The fish were harder to catch."

"I'd suggest using a net this time." Tweaking his cheek, she drifted across the grass, heading toward the house. Harry's gaze followed hers to the deck. "This one's going to be awfully slippery to catch."

CHAPTER 9

"Is everything okay? You looked upset back there."

Kendall kept her gaze on the darkened road ahead, refusing to catch his eye. "I had a nice time. Everyone was very friendly."

Wearily, Harry rested his head against the seat, allowing the silence to lengthen between them. Rather than badger her, he'd begun to realize she never kept things bottled up for long. Eventually, Ken would tell him exactly what was on her mind.

Lord, he was tired. His ankle throbbed fiercely under the confines of his cast. Feeling like an invalid was growing tiresome. He couldn't wait until everything was back to normal– couldn't wait to start running again.

At least he'd finally return home . . . his own bed– though he'd been forced to admit that Kenny's place felt like home, too. It was almost impossible to *not* feel comfortable in her creaky, old Victorian. He'd always been partial to clean, modern lines, but the casual comfort of her house and the peace of her garden had drawn him in. He hid a smile. Just as her prickly personality had proven irresistible. Like a beautifully wrapped gift, the best part was hidden inside. He'd grown accustomed to her moods, her music . . . that smile.

"What's the story between Mona and Linc?"

Ken's voice jolted him back to the cozy intimacy of her truck. "What story?" Glancing around, he realized they were nearly home. "They were married for twenty years and then divorced– for about a dozen, I think. She remarried a guy named George but he passed away two years ago."

"She still has feelings for him."

"No way." Chuckling, Harry shook his head. "That train left the station years ago. We've all noticed they seem to get along much better now, but Linc was the one who never got over *her*. She left him because he wouldn't slow down with work."

"So that's what she meant about business getting in the way of relationships?"

He met her sideways glance. "It's her go-to line. She's always lecturing us not to work too hard."

"That's what broke them up? Work?" Her eyes widened. "After all those years together?"

Hair whipping in her face, an incredulous expression on her kissable mouth, her small-boned wrist balanced on the wheel as though she knew the inner workings of her truck like the back of her hand. Without trying, Ken was just about the sexiest woman he'd ever seen. Unable to stop staring, Harry swallowed around the sudden desert in his throat.

"Back in those days, Linc worked eighty hours a week even though Specialty was pretty well established. We barely saw him when we were kids." Pausing, he considered his words. "My dad was the same way. Only difference was my mother spent those years drunk. At least Jake and Jeff and Andrea had a mother who was involved. Mona was mother *and* father to them."

"I sensed she was that for you, too." She glanced at him, a question in her eyes. "Did she look after you?"

"Thank God for her," he confirmed. "No matter how bad it was at our house, I could go there and pretend *she* was my mother. Something was always cooking on the stove . . . real food instead of pancakes all the time. I don't know what I would've done without her." Frowning, Harry shifted to face her. "Was that how it was for you? You must have felt like you were all alone." The image of her as a lonely, uncertain teenager left completely on her own had anger flickering through him. Kendall was silent for several seconds, leaving him unsure whether he should pursue the subject.

"I . . . uh– yeah. I felt that way," she admitted, her gaze remaining on the road. "Dad and I didn't get along, but I had Jimmy."

"Jimmy?"

"I think you met him— my foreman? He was. . . I guess you could call him a substitute father. That's what it felt like, anyway. I could never talk to my dad, but I could always go to Jimmy."

"That must have been hard on you." Harry carefully stuck a toe in the water. Maybe if he took it slow, she might open up to him.

"I survived." No mistaking the edge to her voice. "It made me self-reliant."

A lifetime of let-downs— spun as resilience. But Harry knew better. He'd never really forgotten the pain of not being wanted. Though endlessly grateful for his aunt's presence in his life— he sometimes wondered whether he'd imposed himself on them. Had Mona really wanted him there all the time? Another son to worry over . . . when she had more than she could handle? Had she ever seen him coming through the door and wished he'd just go away? Even now, Harry sometimes felt like an afterthought— tagging along with a rented family he could never truly call his.

"Most of the time, I prefer being alone."

"Is that a reflection on my shortcomings as a houseguest?" Knowing his words would make her smile, he awaited confirmation.

"You arrived with unexpected benefits." Amusement sparking her eyes, she gave him the once-over. "Despite the circumstances, I think we can assume I greatly enjoyed your stay."

"Next time, why don't we skip the fall . . . and the hospital trip and the fire."

"Deal."

The surprise that flared in her eyes left him a little wistful. As though she couldn't fathom the idea of spending time with him again. But were they really so different? Her frank admission made sense. She kept most people at a distance. Ken could count on one hand those who she trusted— and two of them weren't even human.

"I think we're getting closer. Is this your street?"

Harry's gaze slid from her to the window. "Next street on the left."

Crossing his fingers, he waited until she'd parked in a spot near his building. "Will you come up for a minute? I could show you around . . . maybe try to convince you to stay until morning?" He knew what her answer would be— probably before she knew it herself. Her tension was palpable. After building all afternoon, the energy sat like a boulder between them on the ride home.

"I've got a big mess waiting for me in the morning. I need to head back and face it." Reluctantly, Kendall faced him. The finality of her expression sent unease crawling down his spine. "We still have unfinished business," she admitted. "It's bound to get ugly before it gets better. I think it's best if we don't try to see each other again."

"I disagree." Instead of what he *wanted* to do— haul her against him and remind her why they were so great together— he adopted a neutral tone. "I want to see you. We just need to keep our personal feelings separate from the contract problems."

The light dimmed in expressive eyes. "There's no way this thing will work, Traynor. Even if we resolve the financial issues, we have other problems. Remember Deborah?"

"Leave her out of this."

Wincing, she shook her head. "No. I— I shouldn't have slept with you. I *knew* you had a girlfriend," she admitted. "But . . . everything was going wrong. I'd just lost everything-"

"You slept with me because you had a bad day?" Trying for amusement over her revelation, he failed. His chest tightened, making it painful to breathe.

"A *terrible* day," she corrected. "My entire life is collapsing. And a gorgeous, sexy, *thoughtful* man wanted to sleep with me." She glared at him. "So— yeah . . . shoot me. I figured why not have one beautiful, amazing night before I return to hell?"

"And that's all it was?"

Disgust crossed her features. "I still shouldn't have done it. I'm ashamed of myself-"

"Ashamed?" His stomach plummeted over her choice of words. "Kenny, I meant what I said. I care for you."

"Traynor, you have a girlfriend." Her whisky-soaked voice elevated in the confined truck. " If you cheated on me, I'd work you over with a tire iron."

Harry chuckled despite the seriousness of their conversation. The image made him smile. Kendall would be fiercely loyal to the man she gave her heart. She would expect no less from him.

"Honey, we didn't have that kind of relationship." He hesitated, unsure how much to reveal. Compared to the gut-shredding

uncertainty he was suddenly experiencing– what he'd felt for
Deborah had been pretty damned meaningless. But he hadn't
actually realized that until . . . now. He needed time. To analyze
what he suspected he was feeling. Run the numbers on why he'd
suddenly convinced himself Kendall was somehow different. Give
himself time to come up with a more logical explanation. "It's over
with Deborah. It was over before I met you."

"You thought I was her," she accused.

A brow lifted in disbelief. "Babe, there's no way I'd ever
confuse you two."

She sent him a withering glance. "I'm sure she's very beautiful."

"Gorgeous." He winked. "But . . . no freckles." The confusion in
her eyes made him want to fold her in his arms. But that tactic
wouldn't work on Kendall. "That's a deal breaker now."

"When you were hurt, you . . . talked in your sleep and you
asked for Deborah."

"You're basing our relationship potential on something I
mumbled under the influence of painkillers?" If she hadn't been
serious, Harry would've laughed.

"It didn't sound over." She released a shallow breath, clearly
battling for control. "What we had was . . . amazing. But– it would
never last."

"How do you know?" He gentled his voice.

Her smile was wobbly. "I'm not what you're looking for."

"What am I looking for, Ken?"

"Please-" She brushed a stray tear from her cheek. "No man is
looking for a woman who drives a backhoe for a living."

"Babe . . . you've single-handedly run a business in a male-
dominated industry. Even without that– I wouldn't give a damn if
you drove a garbage truck."

"What does Deborah do?"

"She's an attorney." The exaggerated eye roll she offered was
obviously meant for his benefit. "What does that mean?"

"Clearly, you need an attorney in the family more than a truck
driver."

"Dammit, Ken." Harry finally erupted. How was he supposed to
argue logically when Ken's thoughts were completely illogical? "I
don't require a resume when I date someone. Stop selling yourself
short," he ordered. "You're beautiful and smart. You're

unbelievably talented. Hell, you could probably audition with an orchestra and make the cut."

Golden eyes pooled with tears. "You need someone who's an asset . . . not a liability. Right now, I can only hurt you."

He hesitated, wishing he could argue her point. But– damn it. She was correct. His obligation to Specialty hung like a noose around his neck. He could never turn his back on his cousins. His only family– when his own hadn't wanted him. The Traynors meant everything to him.

Her eyes averted, Kendall seemed to steel her resolve. "I should go."

In a moment of clarity, Harry acknowledged he couldn't have both. With a cloud hanging over them, it wasn't fair to ask for more. But that didn't stop a cold wave of panic from clenching his stomach. "I'm *not* involved with Deborah anymore. You had nothing to do with that decision. It had been coming for a long time."

Her gaze determinedly glued to the steering wheel, she started the engine. "It's probably fixable. You can be pretty convincing."

"There's nothing to-" He released a frustrated sigh. "I like *you,* Kendall. I want to see you. Why is that so awful?"

Ignoring him, she shifted the truck into reverse. "I'll let you know my decision about A & R in a few days."

She was hurting and tired. Overwhelmed with stress. In one day, she'd lost nearly everything. The daunting problems she faced likely seemed insurmountable, especially when assuming she would face them alone. The logical part of Harry's brain suggested he not push when she was emotionally drained. But the flailing, recently unveiled *illogical* portion rebelled against the idea of her shutting him out. This wasn't the soft, loving woman he'd spent most of the last week with. It was fear. Or that damn stubborn pride.

"So, that's it? An amazing one night stand?" Of course, knowing he was being illogical and actually accepting it were completely different equations. Vulnerable didn't feel good. Vulnerable kinda sucked. He didn't want her to leave– not with uncertainty hanging between them.

Her eyes flashed dangerously. "I don't exactly make a habit of one-night stands."

"Ken– you trust me. I know you do." His anger dissipated. "Or you wouldn't have let me touch you."

"You caught me at a weak moment. It won't happen again," she vowed.

"What if I don't want it to end?" The moment the words left his lips, he regretted them. It was the wrong challenge to throw at a woman like Kendall. For a fleeting moment, her expression had softened, her tough outer shell weakened. Now, the beautiful eyes iced over, gleaming like a cornered tiger in the darkened truck.

"It's not enough you're taking my business and ruining my life? You want to string me along, too?"

"I'd like to continue seeing you." He softened his tone. "I care about you."

She snorted. "Yeah, well that and three bucks will buy me a cup of coffee in the unemployment line. Your version of reality differs from mine. Let's see if I have this straight– you get to keep your fabulous life and . . . sleep with me when you get the urge?" Nervous fingers drummed the steering wheel. "While I lose my business, put guys out of work who've never known anywhere else. I get the debts to pay off . . . the sleepless nights wondering whether I'll lose my house . . ." She released a shuddering sigh. "Oh . . . and I get to wait by the phone to see if the rich, successful guy I'm *sorta* seeing can pencil me in for sex on Thursday." Blinking back tears, she turned to stare at him. "Is that about right?"

The torment in her eyes made him sick with shame. The picture she painted was bleak . . . and likely accurate. And he could do almost nothing about it– except be there for her. Viewing it through her eyes– he knew it wasn't enough. "Ken-"

"Yeah . . . that's what I thought. I need to go."

Frustration threatened to swamp him. Where was the loving, talented, mystical woman he'd fallen for? If she would just trust him- He shook his head. *Sure, Harry– trust the guy putting her out of business.* "Ken– let me help you. I know you care about me." He caught her chin, forcing her to face him. "Just like I need you."

Need? Where the hell had that come from? He jerked his hand back. Jesus– he'd meant care. 'Need' sounded desperate– and he sure as hell wasn't desperate. Not for Kendall. For *any* woman. That would never– *could* never happen.

Though her eyes brimmed with misery, he caught the flash of defiance as she seized the bait. "I don't need you or anyone else."

∽∾

Was it nine or ten? Kendall had lost count of the number of times she'd cried that week. "And you're doin' it again." Great, shaking sobs that made it damn near impossible to keep her truck from swerving off the nearly deserted road. What was wrong with her? *She was in love with Harrison.* He'd offered hope. Assistance carrying the burden. And when it was over, he'd hinted at the possibility of a future. Likely short-lived . . . but *with her.* Instead of showing gratitude for the help he could provide– the beautiful, intelligent brain, the strong shoulder to lean on– she'd shoved him away.

Her signature move. *Better to do it first.* Until tonight, it had worked like a charm. All those years ago, when her mother left town, she'd withdrawn into herself. Under her father's bludgeoning criticism, Kendall disappeared a little more. Every humiliation she'd endured in school . . . each hurt thickened the wall she'd built around herself. Refusing to acknowledge pain, she'd discovered the best way to avoid heartache was by keeping her distance.

Now, she'd succeeded in pushing away the only man she'd allowed close in the last decade. Dumping Harrison before he came to his senses and dumped her first. *Why couldn't she trust him?*

She swiped her eyes on her sleeve. Because allowing Harry into her dented heart meant risking him shattering it. Alone was bad enough . . . but alone and heartbroken would be unbearable.

Releasing a sigh, she noisily blew her nose. She'd shut him out the last time, too. Only difference was– Traynor didn't remember it. That long ago night when he'd stopped to rescue the shivering, devastated girl who'd been ditched on prom night. He'd offered his varsity jacket and an unspoken compassion. His beautiful, emerald eyes had glowed with anger over her treatment. He'd demanded names– of the boy who'd abandoned her in the rain on the side of the road. The fact that they'd attended different schools hadn't seemed to deter him.

Mortified beyond words at life's latest humiliation, she'd given him an address several blocks from her own. Then she'd slipped from his car without even a 'thank you'. For months she'd worn his jacket. Slept with it clutched in her arms. Pretending it still smelled like him instead of her. She'd dreamed of tracking him down– to explain what his help had meant to her. Discovering that someone– *anyone*– had cared enough to stop had been eye-opening. She'd tucked his act of kindness away– hidden from anyone who might have demeaned it.

She mattered. Maybe not to most people– but for that brief moment, she'd mattered to Harrison.

She'd never thanked him. Ken had been too afraid he might laugh. Or worse– not even remember her. Instead, she'd worshipped him from afar . . . following his actions from the sidelines through high school and college.

Now– she risked the same mistake. Shutting him out because it was too much to hope that he might care about her. Her father's voice echoed mercilessly through her mind. Why would any man choose someone like her?

"Why the hell not?" she muttered. "*He* thinks he likes me." Head swimming, she swung her truck around. Before her brain talked her out of it, she had to go back. Had to at least talk with him. For the first time in forever, she would be honest. With the man she loved.

∞

Head pounding, Harry trudged up the steps, leaning heavily on the rail. His brain swirled with unanswered questions. What if Ken ended up hating him? Fatigue weighting him, he knew he wouldn't sleep. Even the anticipated pleasure of finally returning home didn't lift his spirits when he turned the key. His steps echoed through the tiled foyer. In the living room, he eyed the glass-topped coffee table, sparkling from a recent cleaning. Despite being gone nearly a week, his house smelled fresh and clean. *Sterile.* He missed the earthy scent of basil and rosemary– and Lurch.

Like clockwork, the cleaning service had stopped by, not knowing he'd been in the hospital. Books and papers were neatly stacked on the sleek chrome desk in the corner. No cushion out of place on his monochromatic sofa. Each decorator-selected piece of furniture had been purchased for its soothing neutrality. His home was in perfect order.

Harry waited for the sense of calm to slide over him– the way it always had in the past. To restore order to his jumbled thoughts. But his tension only increased as he wandered room to room. Though he'd never noticed it before, everything looked the same. Where was the color? The personality?

His home was a haven after stressful days at work. But tonight, the noisy silence mocked him. In the center of his bedroom, Harry slowly turned around. Nothing stood out. Nothing to indicate human existence except the water bottle on his dresser. His home was just a unit– like the one next door . . . a space he happened to occupy. If he were a color . . . he'd be beige.

Swaying on his good leg, he dropped to the perfectly made bed. Heart pounding with sudden awareness, Harry glanced around the colorless room. His gaze fixated on the artwork hanging opposite his bed. For a year, it had hung there. Until today, he'd never noticed it.

The designer had performed to his exacting specifications. Neutral. No drama– no garish colors to draw his attention. The boring landscape fit the bill. The painting was perfectly acceptable and perfectly dull. "This is your life." Efficient and organized and functional. And completely empty. His gaze sweeping the sterile room, his thoughts flew to Kendall. On her way home . . . probably crying. His mouth curved in a smile. More likely, she was cursing him. One of the many things he liked about her. He might not know what she was thinking, but he always knew how she *felt*. Her emotions were always right there in her eyes . . . confusion, sadness, passion.

She was the color. The warmth his life needed. His thoughts drifted to her cozy house. The smells and sounds. Kenny and her damned three-legged dog. Her one-eyed cat. Her gardens and her music. The lively chaos that made her house *home*. The harsh sound of his suddenly labored breathing broke the silence of the still room. Christ, maybe he *did* need her.

The briefcase clutched in his fingers slipped from his hand, hitting the carpet with a muffled thud. When his phone rang a moment later, his thoughts scattered. *Kendall*. Heart pumping, he nearly stumbled in his hurry to pick it up. Thank God, she'd come to her senses.

"Kenny?" His heartbeat slowed to a painful thud when he recognized the voice on the other end. "Hey, Charlie." The brief flare of hope slid into disappointment. "You've already found something?" Harry rifled through his desk for a legal pad.

"Uh-huh. I can handle that. Anything on Barker?" Frustration creased his forehead. "Are there other sources?" He released a deep breath. "I know I'm asking a lot, but if what you're saying is true– I don't like where it's heading."

Ending the call, he stared at his desk, his mind already ticking through his to-do list. Whenever there were problems to work through, his brain became too restless to simply think. Throwing himself into a project worked to clear his head. As pieces of a puzzle fell into place, so too, did the issue he was avoiding. Clarity in one area seemed to lead to clarity in the other.

Wandering back to the bedroom, he retrieved his briefcase. Seeking the flashdrive he'd filled at A & R, he plugged it into his laptop, eager to work. Discovering answers to his questions about A & R would determine Specialty's financial exposure. The sooner he learned Ken's fate, the sooner he could develop a plan to help her– fixing the damage and righting the ship . . . or helping her unwind from the business in a way that left her solvent. But before he immersed himself in what would likely be an all night project, he picked up his phone.

One last piece of unfinished business. "Hi, Deb. Yeah. . . I'm finally home." Harry forced a smile into his voice. Though she'd asked him to call, he hoped it wouldn't be a conversation about getting back together. Though it might have been easier to conveniently forget her message, Deborah's firm still handled Specialty's business. But any doubts he may have held about their relationship were answered.

Though they'd talked several minutes, she never mentioned his accident. As she chatted about the legal conference, Harry felt– *nothing*. Not disappointment. Certainly not love. Only impatience to move forward.

"Think you could swing by tonight?" Fingers restless, he drummed the legal pad. "Great. I don't have my car back yet."

❧

Kendall held her breath when she pushed through Harry's door. She'd waited on the steps for what seemed like an eternity before working up the nerve to knock. When she'd tapped on the solid oak, it had swung inward. Hearing Harrison' reassuring voice, her stomach went liquid with nerves. *What was she doing there?* She was so damned far out of her league.

Releasing a shuddering breath, she steadied herself. No matter how confusing her words might seem . . . she had to tell Harrison how she felt. Waiting for her pulse to stop galloping before making her presence known, she concentrated on his voice, on the husky timbre that sent her heartbeat through the roof every time he spoke. He was on the phone.

With Deborah.

Clapping a hand to her mouth to catch the gasp of betrayal, Ken prayed he hadn't heard the sound. Pain sliced through her heart as she overheard him ask her to come over. Thirty minutes earlier, he'd asked *her* to stay. Now, Deborah would spend the night– a far superior substitute. Staggering back against the door, the varnished oak blurred in humiliated tears.

Crossing the parking lot at a run, she fumbled with her keys before shoving them in the ignition. "Please, God– don't let him look out the window." Her prayer was fervent as she gulped in air, blindly wiping her eyes on her sleeve. She repeated the mantra as she pulled out of the parking space, slowly regaining control as humiliation dissolved to anguish. Please don't let him see he'd hurt her.

She drove through the night, her heart burning where his arrow had slashed an indelible mark. Her eyes eventually dried, leaving a bleak, red-rimmed reminder of her foolishness when she glanced in the rearview mirror.

～∞～

"You okay? You don't look so hot this morning." Frowning, Jimmy shoved a cup of black coffee into her hands, hovering over her like a concerned father.

"My business went up in flames two days ago. How is that supposed to look?" Lifting her head from the desk where she'd sat for the past two hours, Kendall scanned the room, her eyes gritty with fatigue. "This is it . . . this trailer's all we have left. I'm meeting with the arson investigator in an hour. The way our checking account looks, I'm probably gonna have to let most of the guys go end of the week."

"Kenny– let them decide. Everyone knows what happened. The boys– they all wanna help. Where's Claire?"

"Hasn't shown up yet. Most people don't work for no pay." Ken sighed. "I can't let the crew work when I might not be able to pay them. Truth is, I don't know how much money is left. With all the records gone-" Dragging in a ragged breath, she fought the burn of tears. "I'm meeting with the bank later today to see if they can help me recreate some of the records."

Jimmy placed his beefy arm around her shoulders and squeezed. "Some of us can stick it out longer than others. And we ain't leavin' until you don't have this trailer anymore. We're in this for the long haul."

She offered him a watery smile. "You might regret that decision." His eyes appraised her long and hard– as though he had something to say but was holding back. "What's bothering you, Pop?"

"What about the other thing?"

"Other thing? Isn't it enough we're bankrupt? That I nearly burned up in a fireball? That Lance might be an arsonist?"

"There's nothin' bad about him possibly ending up in jail," he admitted. "What about the guy? Where's Traynor?"

The unease that had strummed through Ken all night returned with a wallop. Unable to hold his knowing gaze, she glanced out the window to the bustling site. Even she could've been fooled by the symphony of construction noise outside her window. Production was at full force. For now.

"He's gone. Left yesterday."

"Uh-huh. Didn't I tell you not to get involved with him?"

"I'm fine."

"Don't give me that." Rising from his chair, Jimmy crossed the room. She was encased in his beefy arms a moment later, her nose pressed to his chest. He smelled faintly of cologne, dust and cigar. Despite her misery, she couldn't help smiling.

"Dammit, Kenny– I warned you. Guys like him-"

"I'll be okay." A flicker of warmth lit the cold, aching spot in her chest for the one man in her life who'd never hurt her. Jimmy was angry. With her, for being stupid. And with Harrison–for hurting her. In all the years she'd known him, Pop had never told her he thought of her as his very own daughter. He'd never said he loved her. But she'd always known the truth. She came first with him– even before his friendship with her dad. Jimmy had protected her.

Ken gave him a friendly squeeze. "Don't be angry, Pop. At least not today."

The burly foreman wasn't easily placated. "He better not show his damn prettyboy face around here or I'll take a shovel to it." His body stiffened when she chuckled. "You think I'm kidding? Woody wants to rip his arms off and plant them in the first concrete pour."

Kendall froze. "Woody knows?"

"Honey . . . everyone knows."

Could this day get any worse? "The boys'll think I'm pathetic."

"Hey– they answer to me." Tweaking her chin, Jimmy forced a smile that looked more like a snarl before heading for the door. "The way I feel, I wouldn't mind crackin' a few skulls today."

CHAPTER 10

Tossing his phone to the desk, Harry sighed. Three days of trying not to think about Kendall. He'd lost track of how often he'd called. She still wasn't answering. At least not for him. But he was tired of being ignored. Annoyed, his lips twitched over the unfamiliar feeling. Whether Kenny was ready or not, this time he'd play to win. First, he would kiss her senseless . . . watch the way her gaze would soften when he finally won her over. He'd dreamed of those molten eyes– how they glazed with passion when he touched her . . . shimmering like burnished gold when he was inside her. When he'd managed to sleep at all, his dreams had been laden with images of her.

At least she was safe. The security company he'd hired provided daily reports. When Kendall wasn't at work, she was digging in her garden or playing the *violin* on her deck. His forehead creased in thought over the information. How many instruments did she play? How many more secrets did she hold? His pulse quickened with anticipation. How long before he learned them all? Armed with the information Charlie had dug up on Lance, he'd asked the guards to stay a few more days. Until he could get back out there, he wanted someone watching her every minute. With any luck, it would be today.

It had taken a day to clear his desk of problems that had accumulated during his absence. But Specialty's accounting department ran like a well-oiled machine. Three days earlier, it had taken under an hour to speak with Deborah. She hadn't been upset by the news that he'd met someone . . . only shocked that 'someone like him' could move so fast. Her remark inferred he wasn't thinking clearly. It hinted at a lack of control that just plain didn't exist. Relationship-wise, Harry was in the driver's seat . . . and he intended to stay there.

Deb liked him enough to wish him well. She also appreciated Specialty's billable hours and the resulting connections she gained by being associated with the array of Traynor businesses.

Checking his watch, he rose from his desk. In five minutes, the partners would meet. Once he'd explained the situation to Jeff and the newlywed, Harry planned to head back out to the site. Aware of his need to justify it– Harry frowned. It wasn't just for Kendall. *Specialty* had a vested interest in making sure Charlie's plan went off without a hitch. And the only thing that could go wrong with a foolproof plan was a woman hell-bent on proving something. In this case, a feisty, hard-as-nails woman who was seriously ticked off. At him.

⌒⌒⌒

"So . . . we'd be part of a state police sting operation? Tell me again why we need to get involved?"

"Jake . . . the honeymoon's over. Try to focus."

"Even I get it," Jeff interrupted. "And I'm supposedly the one who never pays attention."

Jake blinked at that truth and sat back in his chair, a reluctant smile twitching his lips. "Okay, hotshot. Explain why the hell we need to go to all this trouble when we could just pull their bond and get another contractor out there to finish."

"Haven't you been listening? Harry's got the hots for Ken Adams."

Jake's head shot up, the infamous laser beam eyes zeroed in on him. "She's not your usual type."

"No– yes. . . I mean, no." Harry tried not to take offense when his cousins cracked up.

"Jake– did you babble like this when you fell for Jen?" Jeff's grin was smug.

"Can we please focus?" He expelled a breath of frustration. They were wasting valuable time. "How I feel about Kendall is irrelevant. My loyalty is with you guys– lord knows why." Feeling Jake's gaze on him, Harry reined in his impatience. They had to be united before Charlie could move forward.

"Give us time to absorb this, Hoss," Jake answered. "I'm accustomed to you thinking with the head that's . . . attached to your shoulders."

Jeff's eyes held curiosity. "What happened with the skinny lawyer?"

"This from the guy who's elevated the one night stand to an art form?" His cousin's exploits were legend around Specialty.

"What can I say? Chicks dig me." Jeff joined in the laughter at the table.

Jake glanced at his watch. "I'm taking off a little early for Megan's first softball game." His gaze shifted to his brother. "Lay off Harry. Let him explain."

Finally. "This plan protects Specialty. It will be quicker and easier than pulling the bond."

"How do you figure?"

"Because the schedule's tight. You lose even a couple weeks and we risk being late on the whole project. If we pull Kendall's bond, we shut down the job. There's no telling how much escalation we'll pay to get another sub out there to finish," he explained. "Plan on double what we're paying A & R. Add that to the shutdown time *and* the time we'll spend negotiating with the bonding company and you're looking at a minimum eight week delay. Probably more like ten or twelve."

Jeff nodded in agreement. "He's right. Everyone's busy with other digs. They don't need our work– not a rush job like this." His faraway expression indicated the wheels were finally turning. "Why don't we just bring 'em all on our payroll?"

"Yeah," Jake agreed. "Why would we want to buy A & R?"

"That's where Charlie comes in. His taskforce has been investigating an equipment theft ring for months."

"Tools and equipment walk off the jobsite all the time," Jake interrupted. "They'll never be able to stop it, not with the number of people on site each day."

"Jake– this is different. They're highly organized. They travel to big construction projects and steal the expensive stuff," Harry explained. "Then it's resold overseas. Charlie says they've stolen close to thirty million bucks in heavy equipment . . . and that's only what he's tracking here in the Southeast. I did some checking here. Donna told me we've filed eight claims for equipment theft this year . . . and it's only June. She said our insurance rates tripled last year."

Jeff whistled. "Not a bad way to make a living."

"Insurance companies are funding investigations all over the country. Manpower and cash. Most of the big carriers have paid out millions in claims. The taskforce thinks the operation is centered in south Florida– easy access to ports . . . miles of unguarded coastline. The equipment moves through the Bahamas and then to Mexico to fudge the serial numbers. From there it gets distributed all over the world."

"So– how do we figure in this?" Jake interrupted.

"Charlie thinks Kendall's step-brother is involved with the thefts.

Jake leaned forward in his chair, his interest whetted. "Why?"

"Timing. Barker's been here six months," he answered. "The taskforce has retraced Barker's movement since he left Florida." Fingers restless, he drummed the table. "Shortly after he arrived, equipment began disappearing from sites. The insurance carriers indicate a thirty-seven percent spike in mid-Atlantic claims for the last six months." He tugged a thick file from his folder. "Hell, Kendall's had four claims from our project alone. She thinks its bad luck."

"I'm failing to see the connection between Charlie's investigation and us having to buy a site contractor." Jake stopped scribbling. "Why are we part of this?"

"We're involved either way." Harry reigned in his frustration. He couldn't help Ken without his cousins on board. "Charlie's theory on the fire is that Barker's getting desperate. His sources say Lance ticked off the guy in charge. Apparently, embezzling from Kendall wasn't in the master plan. A & R should have been perfect cover for him."

"But his greed got in the way," Jake concluded.

Harry nodded. "Don't forget, Barker needed a reason for being in Virginia. Instead, he used it as an opportunity to double the score."

"So– you think he's in trouble for stealing too much?" Jeff stopped drumming his pencil.

"If you were the mastermind of a hundred million dollar scam. . . would you risk blowing your cover for the few hundred grand you could siphon from a small business–especially if that business served a vital function to the operation."

Jake released a low whistle. "People get killed for less."

"From what I've seen, Barker's not the brain behind the operation. A & R was a cash cow for him, but he's bled it dry."

"You know this how?"

"I've analyzed A & R's financials. Initially, I was tracing the problems on our project, but it wasn't hard to see what Lance is doing. Old fashioned embezzlement . . . nothing fancy."

Jake tossed his pencil on the table. "So– Barker's blown his cover. . . he's got the feds breathing down his neck and he's exposed a hundred million dollar operation that until recently, was running smoothly. If I were his boss, I'd be pretty pissed."

"The embezzlement might have been fixable, but nearly killing two people in a fire-"

"He's out of free passes," Jeff concluded.

"That's where Specialty comes in. Charlie needs a legitimate company to make an offer for A & R. The taskforce can set up a dummy company– but it'll take several weeks. And since the fire . . . Lance doesn't have much time left."

"Got it so far."

"The taskforce wants Barker before his own organization gets him first. Charlie wants to grab him in a quick sting, then offer immunity if he rolls over on the head of the operation. Charlie's asking us for a favor. We're here– already established. It wouldn't take any time for our lawyers to draw up papers that look legitimate."

"What does that accomplish?"

"It flushes out Barker," he answered. "With an easy score dangling in front of him, the logic is he'll try something stupid– like forge Kendall's signature on the sale papers."

"So– they don't nail him on the equipment thing?"

That had been one of his questions, too. "I'm not sure how it works. Charlie says they use one charge as leverage on the bigger score."

The particle accelerator in his brain already firing, Jake gazed at a spot on the conference room wall. Familiar with the expression, Harry waited him out. "So– we buy A & R– on paper? Charlie arrests Barker. Kendall gets her money back– and we finally go back to digging the damn job?"

Jackson Traynor wouldn't be talked into anything. Either he agreed with a plan and threw his full support behind it, or he declined and didn't spare the matter another moment's thought. Jake was the final say on all business matters, ultimately responsible for the entire company. Harry respected his caution. "Due to the size of their losses, the insurance fund has agreed to replace Ken's embezzled funds until her carrier steps in with a settlement. Ken stays in business. We tear up the fake buy-out agreement and the project gets back to normal."

"What do we get out of this?" Jake finally asked.

Harry didn't bother sugarcoating the truth. "Not much. Charlie makes a splashy arrest. We complete the project with only the normal amount of aggravation." Loosening his tie, he tugged it free, the first indication he was feeling any stress. He ignored Jeff's smirk. "The alternative is probably worse. Charlie is convinced Lance is a key suspect. That means the taskforce will be at the site, getting in everyone's way. We can cooperate and end it quickly– or we can watch them disrupt the entire project. If that happens and A & R can't finish . . . we still lose. Pulling the bond virtually guarantees we'll miss the completion deadline."

"What's your take on Barker?"

"I think he's a pretty good thief. That's why Kendall's in such bad shape. Without the embezzling, she'd be solvent."

"Does Ken know any of this?" Leaning back in his chair, Jeff stretched.

"She's– not taking my calls." Harry waited for the eruption of laughter to subside. "She knows Lance is a huge problem, but it hasn't occurred to her he's stealing– at least not to this extent."

"Why doesn't Charlie just nail Barker on the embezzling charge?"

Harry's smile faded. "Because busting up a nationwide theft ring would be a gigantic score for the state police. Charlie's getting heat from his higher ups. And they're being pressured by the insurance companies. They want a big splashy arrest– to scare off other gangs with the same idea. That's why the taskforce won't go away."

"How much of this are you going to tell Kendall?"

His face heating, he jerked a hand through his hair, ignoring the warning in the pit of his stomach. "As little as possible. Charlie doesn't want to scare off Barker. He thinks if Ken knows too much she might start acting different."

"Is Barker dangerous?" Jake returned to the conversation, an indication he'd made his decision.

"He has a criminal record in four states. Charlie thinks the pattern and his timing fit just a little too well. And maybe. . ."

Harry swallowed around the lump of uncertainty. It felt wrong to voice his suspicion— even to the men he considered brothers. Worse, it felt disloyal to Kenny.

"Maybe what?" Jeff stopped tapping his pencil and tucked it behind his ear.

"I'm beginning to suspect her old man might be involved, too."

Harry was performing an illegal act and it felt damn good. Worst case, if he got pulled for driving with a casted foot, he'd namedrop Charlie's name. A shade past noon, the day was finally falling into place. After more grilling from his cousins, he'd received the go-ahead to proceed with the fake purchase of A & R. Thirty minutes of finagling and he'd cajoled Deborah to begin drafting the documents Charlie needed. Another hour to drive home, pack a bag and hit the road.

Mentally replaying the conversation with his cousins, Harry realized Jeff had been right. Kendall *was* different from the usual women he dated. He *felt* different when he was with her . . . less like himself. Less like the self he'd always assumed he should be. Less like the man everyone had come to expect.

Through Ken's eyes, he was human— incredibly so. And he hadn't felt that way in a long time. Truth was, he'd felt hollow inside . . . as though there'd been a computer chip implanted in his chest instead of a heart. For the longest time, he'd isolated himself from everything except the bottom line. Both Specialty's and his own. In his mind, his blueprint had been cast in stone. No whims allowed. No eraser marks. No emotion in the decision-making process.

But Kendall didn't think that way. And that was probably half the fascination. She wasn't impressed with the suit or the status or his connections. When she looked at him, she saw a man— a funny, aggravating, flawed man. For the first time, Harry felt . . . real. Instead of a boring guy playing a dutiful role. He wasn't a robot anymore. His life had changed when he'd taken a header into that parking garage– when he'd fallen for Ken. And he wasn't ready to relinquish the light, happy feeling of being alive. At least not yet.

Another few months and Miss Hardhat's fiery disposition would probably wear thin. They'd both be ready for a change. The sharp jab of possessiveness caught Harry off guard. Okay– so for now, that notion didn't play well. For now . . . she was his.

His pulse ratcheted a notch in anticipation. Hell– he'd missed her. It had only been three days . . . but she'd tangled in his thoughts a thousand times. Her refusal to budge had frustrated him at first. By the second day, it made him smile. He'd gotten used to her smoky voice teasing him. Arguing with him. Harry couldn't decide what he missed more– kissing Kendall or debating with her.

One thing was certain. She was so damn stubborn that if he ever won her over, she'd be his for the taking. Assuming she'd ever lower her guard enough to trust him. His hands tightened on the wheel. *Did he want her trust?*

Harry wanted a whole lot more than that. His gut fisted with an emotion that felt surprisingly like determination. He wanted to win. He wanted– her. For as long as it needed to last.

∞

"What the hell do you mean, Floyd?" Kendall slapped her hands down on the cluttered desk, barely resisting an urge to strangle the old coot standing before her. There were days when she longed to be in a bigger town– a place where people didn't know every last damn thing about her.

Like her lapse with Harrison Traynor. If one more person asked how she was feeling . . . always accompanied by a long pause and that *you-should've-known-he'd-dump-you* expression in their eyes– she would scream. Jimmy's bull in the china shop method of compassion was hard at work. He'd probably warned the crew, his well meaning attempt to protect her from the prickly subject of Harrison. Of course, that had only drawn more attention to her.

"Nothin' to be alarmed about, Miz Adams." The fire marshal shifted awkwardly from one foot to the other. "We just don't want you takin' off anywhere sudden-like. You don't have any plans to leave the state now, do you?"

She stiffened at the insult. "What possible reason would I have for torching my business? It's been in our family nearly thirty years. For God's sake, Floyd— you grew up with my daddy."

"Now, Kenny," he whined, "everyone knows you bin' havin' financial trouble. Maybe you just got tired tryin' to make ends meet."

"If you believe that, you deserve that reservation at Shady Oaks your kids are saving for you, because you're losing your marbles."

"Kendall Renee— if your daddy heard you, he'd take a bar of soap to that sassy mouth."

She ignored the sting of truth. A bar of soap would've been child's play. A whipping was more her father's style. "Is there anyone else on this so-called investigation team, Floyd? Anyone who's actually looking for clues— like a faulty heating system . . . maybe some bad wiring?"

"Kenny, no one's accusin' you of anything yet." The old man gentled his tone. "For Pete's sake, the lab boys don't even have the test results back yet."

"But you've found a canister of accelerant near the scene and you think I left it there." Jerking from her chair, she paced the length of the trailer. "Do you think I'm stupid? Don't you think if I started the fire, I'd make sure I had an alibi? That I'd get rid of the evidence, for God's sake?"

The fire marshal opened his mouth, shutting it again when he realized she'd only come up for air. "Don't you think I would've avoided getting myself killed in the process?" Kendall whirled around, stomping back. "What about Lance? He was in there after I left. *After*— get it? As in— later than me. That moron throws his cigarette butts in the trash all the time. Have you checked? I told you when I went back upstairs to my office, the fire was already going."

"He said y'all left together."

"And you believe him?" She glared at him. "Hell's bells, Floyd! You've known me thirty-one years. He's been here six months," she pointed out. "What about Traynor?"

"Yep— I heard about you two. Sorry about him dumpin' ya like that."

"The fire, Floyd." Gritting her teeth, she resisted the urge to hurl something at his head. "Harrison was there. We reviewed files for several hours and then we left together. Have you interviewed him?"

"There ain't been time, Kenny. I figured I'd stop by and talk with you first."

She glared pointedly at the door. "To answer your original question. . . I'm not going anywhere. Now, if you don't mind, I still have a hole to dig."

She'd barely laid her head on the desk when she heard the outside door open again. *Mother of God*– now what? Resisting the urge to pound her forehead on the cool Formica top, Ken reluctantly raised her gaze to meet the next nightmare sticking its ugly face around her door.

"You busy? You must be– since you can't find time to return my calls."

Ignoring the cold lump of despair suddenly strangling her chest, Kendall forced a shallow breath. And discovered it hurt to breathe. "Nothing goin' on here, Traynor. Burning down my business left me with loads of free time. I'm getting a manicure later today."

Harrison had the gall to smile. "Ah, it's take-no-prisoners Ken. Where's your twin? The one I like so much?"

"Go to hell." What was it about him? Half the time she wanted to swing a Louisville Slugger at his head. The rest she spent wishing for foolish things she had no business hoping for.

He moved stealthily closer. "Where's the other Ken? She has beautiful, golden eyes I can't stop staring into. And this incredible, argumentative mouth– I just want to kiss into silence."

Kendall was helpless to control the shiver of awareness forking through her. The bastard actually grinned. "If you think I'm falling for your sweet talkin' bull-"

Her nerve endings sizzled under his perusal. Fisting suddenly restless hands, she scowled when her stupid heartbeat accelerated

"Her skin is like satin under my fingers." Continuing as though she hadn't spoke, his gaze burned steadily, seeming able to peer inside her. "She has this incredible throaty moan when I'm inside her."

"H-harrison-" Swallowing, she staggered back a step. Her face had to be flaming.

His voice dropped to a whisper and he took another step. "Is she gone for the day?"

"I didn't return your calls because . . . I w-wasn't . . . interested in talking." If he heard the desperate little squeak in her voice, he chose to ignore it.

"You're right," Harry agreed, closing the distance between them. "Talking doesn't seem to work with you." The last was whispered against her lips before he sealed them with his own. Kendall struggled against him for a moment before giving in to the temptation of his mouth, relinquishing to the haze of memories she couldn't make herself forget. She'd thought of nothing else–

She fell against him with a soft moan of frustration mingled with desire. The moment he touched her, her limbs seemed to lose their bones. Wrapping her arms around his neck, she fell headlong into his kiss. Lord, how she'd missed him . . . ached to feel him in her arms again. Hell– she could return to her senses later. She'd be lying if she didn't admit she needed comforting. Right now, she needed his touch. Desperately.

It was several minutes before reality began seeping under the edges of passion and Ken jerked away from him. The slumbering satisfaction in his eyes made her stumble back against the desk. Mortified, she discovered her hands shaking. "Damn you, Traynor. You'd better leave before Jimmy catches you. He's got a shovel with your name on it."

An enlightened smile creased Harry's face. "A price on my head? That's promising." When he reached for her again she bolted around the desk, relieved to have something sturdy between them.

"Don't flatter yourself. He's protective, that's all."

He nodded with approval. "Good. You need taking care of."

Despite her frustration, Ken chuckled. "Maybe I wasn't clear. He means to protect me *from* you."

"That should be easy enough to clear up." Apparently deciding that any attempt to catch her would prove futile, Harrison pulled out the chair to her desk and flopped into it, a smug expression in his beautiful, brilliant, lying eyes.

Wary, Kendall pulled up a side chair, keeping an eye on the door. Forcing a neutral expression she sure as hell didn't feel, she prayed he couldn't see the pulse ricocheting in her throat. "How will you explain away your girlfriend?"

"I'll tell him the same thing I'd have told you if you'd answered the damn phone." The first trace of annoyance crept into his voice.

"That I broke it off with Deborah two weeks ago– before I ever met you."

"That's a lie." Kendall bolted to her feet. "You were talkin' to her Tuesday night-" When Harrison stilled, she realized she'd revealed more than she'd intended.

"How would you know . . . unless-"

"I came back to apologize. That's all." Better to set him straight before he leapt to conclusions. She flopped back in the chair, feigning an indifference she didn't feel.

"And you heard me on the phone." Stacking his hands behind his head, he leaned back in the ancient chair, grimacing at the harmony of squeaks. "I told you my personal relationship with Deb was over– but she's still Specialty's lawyer."

"Not my business." She was too tired to win an argument with him today. And it was damn near useless to try when he had that annoying habit of reading her thoughts.

"Why didn't you stay? If you heard that call– we only spoke a few minutes."

Her gaze slid away. Because he'd asked her to come over. That phone call had gnawed away at her all night. As dawn filtered through her windows, she'd arrived at the miserable realization that . . . she'd trusted him. He'd crawled under her skin and wormed his way into her heart. And if she felt this miserable now, then how would she feel later– when he abandoned her?

"I wish you'd stayed. I missed you, Ken." His voice was softly persuasive. "Being away from you these past few days made me realize how much I like being *with* you."

A foolish flame of hope ignited in her chest before she resolutely doused it. She couldn't take the strain of loving Harrison. Couldn't live with the uncertainty. She could bear the weight of losing everything else . . . the business– her crew, her livelihood. But not Harry. She had to guard her heart against him. Lock it away in a steel box. Because loving him would shatter her when he decided to move on.

"Nothing's changed, Harry," she warned. "We're too different. I don't want to see you anymore."

"You sure about that?" His smile twitched. "Five minutes ago, I could've taken you on this desk." His gaze heated as his checked the open door. "Against that wall." His voice dropped to a caress. "Swallowing your moans . . . so no one hears when you-"

"Traynor-" Releasing a shaky breath, she fought the erotic image in her head. Her face burning up, Ken knew he was trying not to laugh.

"I've finished reviewing your financial records." Deliberately changing the subject, Harrison dangled the carrot just beyond her nose.

Sliding her chair closer to the desk, she leaned her elbows on the edge. "What did you find? Was there a mistake?"

"Several. But not the way you're thinking," he warned when her mouth curved upward.

Her smile dissolved. "You're still insisting I got the payment from Specialty?"

"Yeah. The mistakes I'm talking about are internal errors— you've got a bunch of misapplied payments and if you ask me— a couple pretty suspicious looking vendors you've been paying quite a bit of money to."

"How could it be that screwed up? I coded everything for Claire before she entered anything into the system. It's not like we're running fifty jobs," she reasoned. "More like two or three big ones and half a dozen small projects."

"Well— someone botched the entries pretty well. I've got the file out in my car. We can review it later."

"Why don't we look now," she suggested, caution seeping into her voice. "No need to hold you up."

His grin told her he was doing the damned mind reader thing again. "I'm not in any rush. I planned to stay a few days. My bag's in the car."

"Harrison. . . I've got enough problems without having to deal with you on top of-"

"I'm here to volunteer my services," he interrupted smoothly. "I don't have a place to stay. I thought I'd bunk down with you."

Kendall didn't know what to feel anymore. She'd just about exhausted all the anger she had left. Her supply of tears had thankfully dried up, too. Fatigue, she had plenty of. Her body wanted to sag into the chair and never move again. And their conversation wasn't helping. If ever there was a man worth leaning on, Harry was the guy. Her brain knew better than to hope for love.

But the ice around her stupid heart was cracking– softening toward him.

Falling for Harrison meant relinquishing control of her ironclad will– the one force that had propelled Ken rather nicely over the past dozen years– through turmoil and heartache. She'd be forced to wait him out– always on guard . . . never able to relax. The only question was how long. A month? Six? A year? The not knowing would kill her. Because it wouldn't be a question of *if* he grew tired of her. Only when.

And what would be left of her when he decided it was over?

"As I'm about to be arrested shortly, you can have the whole damn house, Traynor. I don't care anymore. Just remember to feed Lurch and walk him at least once a day. Wink can take care of herself but she gets ornery if you don't pet her."

Leaning back in her chair, Ken hoisted booted feet to the desk, weariness crashing over her. The sun beating through the window heated her skin. A nap would feel so damned good right now.

His amusement disappeared in a flash of disbelief. "What are you talking about?"

"The fire marshal is suggesting I set the fire Tuesday. According to Floyd, I planned this."

"You're not joking?" Harrison stared, eyes wary over her deceptively calm demeanor. "Who the hell is Floyd?"

"The fire marshal. You probably saw him leave." Her lids felt weighted as she sank deeper into her chair.

"And he learned this . . . without talking to witnesses?"

She smiled when his eyes sparked. When she grew too weary to battle . . . Harrison could get angry for her.

"Babe, you're scaring me. Is he the best this town has?"

"Just about," she admitted on a yawn. "Floyd's not a bad guy. He just needs to retire."

"You don't sound terribly upset about going to jail."

"Like you said, they haven't interviewed anyone yet." She shifted her gaze back to him. "You were with me. It's not like I don't have . . . an alibi." She closed her eyes for a minute. They were so heavy. "Now, if you decided to turn on me . . . I'd have a problem."

CHAPTER 11

Harrison eyed her drooping lids, his lips quirking in a thoughtful smile. Slumped comfortably in the ancient upholstered chair, Ken released a husky sigh, sliding into sleep. Her long, silky hair was caught up in a lopsided ponytail that slipped over her shoulder, covering half her face.

For several minutes he watched her, listened to her breathing deepen as she finally lost the battle to remain awake. The dark smudges under her eyes made his smile fade. His chest constricted on a sudden wave of frustration. How could such a little body absorb so many blows and remain standing for as long as she had? How much longer could she continue this way before she collapsed under the weight of stress? Kendall was running on empty and had been for a while. Staring at her slight frame, Harry vowed to change that.

It didn't take much convincing a half hour later to get her loaded into his car for the drive back to her place. It had, however, taken a full twenty minutes to convince Jimmy not to brain him with a lead pipe. The only thing saving him from a beating was the warm, slack body nestled in his arms. Kendall came first with the old man. His affection for her was obvious . . . though Jimmy buried it under a hide as thick and tough as an elephant's. Harry was grateful to him.

All those years, he'd protected Kendall. The soft, silky woman in his arms had been a soft, sweet, little girl. And Jimmy had ensured that no matter how her father mistreated her, she'd always had him to turn to.

Glancing to his right, he found his smile again. Kenny was peacefully asleep, curled up on the seat, oblivious to the breeze wafting through his car. He remembered Jimmy's grudging words when he'd reluctantly allowed him to pass.

"This ain't finished. You hurt her and I'll make you sorry for the rest of your days."   It wasn't finished. Not by a long shot. He remembered Kenny's insistence that if she were destined to meet the man of her dreams, fate would lend a hand. He'd laughed at the ludicrous suggestion she would simply bump into the man she was meant to spend her life with. How could she operate without a plan? A blueprint? How could she leave everything to chance? Harry had made it his business to plan for everything.

His parents' marriage had taught him only that loving someone hurt . . . that everything and *everyone* else was sacrificed when you loved someone. He'd taken that knowledge and run with it, distancing himself from any relationship that might leave him vulnerable.

But Harry didn't know how to distance himself from the ache of compassion he felt for Kendall's lonely childhood. From the hot, bubbling anger toward parents who hadn't cherished her. He hadn't expected the . . . longing he experienced every time he looked at her. As though he could spend the rest of his days just . . . being with her. He sure as hell hadn't planned for the deep, stirring certainty taking root in his chest.

He thought about his blueprint . . . the meticulous map he'd drawn for his journey through life. And forced the question that had nagged him for days. What would his blueprint look like without Kendall in it?

≈

Kendall blinked owlishly and pulled herself upright in the seat. "Where am I?" She winced at the raspy sound of her voice, still sluggish from sleep.

"We're nearly home. You're going up to bed for a nap."

"Traynor– I have a hundred things to do and you want me to nap?" He'd only been back an hour and already he was telling her what to do?

"Yeah. And if you don't give me a hard time, I might be convinced to join you for a little while."

Glaring at him, she realized her heart wasn't in the argument. It was too busy careening around her chest, tripping like a rapid-fire machine gun.

Traynor. In bed. With her.

In seconds, she went from unconscious to throbbingly aware of him. One subtle glance at his knowing grin told her he'd just finished reading her every thought. "Quit doing that."

"What have I done now?" Pulling into her driveway, he switched off the engine before turning to face her.

"You're pretty sure of yourself all of a sudden." She eyed him suspiciously.

"In matters of the heart, it's important to appear confident."

"Name one time in your life you weren't positive of the outcome," she challenged. How could someone like Harrison understand what it was like for everyone else? He'd been one of them– the 'has-it-all' crowd. Despite his mother's alcoholism . . . despite his father's emotional abandonment . . . he'd still managed to be popular, well-liked and ultimately, successful. She, on the other hand, had spent her life outside the candy store window, nose to the glass, watching everyone else eat sweets.

Startled when he tipped her chin up, Harry forced her to make eye contact when she would have turned away– when she wanted to look anywhere other than into those knowing eyes.

"I'm not positive now," he admitted. "I know what *I* want– what I've wanted from the moment you left me Tuesday."

Rather than struggle against the walls of her chest, her heart leaped straight into her throat. "W-what's that?"

"I want to make love with you again. I want to see your eyes . . . that beautiful flashing gold. I want to feel your luscious body-"

"H-harrison-" she croaked. Heat flooded her body, leaving her shaking in its frothy wake.

"But most of all, I want to hear you . . . when you say my name. It's the most incredible sound I've ever heard."

Her eyes widening with shock, she struggled to pull in a breath. When Harry released her, she rocketed from the car. She had to stop twice on the way up the porch stairs, grasping the railing when her knees threatened to collapse. Risking a glance over her shoulder, Harrison trailed her by a step or two, deftly mastering the steps with his cane. Ken acknowledged that his broken ankle had been reduced in status to a mere nuisance. Whistling softly under his breath, he winked in acknowledgment and her pulse soared to what was surely a dangerous level. With his injuries nearly healed, spending time with Harrison was about as safe as juggling a sparking stick of dynamite.

"We'll see about that, Traynor."

∞

They made it to her bed, but only barely. Kendall's intent had been space . . . lots of it. This thing with Harrison– was too dangerous to start up again. But he caught her in the kitchen. All he had to do was touch her. Those perfect, capable hands. . . And that smile– the one that tricked her into thinking she was the most gorgeous woman he'd ever seen.

She was done for.

She'd lost her hairband in the kitchen when he'd tugged her hair free of the ponytail. Their shirts had been discarded on the landing halfway up the stairs, leaving Lurch in a jumbled pile of clothing. Kendall couldn't be sure, but she vaguely remembered leaving her bra on the banister at the top of the stairs. And by the time Harrison rid himself of his pants, she wasn't able to think at all. Skin on glorious skin. She ran trembling hands down his back, reveling when his muscles corded under her fingertips. Lord, she'd missed feeling him next to her. She'd missed his quiet presence.

All these years, her solitary life had never felt lonely. Until this week when her house had seemed shatteringly empty without him in it. She'd missed his teasing remarks. The only time she'd heard his easy, bantering voice had been on her voicemail. She'd missed everything about him.

"Kenny . . . you're so beautiful." She shivered when he traced the length of her arms. They stood facing each other at the foot of her bed. His touch was soft, the caress gentle, as though he was fascinated by the texture of her skin. "So soft and beautiful. So responsive. I love watching you."

She only had to lift her gaze to Harrison's eyes to see the conviction behind the words. In his unwavering gaze, she was beautiful. For as long as it lasted, she would choose to believe him.

"Kendall. . . I missed you this week. Did you think of me? Even once?"

The last week had been lonely . . . so unbearably lonely without him. She slowly nodded, too mesmerized by the smoldering expression in his eyes to look away, her heart too giddy with joy to remember she wanted to be cautious. "I thought about you all the time."

Harry released the breath he had been holding and acknowledged the first trickle of relief. It bothered him that he was even a little nervous. And while part of him was shouting with the rough need to pull her against him, with the overwhelming desire to touch and be touched, another part of him had iced over with fear. He was supposed to be the one in control. But when he held Kendall in his arms . . . when she swayed toward him the way she was now, he felt anything but control. He felt only desire . . . a dark, desperate need that threatened to spiral out of control. He'd tried to keep himself separate from it and when that hadn't worked he'd tried to run from it. And in the end, he hadn't really wanted to leave.

When Ken's lips curved in a tentative smile that ignited her golden eyes, an answering stab of possessiveness clenched his gut. When she leaned in to brush his lips with hers, Harry felt only the liquid pull of heat. And knew he would never have enough of her. Not today. Not in six months. Not in a dozen years.

His hands shaking, he tugged her closer, groaning with raw pleasure when their bodies collided. Sinking into her sweetness, he deepened the kiss until they were both trembling with need.

"Harrison. . ."

His name was a soft breathy moan that spilled from her lips when Harry found the fluttering pulse in her throat. She melted against him like soft, pliant wax, her head falling back against his shoulder when his mouth latched on to her breast. His heart thundered in primitive response to the sheer wonder of her surrender. Her nipple tightened against his tongue and he nearly exploded with the need to be inside her. He lowered his hand to her waist and still lower to her smooth, flat stomach. Ken's knees actually buckled when he cupped her with his hand. Harry's smile was fleeting at best when he discovered her hot, wet center. What was left of his control simply shattered.

"Kendall, love. . . I need you. Tell me you want me." Raising his gaze to hers, he found his first real smile. Huge with wonder, the beautiful golden flecks on fire with passion. If his own need wasn't so painful, he would have given anything to simply watch her beautiful, expressive eyes, watch them glaze over when he took her over the edge of the precipice they both clung to.

"I want you . . . now, Harry." She tugged him down on the bed, her hands trembling when she sheathed him with a condom. He groaned low in his throat while he tried to capture her hands. But the pull of her heat, the sheer wonder of her skin against his own was too much for him. He couldn't wait a moment longer.

They sighed in unison when he finally slipped inside, filling her. Her smile was one of delight. Harrison felt a corresponding ache of acknowledgment in his chest. His thoughts grew disjointed with each thrust until his sole focus was pleasure. And when Kendall moaned, when the shivers of her release rocketed through him, the throaty rasp of her sexy voice sent him beyond the edge of reason. His mind splintered into a thousand tiny pieces.

She was still quaking when he collapsed next to her, her eyes still dazed when he leaned in to kiss the satiny sheen of her shoulder. As he stared down into her face, his heart tripped along like a freight train. And when she smiled up at him, Harry was lost all over again.

How had desire turned so quickly to need? It should have troubled him that he could no longer separate the two. But she'd slipped inside his head. She'd taken ownership of his heart. He'd felt the connection and tried to dismiss it. But there would be no more denial. At least not on his part. Because in the dusty corners of his muddled brain, an increasingly persistent voice whispered crazy words like forever. Holding Ken in his arms felt as natural as breathing. Protecting her, helping her. . . He wanted it all. And he wanted it with Kendall. She was the light and the warmth in his sterile, lonely world. She was the woman who would bring color and dimension to his flat blueprint. The only woman who could bring his plan to life.

He needed her. And right now, forever didn't seem like nearly enough time. With a thunderbolt of certainty, Harry knew he could spend the rest of his life coming home to her. On the good days and bad. Especially the bad days– because she would make them better– just by being there.

"Kenny?"

"Mmm?"

Her sleepy, sated voice dragged over his nerve-endings. Even now, only moments later, he wanted her again. "I love you, Kendall."

"That's nice." Sighing, she burrowed into his neck.

The silence ticked on for several long seconds. Harry was just beginning to wonder whether he would have to wake her up and summon his courage all over again when she bolted up.

"What?" All trace of sleepiness gone from her expressive eyes, his heart stumbled when he read her panicked expression.

"I love you." When she would have leaped from the bed, he quickly blocked her escape, pinning her trembling limbs with his good leg. "I'm sorry to spring it on you like this, but you're just gonna have to learn to live with it."

"Harrison. . . y-you don't have to say. . . that." She hesitated, seeming to choose each word carefully. "My eyes are wide open. I know what I'm getting into. You don't have to pretend to feel something-"

"But I *do* feel it. I know it's too soon," he admitted. "I'm not looking for you to say anything, okay?"

"Harrison– h-how can you . . . how can you know-"

"I've spent thirty-three years on the planet never feeling anything like this," he explained, frowning over the trace of annoyance he heard in his voice.

"But-"

"Look– I know you don't want to trust me, but you're going to have to make an exception." He cut off her stammered reaction, his heart skipping erratically in his suddenly constricted chest. Hell– he shouldn't have told her. Not so soon. He felt the crackling tension in her body, felt the shockwaves radiate out to encompass him, too. He should have waited– until he could make her realize she loved him, too.

"But– where did this come from," she whispered.

"I've been fighting it . . . nearly from the beginning." He nodded over her expression of disbelief. "You don't see what I do when I look at you . . . when I spend time with you."

"I'm just . . . a novelty. Those feelings won't last."

His heart sank with the certainty of her words and nearly broke over her bewildered expression. Of course love didn't last . . . not in her world. No one had ever loved her enough to stay. How could she believe in someone like him– when her own family hadn't been worthy of her trust? "I know what I feel, Kenny. My heart knows."

"Harrison . . . you don't– if you knew the real me . . . you wouldn't want me."

Amber eyes bright with unshed tears, the pain flaring in their depths made Harry's chest ache. He brought his fingertips to her lips, silencing her confusion. His feelings were too new . . . too raw. He didn't think he could bear to hear her uncertainty. It would be better to simply wait her out. She cared for him. They couldn't be so connected without her wanting it too.

He would reassure her what he felt was real. Through whatever happened, he would be there with her. That together, they would be happier than he'd ever dreamed possible.

"Don't say anything," Harry whispered before he dropped his gaze to her lips and smiled. "Let's just wait and see what develops, okay?" He brushed his mouth against hers, his heart soaring over the telling shudder she couldn't seem to contain. Ken opened to him on a soft sigh of wonder and he stepped willingly back into her warmth, tumbling back into love all over again. He finally had a plan. The blueprint was clear. He would gain her trust . . . and her love . . . one kiss, one stroke, one loving word at a time.

Kendall would learn just how patient he could be.

There'd been no more talk of love, only the actions of a man in love. They'd driven each other crazy for as long as Harry could bear it before he'd experienced the most powerful release he'd ever known. Then he'd held Ken until she'd stopped trembling, until his own heart had finally slowed to a dull, reassuring thud. He'd watched her slip into sleep, enjoying her soft smile when she stretched against him.

He watched her now from the doorway, lingering over the task, reluctant to leave for even an hour. But keeping up with Charlie's schedule meant he had calls to make. Once downstairs, it only took a moment to retrieve the number he'd scribbled in Kendall's office a few days ago– mere minutes before the place had gone up in flames. He dialed the number, gathering his thoughts while he waited. The phone rang several times before it was finally answered.

"Yeah?"

"Lance? This is Harrison Traynor. We met last week?" He
frowned when the oily little weasel cut him off– rambling about
the fire and the cause. His blood pressure spiked when Barker
immediately tried to pin the blame on Kendall. With effort, he
forced back the contempt surging through him. Charlie had given
specific instructions. He couldn't mess up the plan just because he
was furious.

"I was calling about the offer you made a few days ago– you
know. . . about selling? Is that something you're interested in? The
way I see it– you and Ms. Adams don't have much choice. I need
that sitework completed in the next month– otherwise, Specialty
will be in a bind with the schedule." Biting his tongue when Barker
interrupted him, Harry forced back the words he wanted to let fly.
For Charlie's plan to work, he had to bait the hook just right.
Scanning the bulleted items in his notes, he checked them off.

"Lance– if we buy A & R, that saves us the time and trouble of
you going into default. There's no sense involving the bonding
company. Hell, we'd lose a couple months negotiating a
settlement." Harry listened carefully, jotting notes on the legal pad.
So far. . . everything was proceeding according to plan. If Barker
seemed eager, it would confirm Charlie's intelligence– that he'd
exhausted his chances with the people higher up the food chain.

"Great. I'm sure we'll be able to do business. Why don't you
discuss my offer with Miss Adams and I'll call in a few days."

∽∾

Later that night, when they were both comfortably seated on her
deck, Harry took the final step off the plank and put Charlie's plan
into action. Kendall was relaxed and happy, her bare feet tucked
under the fluffy folds of her robe, her violin still loosely clasped in
slender fingers. She'd played for him. . . shyly at first. . . then with
certainty. And she'd taken him on a mystical, lyrical journey that
left him breathless. The arrangement was moody yet hopeful,
gently optimistic but cautious. And the musician herself was
absolutely magical. Harry watched, mesmerized while she wove
his heart through her fingers, binding him more tightly to her with
each passing second.

She was quiet now, gazing softly into the growing dusk as it
settled peacefully over them. The heady scent of her sleeping
garden washed over him, leaving Harry more content than he'd

ever dreamed possible. But the moment he dreaded had finally come. His heart stuttering an erratic beat, he prayed he wouldn't regret the words he was about to speak.

"There's been an offer for your company, Kenny."

Her luminous eyes were startled when she raised them to meet his. "How can that be? Who would know about-" Understanding dawned in her expression. "Everyone knows I'm in trouble, right?"

Harry ignored her question. If he hesitated now, he might change his mind. "It's not bad for a first pass. But we could probably get them to raise the offer a little . . . get enough so you can pay off all your debts. Maybe walk away with a little money left over."

"How did you hear about this?"

He'd anticipated that question. "They contacted Specialty . . . they know about the bond. Probably figured we'd be working some kind of deal with you."

"Who are these people?"

He cringed at the stiffness that had crept into her voice. Dammit, he wanted this to be over with. The sooner they moved beyond the mess with Lance, the sooner he could devote himself to their future– to the more daunting task of earning her trust.

"They– they didn't say. It's some kind of joint venture. A few different interests. . . their attorney contacted us."

Ken turned to him, her expression unfathomable in the growing darkness, but something flickered in her eyes that tightened the knot in his stomach. "How could I take any offer seriously if I don't know who they are?"

Harry shrugged, forcing a casualness he sure as hell didn't feel. "If the money's right . . . the rest usually falls into place pretty quickly."

She shook her head, a frown forming in her eyes. "What about my crew? I'd want to know they'd be protected. Would they still have jobs?"

He weighed his answer carefully. Relaying too much information at this stage would only raise her suspicions. "I don't know. These are all questions I can present to them."

"If not, I'd want enough money to pay them for their loyalty. They deserve a severance after all these years."

"Kenny, you may not have that option."

"Then I'm not interested." Setting her instrument on the weathered teak table, she clasped her hands in her lap. Flickering candlelight cast exaggerated shadows on the deck. Releasing a sigh, Harry worked to bank his frustration. Why did she insist on carrying the burden of everyone else's problems?

"Don't you have enough to worry about?"

"My crew has always been there for me, Harrison. They've always had my back. I won't desert them now."

"What about the fire? This is the poorest excuse for an investigation I've ever seen. You said yourself he wants to arrest you."

"I've got you for an alibi, remember?" She expelled an angry breath. "And there's the little matter of the truth. I didn't start the damn fire– Lance did."

"We're not off the hook yet," he muttered, shaking his head.

"What's this 'we' business?" Ken sat up straighter in her chair, her voice lowered in anger. "These are *my* problems, Traynor, not yours."

Harry hoped the despair didn't show on his face. Armed with the knowledge that he loved her, she was still keeping him at a distance. Swallowing the stab of disappointment, he carefully schooled his voice. "Kenny, I want to help. Whether you ever decide you love me-"

She flinched as though he'd struck her and his heart tumbled the rest of the way to the floor. Proving himself trustworthy would be a full-time project. How long before she realized he wasn't going anywhere? How much time was required to undo a lifetime's worth of damage?

"Let's take this one step at a time," he repeated. "I love you– and I want to help."

"Stop saying that!" Her expression worried, Ken's glance slid away. "I don't need you to say that. And I don't want your help."

"Well that's tough because I'm not going anywhere." He chilled his voice to match hers. "We can work together, or we can get in each other's way. But the end result will be my assistance."

Whether she liked it or not, he was speeding up the process. She would trust him, dammit. And soon. Harry wasn't about to let her go off in a huff. Not with her psycho step-brother on the loose. "So, think it through that damn stubborn head and let me know which way you prefer." A headache forming behind his eyes, he stalked to the patio door.

"Harrison. . . wait."

Her soft, husky voice stopped him in his tracks. The thread of fear was unmistakable in her tone. Hope flared briefly, making him hesitate, his fingers still on the handle. At least she wasn't completely immune to him. As the silence lengthened, Harry felt her tension coil around him. Heart pounding, he waited.

"I-I have to tell you. . . I have to thank you for something," she corrected.

He wanted to face her, but feared she would clam up if she knew he was watching. Instead, he released the handle, his back still to her. "I'm listening."

"I– we've met before. A l-long time ago. You helped me. . . and I never thanked you. I always wanted to. . . but I was too ashamed-"

His body rigid with tension, he trekked swiftly back over the years. When? When had he helped her? And why didn't he remember? Those eyes. . . he wouldn't have forgotten her.

"You. . . probably don't remember." Ken's voice was thick with unshed tears. "But I've never been able to forget."

"When did we-"

"It was cold that night," she interrupted, not seeming to hear him. "I didn't wear a coat. I wanted to show off my d-dress. But April nights are so unpredictable. . ." Her voice trailed off. "I didn't know it would rain."

An electric current jagged through his chest, leaving him swaying. Spinning around, Harry had crossed the deck before he was even aware of it. Dropping to his knees before her chair, he reached out, his hand tentative. And caught the tears sliding down her smooth cheek.

"You were the girl– the girl in the prom dress. I gave you a ride." The images from that cold, black night returned as vividly as though it had happened yesterday. "When I first saw you– I thought you were hurt."

Her smile was so sad it made him ache. "No. . . just pathetic. But you helped me that night. . . when no one else would. I was so humiliated. . . I almost wished you hadn't stopped." She released a ragged breath. Emotions waged a war across her face in a battle to regain control. "But you *did* help. . . and I never thanked you."

"You didn't need to."

"I'd been invited to the junior prom. *Me.*" She shook her head derisively. "I should've known it was a set-up. I should've r-realized he meant it as a joke."

Suddenly, Harry knew exactly what had happened. "He was an idiot, Ken. Teenage boys are cruel, selfish idiots." His hand fisted at his side, the knife in his stomach twisted tighter. He'd always wondered . . . The girl in the rain. Her hollow eyes. The empty resignation in her expression— had reminded him so much of himself. She had *looked* that night how he'd felt on the inside.

"I was so hopeful . . ." Ken stared out into the darkness, not seeing him. "That maybe I finally fit in. . . that— someone wanted me." Her knowing glance destroyed him. "I chose to overlook the obvious."

"You were sixteen."

"I should have known." She shook her head. "My father. . . was right. Damn him."

Hot, angry blood pumping through his heart chilled with warning as Harry sensed something awful approaching. "What did he say?"

Her eyes were lost in memory, but pain flared visibly in the golden depths. "That no one in his right mind would want me . . . I was the d-daughter of a whore— and everyone knew it."

"Kenny. . . I'm so sorry." His heart hammered relentlessly in a futile drumbeat. Her voice had gone cold and sterile, nearly unrecognizable. She began to shiver, her eyes bright with unshed tears and it took every ounce of control Harry had not to reach out and fold her against him. Instead, he relived the same helpless rage he'd experienced that cold, stormy night— when he'd been unable to lessen the hurt that had been inflicted upon her.

"Turns out he was right. My date never planned on taking me to the prom. I was just the entertainment. After he picked me up, we stopped for several of his friends . . . and h-his girlfriend. That's when they dumped me out on the side of the road."

"I wanted to hurt him." Tentatively, Harry reached out to stroke her face. When she didn't flinch, he released the breath he'd been holding. "I'd *still* like to hurt him . . . and your father, too."

Ken raised her hand to capture his. "Fifteen years later. . . I'm finally thanking you. Your kindness that night. . ." Her voice dropped to an anguished whisper. "Do you know how long it had been? Since anyone had worried about me? Wondered what happened to me? Only Jimmy cared whether I lived or died. You were the only person who stopped– the only one who cared whether I got home safely. And I was too embarrassed to t-thank you. But I never forgot."

"I never forgot you either." Harry swallowed around the lump in his throat. "I always wondered who you were. This'll probably sound weird . . . but I used to scan the crowds– every soccer game– I'd look for you." He shrugged, feeling faintly embarrassed. "I guess it became a habit."

The ghost of a smile twitched on her lips. "I looked for you, too. You had a State sticker in your window. I became a fan that night." She lowered her gaze. "I held on to that memory for so many years– whenever I was lonely . . . or scared . . . or ashamed. I'd think of you– rescuing me in the rain. And it carried me through another day."

Her confession humbled Harry, cleansing him. Unable to contemplate that his simple act of kindness could have meant so much to another person. It made him wonder what other actions he'd taken that had reverberated through someone's life. And the actions he could have taken . . . but hadn't. Weaving her fingers through his, he drew her close. Her lips were whisper soft, still tasting of the tears she'd shed when he brushed them with his.

"Harrison . . . please understand– when you tell me I'm beautiful . . . when you say-"

He tried not to wince over her hesitation to say the words he desperately wanted to hear. "I love you?"

She nodded slowly. "I *want* to believe you. Really– I do. But this voice in my head . . . tells me it can't possibly be true."

Instead of embracing his words, she deflected them. But discussing the issue, he realized– was a positive step. "So . . . what's it going to take to muzzle that troublemaker?"

She smiled, but the warmth didn't reach her eyes. "It's been with me for as long as I can remember."

Understanding finally dawned, as though someone had flipped the light switch in a very dark room. Before someone could hurt her, she moved out of the way. Instead of opening herself to possibilities, she ran in the opposite direction.

The only answer to a great defense was an even better offense. The only way Harry could hope to win would be an end-run around her. His actions would have to speak louder than his words.

"Did you ever think maybe we were fated to meet again?" A fleeting dimple winked in one satiny cheek and he was again blown away by her fragile beauty– and the gutsy determination that shimmered just below the beautiful surface.

"It crossed my mind," she admitted with a flicker of amusement. "But what's a Traynor doing talking about fate?"

The opportunity was too good to pass up. Scooping her up from the chair, he smiled over her startled yelp. Kissing her again, Harry savored the sweet, warm taste before his mouth drifted to her delicate collarbone. She allowed him access with a soft sigh of satisfaction. Together, they managed to push the patio door open before he staggered through it with Ken still locked in his arms. Leaning back against the door, he heard it click and nodded with satisfaction.

"You don't believe any of that stuff," she insisted, her whispered voice already ragged with desire. "You've got your blueprint, remember? Your plan."

His mouth sought the fluttering pulse in her graceful throat before trailing back up to capture her luscious mouth. His last coherent thought before he set her on the kitchen table was that impressing Kendall just might be the end of him. As she stripped him from his shirt, a satisfying tremor rippled through her when he whispered his answer in her ear.

"Because I'm the one you're waiting for." Tugging the robe from her shoulders, he pulled her satiny body against his. "I'm the . . . accountant of your dreams." Swallowing her gasp of laughter, he proceeded to remind her how perfect they would be together.

CHAPTER 12

Harrison Traynor *was* the man of her dreams. Kendall tried to push the thought aside. But like the man himself, he just kept coming back. She wanted so badly to believe him, had thought of little else over the next several days. It was too easy to see what life with him would be like. They laughed and talked. About important things and nothing at all. Each morning, he rose early to make breakfast before he would slip back into bed to awaken her properly-

"Do these terms sound like what you're looking for?" The discreet cough jarred her back to the present. Thoughts scattering to the wind, Ken forced her attention back to the banker seated across the mahogany desk.

"Those terms sound fine," she assured him, wondering what she'd missed.

"You're certain this is what you want to do, Miss Adams?"

"Very sure, Mr. Baxter." She signed her name with a flourish and shook his hand. As soon as she reached the door, she dragged in a breath of fresh, sweet air. How could anyone spend their days inside when it was as nice as today?

Her mind wandered back to Harrison on the ride home from the bank, thinking of the night ahead. Evenings were spent on the deck, stargazing and holding hands. Or in the garden where Harrison drank in another lesson about the different plants she had coaxed to life. Or she played music for him. At his suggestion, she'd begun writing it down. To her surprise, instead of inhibiting her musical ability, it only seemed to enhance it. Ken's head was swimming with lush arrangements that simply begged to be developed. She had no right to feel this happy. But that didn't stop the foolish grin she knew was etched on her face.

The buyout offer for A & R was still alive. With Harrison's advice, she'd countered the first offer. She'd begun envisioning a life beyond the business she'd spent the better part of her life worrying over. The future seemed bursting with possibility, thanks to Harrison. His confidence in her seemed to magically buoy her own.

Cracking the window in her truck, she inhaled deeply of the fresh scent of summer hay. All in all, it hadn't been such a bad week. Her life was humming along . . . the pieces falling slowly back into place.

And she was in love with Harrison Traynor. For fifteen years, she'd been in love with the memory of a boy. But it was the man he'd become who'd captured her heart. In a hundred different ways, he'd shown how much he loved her. Now that she'd summoned the courage to admit the truth to herself, she planned to enlighten Harry. He'd waited patiently– smiled when she knew he was hurt by her inability to trust him. Harrison wanted to hear her say the words.

Tonight, she would take the final step. Tonight, her heart would take a giant leap of faith into his steady hands. She would finally tell him how much she loved him.

Kendall should have been thrilled.

Instead, she was terrified. Experience had taught her that when life started running smoothly, disaster loomed just around the corner. But hope was a dangerous thing. Too often it had led to disappointment. But it was there, flaring in her chest. About a future with Harrison– that they would always be happy together. Hope she could pull a miracle out of her hat and finish the dig.

Her entire crew, including Claire– had agreed to stay on without pay until she received the fire settlement from A & R's insurance carrier. She hadn't been surprised by the men of her motley crew– they'd been with her for years. But Claire's loyalty left her with a warm feeling of pride. She'd only been an employee for a matter of months.

Despite their show of loyalty, Kendall refused to wait for the insurance settlement to do the right thing. Her crew deserved to be paid. . . handsomely. They'd been working like demons. Four more weeks and she'd be substantially complete. Under the terms of her contract, she'd meet her obligation to Specialty– and to Harry. An emergency loan from the bank would float her payroll for three of those weeks. The loan would buy her twenty-one days to reach an agreement with the insurance company. And it bought negotiating time with the party interested in buying A & R.

Swallowing nervously, she avoided thinking what this latest risk would cost if she failed. Then she'd gone ahead and signed the second mortgage on her beloved Victorian.

"Yo– Woody. . ." Harry waited for Gigantor to acknowledge his presence. He did with a wave and a friendly smile. It was hard to believe there was a soft-hearted human inside the imposing bulk of Woody Cutler. He'd entered into a wary truce of sorts with Jimmy– and by default– with Woody.

"What's up?" He swiped a grubby fist across an equally grubby forehead.

"I'm heading out. Kendall's probably already home."

Concern flared briefly in his eyes. "She's okay?"

"I'm sure she's fine, but with Lance MIA. . . I don't want her there alone. It's tough enough trying to keep the investigation from her. If I told her she was in danger, I'd probably have to tie her down to keep her away from Lance."

A knowing grin replaced Woody's worried frown. "I don't know why you're keepin' it from her. She'd probably love to take down that jerk."

Talking about Barker made his stomach knot. Harry didn't want him within a hundred miles of Kendall. But the thought of her with a scowl on her face and revenge in her heart caused a flicker of a smile to cross his lips. "She'd take him out before the police could get him." Under the circumstances, he wouldn't want to be in Barker's shoes. Hell, he didn't want to be in *his* shoes if she ever found out.

Woody nodded. "I'll tell Jimmy you're leavin'."

Knowing the operation held little hope of success without their cooperation, Charlie's team had briefed Kendall's crew leaders on the sting operation.

"See you tomorrow." Since moving in with Kendall, Harry drove out to the site each day to pitch in with A & R's crew, doing whatever he could to facilitate the project. Always a man with a plan, Harry figured that becoming a fixture at the site could only help– with the project, with the investigation and with Ken, who'd assumed he'd taken leave of his senses.

Jimmy hadn't been crazy about the idea either. But what had started as barely restrained hostility had morphed into mutual respect. He'd pushed back against Jimmy's initial dislike– slowly winning him over. The old man had been in full agreement on keeping Ken in the dark about the investigation.

Harry was making headway at home, too. Like a tightly budded flower, Kendall was slowly, painstakingly opening up to him. She was learning he could be trusted . . . that his actions equaled his words . . . that he could be relied on. All it required on his part was an infinite supply of patience and an endless calendar.

But with the sting underway, Harry felt like a juggler with too many balls in the air. It would be terribly easy to drop one. The knowledge that Charlie's team had already dropped the most critical ball– Lance's surveillance– gnawed at him. How could they have been so careless?

Barker had already been AWOL for two days. There'd been no contact about the deal to sell A & R. Charlie's team had been so damn certain Lance would take the bait, they hadn't considered other options. With a price on Barker's head, the team was running out of time, too. No one seemed to know what to do next.

He scowled in annoyance when his cell phone rang for the hundredth time. Nearly sunset, the jobsite was still in full swing. Jimmy had rallied the troops and the crews were making more progress than he'd dreamed possible. The sooner they wrapped up this dig. . . the sooner his new life with Kendall could start.

"Traynor." His pulse quickened when Lance's oily voice interrupted his thoughts. *Finally.* Relief poured through him. If he could just keep him on the line long enough, Charlie could trace the call and find out where Barker was hiding.

"Hang on a minute. . . all my stuff's in the car."

Relief turned swiftly to panic. "No– don't hang up. You're a hard man to reach these days. Have you come to any decision on my offer?" Crossing the site in angry strides, he jerked open his car door. Tossing his hardhat on the empty passenger seat, he waited for the sleazebag to ramble his way to making a point. "What do you mean. . . don't involve Kendall? How do you propose we do that? She's the majority-"

Lance's falsetto voice buzzed in his ear, his brain taking several seconds to process Barker's suggestion. It took another moment before the pencil he was gripping snapped between his fingers.

" Well, why– why don't you think it over." His knuckles whitened around the receiver. "Maybe we can work out an arrangement that will benefit both of us."

His heart still pumping like a locomotive, Harry disconnected the line. Before he could stop his hands from shaking long enough to punch in Charlie's number, the phone rang. "Yeah . . . did you get that? Where the hell is he?" Hot fury pumped through his veins, replacing the icy shock of panic. "How long does it take to trace the call?" He threw the jagged stub of pencil to the ground. Dammit, he was tired of waiting.

"The bastard wants to kill her– and you're telling me to stay calm?" he shouted before glancing around the parking area and lowering his voice. He flexed trembling fingers into a fist, wanting badly to hit something.

"Barker didn't suddenly think of this idea. He's been planning it." A bolt of clarity sizzled through him, rocking Harry to the core. "The fire. . ."

Never for a moment had he believed the fire to be accidental . . . but it hadn't crossed his mind that Barker wanted anything more than the insurance payout. His grip tightened around the phone as he flashed back to his own nightmarish plunge to the bottom of the construction pit . . . just as he'd clutched the loose railing. Had the loose railing been a deliberate attempt on Kendall? Or simply a warning to sell out before something worse happened?

His heart on overdrive, Harry had the distinct certainty that Charlie's team had miscalculated badly.

Kendall- His instincts screamed *move* and his limbs were eager to comply, already in motion as he dove into the car when he heard Charlie's muttered curse on the other end of the line.

"Dammit, where is he?" A heartbeat later, he squealed from the gravel lot, his blood icing with fear when Charlie finally confirmed his worst nightmare.

A ping from a cell tower– five hundred yards from Kendall's house.

Kendall jumped down from the truck, the loan papers still clutched in her hand. The driveway was empty. That meant Harrison was probably still out at the site. More amazing than getting used to his presence in her home, was the idea that he was helping out at the dig.

She shook her head as she stuck her key in the lock. Who would've thought a man like Traynor could win over a stubborn old goat like Pop? It was yet another puzzle piece that had fallen miraculously into place. For the first time in her life, the stars had aligned themselves behind her.

Just like the fire. Floyd had finally wrapped up his investigation. And while it didn't appear she was about to be sent to jail, it didn't appear likely Lance would be either. Essentially, Floyd had given up. . . finally listing the cause of the blaze as suspicious. While she was relieved not to end up behind bars by mistake, Floyd's non-committal ruling meant her insurance carrier had an excuse to delay paying her claim.

Her stepbrother had pulled his usual disappearing act. For two glorious days, he hadn't shown up at the site. Ken knew better than to believe it could last, but was grateful all the same for the break. Loving Harrison made her realize she didn't want to waste another moment of her life. She wanted to get the sale over with. The sooner they came to terms, the sooner Lance would be out of her life forever.

"Lurch? Here boy. . ." She whistled, waiting for the familiar hop-a-long footsteps to scramble through the house. Frowning, Ken took a step into the shadowed foyer. "That's funny-"

Her gaze wandering through the foyer to the kitchen, she gasped. Her brain snapped pictures while the rest of her went into shock. Broken shards of glass glittered like diamonds across her tiled floor. What remained of the shattered French door listed to one side, tilting drunkenly in the frame.

"Lurch!" Her heart hammering, Kendall passed swiftly through the kitchen, dropping her papers on the table before she ran to the door. Please God, let him be all right. Stepping carefully over the glass, she scanned the living room for signs of her dog. And where the hell was Wink? Jerking the broken door open, she ran out on the deck. Calling his name, she stumbled toward the darkening woods. She was a few steps into the trees when she heard the distinct sound of whimpering. Frozen in her tracks, she spun to the left, scanning the dusk-shrouded path. Where had the sound come from? She whistled again, waiting for a sign.

A soft, listless breeze ruffled her hair, breaking the eerie stillness. Her senses prickled, goosebumps raising on her arms. The forest felt unnaturally quiet, the swaying branches crackling with wild energy, reminding her of a looming summer storm.

"Lurch? Where are you?" The reverberation of another whimper and then three staccato barks had her body in motion toward the noise before it fell silent again. Someone or something was hurting him. She was nearly to the clearing when she tripped on a root and staggered to the ground. Her hands grasped fistfuls of moss, but her knee landed on a sharp-edged stone that scraped her skin raw.

"Dammit!" She'd walked these trails dozens of times, but always during the sun-drenched hours of daylight. Biting back a groan, she rose unsteadily to her feet in the rapidly fading light. Ken forgot about her scrape when she heard the unmistakable crack of a dry branch. When the hair on the back of her neck stood at attention, she knew with certainty she wasn't alone. Holding her breath, she waited for another sign of movement. Her blood iced over at the sharp painful yelp from Lurch, but it was the macabre sound of laughing that had her heart tripping in terror.

Sweet Lord, why hadn't she brought a weapon with her? Why hadn't she waited for Harrison? How could she save Lurch when she probably would have trouble saving herself?

Her brain registered a subtle movement to her left. Without questioning it, she swerved right. Her sharp cry of terror was cut off by the looming shadow that swooped over her. Pain lanced through her head as she absorbed the blow, her ears buzzing with the twisted sound of laughter. Darkness crept over her eyes and she sank to her knees, fighting the confusion that had taken over her brain. Sucked into a vortex of spinning color, she let the waves crash over her as the laughter blessedly faded away.

∽∝

Charlie and his partner had screeched up to the house in a pluming cloud of dust. Arriving from the opposite direction, Harry beat them by mere moments. The sound of sirens wailing in the distance told him their backup was minutes away. His heart lodged squarely in his throat, Harry launched out of the car. The three men didn't speak as they took the porch steps two at a time. Kendall's front door was wide open.

"Bill– you take the back. Harry– you know I'm not supposed to let you in here. . . so stay way the hell back and do exactly as I tell you." Charlie barked the order without even glancing his way.

Nodding, Harry would've agreed to anything. "Kendall-"

"We'll find her."

Charlie's terse remark held more anger than confidence, but Harry couldn't contemplate the alternative. He fell into step behind his cousin's bulky frame as Charlie crept into the foyer, gun drawn, his eyes scanning the room.

"Don't touch anything," he reminded.

The shattered patio door had icy shards of panic pumping through him. Chunks of wood lay on the deck where someone– Lance– had violently attacked the frame with a crowbar. Harry's mind quickly filled in the blanks with brutal images that threatened to paralyze him. Had he surprised Kenny in the house? She would have been terrified. But she wouldn't have been caught off guard. Lurch would have warned her. Where was he? His gaze flew to the telephone. She would have called for help. He crossed the room to check the dial tone but remembered as his hand reached for the receiver that it might hold fingerprints.

He was vaguely aware of Charlie moving upstairs, searching the rest of the house when he heard Bill on the deck. Like an automaton, he stepped through the twisted remnants of the swaying French door and met him there. "Anything?"

"Nope. Phone lines are cut." He surveyed the damaged patio door dispassionately. "Looks like he didn't mess around. Just cut the lines and bashed in the door."

"But the bastard took the time to call us." Charlie stuck his head through the shattered door. He was stepping through the door, glass crunching under his feet when Harry felt a jolt of recognition. His pulse skyrocketing, he jerked his head up and raised his hand for silence.

"I heard a dog bark."

"Can't hear much of anything with all those sirens." Charlie glanced at his partner. "Go around front and tell them to cut the noise. Then meet us back here." His glance shifted to Harrison. "What'd you hear?"

He turned to face the woods, his heart pumping with certainty. "There– I heard Ken's dog. . . in the woods."

Without speaking, the two men vaulted over the side of the deck. Charlie called back over his shoulder to his partner. "Bill-"

"We'll be right behind you."

Harry's instinct told him to run . . . to shout her name. . . to crash through the forest leaving no stone unturned. But his brain spoke of caution. He glanced down at the spot where Charlie's fingers bit angrily into his forearm, warning him of the need for silence. Together they crept through the gloom, inching painstakingly along the path. Minutes passed. Without turning back to confirm his hunch, he sensed Bill had rejoined them, along with a handful of officers who quickly dispersed, fanning out through the woods. Harry experienced a moment of overwhelming relief.

It would end well. It had to.

That illusion ended a nano-second later with Kendall's bloodcurdling scream.

⬲

"Kenny!" Harry's hands shook badly as they ran over her prone form. He'd nearly tripped over her in the darkened glen. Charlie dove to the ground, quickly checking for a pulse. Finding a strong, healthy beat, he left her in Harry's care before sprinting off in the dark in hot pursuit of Lance. Further down the trail, one of the team retrieved Lurch. He'd been tied to a tree, and though he appeared stunned, he yipped eagerly, staggering to Kendall's side the moment he was untied.

"Honey, can you hear me?" She groaned in response, her muttered words incoherent to a brain frozen with relief. Harry clutched her hand to his lips and fought to swallow the fear descending over him. He should be grateful. They'd found her . . . and she would be alright. The medic working on her suspected Kendall had been blasted with a stun gun.

Instead of relief, the what-ifs reached out to strangle him. Mental images of his father flashed before his eyes . . . hovering over his mother's bed. At the end, Buchanan wouldn't leave Sarah's side. At forty-seven, the endless years of drinking finally caught up with his mother's slight, malnourished frame. At the time, Harrison had believed his father pathetic. To have wasted his life over a woman who loved alcohol more than him.

Now, Harry couldn't be certain. He was in love with Kendall . . . a woman who might never love him in return. Had his father been in the same boat? Without question, Sarah Traynor had owned his father's heart. Perhaps it had been strength that kept his father by her side. Or honor . . . of the vows they'd spoken decades earlier, before his wife was ravaged by her disease. Or love. Bucky had loved her desperately. And when she died, the part that made his father whole had died right along with her.

The truth punched him in the face as he watched the medic hover over Kendall's prone body. Gripping her fingers like a lifeline, Harry knew with blinding certainty he would die to protect her. He would kill Lance Barker before giving him another chance to hurt her.

"Harrison?"

"I'm here, love. You're safe."

Her brows scrunched in confusion. "My door-"

"We'll fix your door, sweet." Harry found his first smile. She must be alright if she was worried about repairs.

"Lurch?" She tried to raise her head and he gently eased her back to the damp ground.

"He's right here."

"Someone was here. I-I heard laughing-"

The tidal wave of fury awakened deep in his chest and began churning with a violence that threatened to obliterate anything in its wake. Unleashed, it would crest over him and he would drown in the crashing swell. Harnessed, the energy would work to his advantage. Expelling a deep breath, he forced the darkness back.

"He won't hurt you again." He'd make damn sure of it.

⚮

Late the next day, Kendall could only smile over Harry's doting. It was either that, or tear her hair out. His constant hovering would drive her insane. She'd been in bed since arriving home the previous night, despite the fact that she now felt well enough to maneuver around. She didn't know which troubled her more– the vague memory flashes of a shadowy presence in the woods behind her home or the ferocity Harrison displayed every time she attempted to climb out of bed.

The ER doctor had explained that her bruises would heal in a few days and the pervasive soreness she felt would lessen overnight. That diagnosis hadn't worked for Traynor. After five minutes of intense questioning, the poor doctor had been eager to make his escape.

Leaning back against the pillows, she sighed luxuriously. The over-protective thing had benefits. She'd never experienced the delight of being pampered by someone. With a little practice, she could probably get used to it. A distinctive sound on the stairs forced her thoughts back to the present. Reluctantly, she lifted her head.

"Lord, here they come again."

Traynor's casted foot clunked up every step. Then the dishes on the dinner tray rattled precariously. This was followed by a volley of muttered swearing. Lurch finished the series with an odd three-legged thump as he tagged along behind Harry, no doubt getting underfoot. Together, they sounded like something out of a horror movie. Any minute now, she expected Lurch to trip Harrison, the tray to go flying and Traynor to cartwheel back down to the foyer.

When his head appeared around the doorframe she released a sigh of relief. "Harrison . . . you just fed me an hour ago. I can't eat all that."

"But you barely ate. The doctor said you should get lots of fluids." He set the tray down with a decisive thump. "I brought you lemonade this time. And tea. And water."

"This isn't the flu, Traynor. I got zapped by a stun gun."

His no-nonsense eyes flashed a warning. "You'll drink something."

Her gaze ran over the laden tray. "Then you'll finally have to let me up." At his quizzical expression, she smiled. Sometimes he was completely clueless. "To go to the bathroom?"

"The doctor said to keep you in bed."

"He said that out of desperation. You had him cornered."

"You weren't well enough to ask questions, so I asked for you." Harry shrugged as though his over-reaction to minor injuries was completely normal.

"When that Code Blue was announced, I swear he looked relieved," she countered. "He would have used any excuse to get away from us."

Harrison sat gingerly on the end of the bed, frowning when she shifted her feet to allow him more room. "Honey, try not to move around too much."

"Harry– I'm fine." Clearly, she would have to be more firm with him. "Try to understand– I appreciate all the attention. It's just that. . . I'm fine!"

"I know," he conceded, his beautiful face marred by a frown. "I just can't erase that picture of you lying in the woods . . . unconscious. I thought-" He released a gusting breath. "It scared the hell out of me, okay?"

Her heart contracted as the pain in Harry's voice hit her square in the chest. Frozen with shock, she nodded, the teasing remark she'd been on the verge of tossing lodged squarely in her throat. He absently stroked her calf under the blanket and Kendall had all she could do not to sigh over the sheer wonder of it. He was kind. And caring. And so damn dependable it made her want to weep with joy.

Harrison– loved her. If she'd had any doubt, it was written all over his face. He'd shown her his love in a hundred different ways. Like a puzzle piece finally fitting into place, Ken finally understood what he'd somehow known all along. She was worthy of his love– and he was so incredibly worthy of hers.

Her heart pounding, she reached down to clasp his hand. "Harry . . . I'm sorry I scared you. But I think you know by now that I'm tough. I won't break."

He smiled at her description. "I know you can do whatever you set your mind to. And I know you can take care of yourself. You certainly don't need me, but just this once-"

"I need you," she blurted.

"I want you to rest-" Harry's lecture stopped mid-sentence. "What did you say?"

Ken knew she would never forget the flare of emotion she read in his eyes, the anticipation– that she was finally ready to receive all the love he had to give. "I love you, Harrison. I've loved you for such a long time."

"Kenny– are you–" He closed his eyes for a second. "You'd better be damn sure, Adams. Because you can't back out," he warned. His lopsided grin told her he knew, but his hands still trembled when he tugged her into his arms. "Did I hear you right?"

"I think you heard me fine, Traynor." The last was whispered against his lips when he quickly moved to cement the deal. Several minutes passed before he reluctantly released her to draw in a gasp of much needed oxygen. Somehow they'd toppled back against the headboard. Their heads sharing one pillow, she stared into his beautiful eyes and smiled.

"It's too bad you're so concerned with doctor's orders because I can think of several more interesting things we could be doing right now."

He smiled– the slow, sweet grin that made her insides melt like wax. "He ordered bed rest, love. Lots of bed rest. Weren't you listening?"

⬳⬲

Kendall was soundly asleep upstairs. Though he knew he could talk freely, Harry still took the precaution of walking outside with his phone. Unable to reach Charlie since the previous evening, he wanted to talk some sense into his cousin. After last night's close call, he couldn't risk another. Lance was dangerously unstable. Kenny wasn't getting within ten feet of him again.

"We have to tell her."

"She could blow the whole operation," Charlie fired back. "Wasting six months of effort."

"He practically called from her house, for God's sake."

"So– he's taking chances. That's what we wanted–"

"Not with Kendall's life," he interrupted.

For the sting to work, Charlie was adamant she couldn't know she was in danger. Lance's greed was an opportunity to trap him– with her as bait. Harry shook his head. "It's too risky. When I agreed to help I didn't know he–"

"She's been in danger since the beginning." The cop in Charlie voiced his objections over the ruination of a perfectly viable plan.

"What if this were Andrea we were discussing?"

"Then I'd be sweating this op as much as you. But even if she knew the reasons why, she'd still be in danger."

They debated for several useless minutes. Charlie's argument had merit. It was better to know what they were up against. Kendall would be safer now that they knew Barker's true intentions– frightening though they might be.

Harry couldn't shake the gnawing fear that something was about to go terribly wrong. "If he so much as touches her-" Swallowing around a knot of dread, he acknowledged the very real possibility. "There won't be a trial. There won't be any jail . . . because I'll kill him."

Seated at the table, Kendall sniffed appreciatively, watching Harry try not to burn the grilled cheese sandwiches.

"Was it my imagination or did I see one of your relatives here yesterday during all the excitement?"

"You mean Charlie?" His hand hesitated on the spatula.

"Yeah, Andrea's husband, right?" She remembered him from Jake's party.

"Uh-huh."

Fascinated, she watched Harry maneuver at the stove, the reflexive slide of sinewy muscle under firm skin, his strong capable hands equally at home finessing her dinner onto a plate as they had been stroking her body only an hour before. The sweet, dizzy knowledge that he was truly hers made her stomach flip-flop with newfound happiness.

"So, what was he doing here? Is he a cop?"

Harry shifted the sandwich from the griddle to her plate in one deft movement. "State police," he corrected. "He's an investigator."

"And he works out here? In my district?"

"I guess so." He pulled open the refrigerator door. "Orange juice okay for you?"

"Whatever you're having." She waved absently. "That's pretty amazing."

"What?"

"Your cousin. What are the odds he would respond to a call at my house? When I only just met him a couple weeks ago." Ken waited for him to set the plates down before continuing. "You must have been surprised to see him. Did you know Charlie worked out here?"

"I- uh– I don't know. I mean. . . It's never come up in conversation before." Traynor flashed her a distracted look, as though she'd interrupted him in the middle of balancing his checkbook. "Damn. . . I forgot the forks."

"It's okay. The salad will keep until tomorrow. I'm not very hungry." Ignoring her, Harrison returned to the silverware drawer, rummaging for salad forks.

"Babe, dig in or it'll get cold," he admonished.

"I was just waiting for you, Sugar," she teased, testing the word of endearment. She liked the way it sounded, liked the flash of surprise that lit his eyes even more.

"Sugar? I could get used to that." He nodded. "How about Stud?"

"Stud . . . hmmm, not bad," she agreed. "With those stitches you look like a pirate. Maybe toss in an eye patch? I think you'd look hot with an eye patch."

Harry nudged the fridge door shut, his shoulders shaking with laughter. "An eye patch? That would turn you on?"

Blushing furiously, Kendall shrugged. "It's the whole package. All those muscles . . . the stitches. And yeah, maybe an eye patch." She smirked. "Would you prefer a parrot on your shoulder?"

He winced. "Eye patch it is."

"How did Charlie know I was in trouble last night? Did you call him? I'm still fuzzy on the details. I remember going outside to find Lurch."

His easy smile disappeared. "What else do you remember?"

"I heard Lurch barking . . . and then . . . this weird laughter."

"Honey– why did you go? When you saw that door shattered?" He shook his head in disbelief. "And then . . . you went into the woods alone."

She noticed the edge to his voice and frowned. "Harrison, I've been in those woods a hundred times. I wasn't lost in a forest somewhere. I was behind my house."

"You should've waited. I was on my way home-"

"I didn't think," she admitted. "Lurch was gone. That's all I thought about."

"Kenny– do you realize what could have happened?"

The warm glow that had settled over her began to dissipate under his implacable stare. She'd made a mistake. They both knew it. Why was he overreacting? "Can't we forget about it?"

"No, we can't," he insisted. "What if you-" He shuddered. "The bastard who did this. . ." Harry motioned to the boarded up French door. "He's still out there somewhere. What if he comes back?"

Restless, Ken slid her plate back, appetite gone. *He loves you,* she reminded herself. That's why he was angry. And overprotective. But it almost seemed as though he blamed her for getting attacked. His accusation sounded dangerously similar to her father's complaints. How could she be at fault for something beyond her control? Swallowing her trepidation, she forced a semblance of calm. The last thing she wanted was an argument.

"He won't come back, Traynor. It was a fluke. Break-ins don't happen out here. Maybe once every ten years." Something in his eyes seemed to shutter and Ken nearly shivered at the bleakness she found there. As though an invisible wall had erected between them.

"What if it was Barker? Do you think he'll stay away?"

Releasing a sigh, the throb of unease subsided a bit. *That's* what he was worrying about? "Lance? Gosh, you had me nervous– I thought something was really wrong."

"Why don't you take him seriously, Ken? After all he's done . . . why do you have such a blind spot toward him?"

Standing beyond her reach, she stretched to touch his arm and felt the muscle jerk against her fingers. "Because he's getting everything he wants. I'm selling the company. When the deal goes through, he'll get his cut," she explained. "He doesn't deserve it. . . but I don't care anymore. I'm tired of fighting. I'm tired of carrying the weight of the world on my shoulders." Her heart brimming, she raised her gaze to his. "I finally realize that selling doesn't mean failure. I have *you* to thank for that."

"Don't-" He winced. "I don't deserve it."

"You made me realize I have options. With the deal you struck for me, I'll have the freedom to explore something else. And you made sure I'll be able to take care of my employees. With the money from the sale, I'll be able to pay off all the suppliers and my crew."

Glancing up, Kendall smiled, embarrassed. But he'd helped her immeasurably– with no strings attached. Harrison helped people because he was able, not because he expected something in return. Even though the deal would help Specialty finish the project on time, he'd negotiated as though A & R belonged to him.

"I never would have haggled like you did. Because of you, my crew will have severance– enough to get back on their feet." Tears welling in her throat, she resolutely pushed them back. "For so long, I've had to do everything . . ."

He didn't appear to be softening. "I didn't do anything you couldn't have done on your own."

He was wrong. "I would have been too emotional." She shook her head. "For months, I've been devastated about giving up A & R– before you ever arrived," she reminded. "This company has been in my family for thirty years. As much as I've loved it . . . it's also been a noose around my neck."

No longer able to fight the tears, they spilled down her cheeks. "I don't want to waste any more time. The sooner I pay off Lance . . . the sooner he leaves." Her heart full after so many years of emptiness, Ken didn't know how to explain what she was feeling. "I want to get on with life. *Our* life."

"Even though, he's likely the one who stole from you? Even though he's practically forced you into bankruptcy?" Arms crossed defensively over his chest, the salad forks were still clenched in Harry's hand.

Her heart skipped several beats as she absorbed his belligerent tone. The silence lengthened as he stared at her, his expression one of frustrated disbelief. "When you say it that way, I sound stupid." Her face heated with anger. She'd just laid her heart on the table for him. She'd never confided in anyone before . . . had never trusted anyone enough to open up the way she had with Harrison. "What's your point?"

"That he's dangerous, Kenny." His eyes sparked with anger. "He nearly killed us both in that fire. I don't like that he's out there . . . somewhere."

"Somehow it's my fault Floyd didn't arrest him?"

Tossing the forks on the table, he stalked to the window, shocking her. His back rigid, she watched his reflection in the glass as he stared broodingly out into the night. Her heart pounding, she rose from the table.

"What is this really about, Harrison? Have I done something–already . . . to upset you?" She waited, the warm flame that only an hour earlier had burned happily in her chest, now sputtered in the sudden chill. *Had he already changed his mind?* Was he having second thoughts?

Dragging in a deep breath, she summoned the courage to endure the next few minutes. Praying for calm, she schooled her features blank, a defense mechanism she'd perfected the hard way at thirteen. If bullies didn't see their words upset you, they couldn't win. It had worked like a charm on the unmerciful kids at school–and her belligerent father. When he failed to get a rise, Ken, Sr. had quickly bored with tormenting her.

"Do you know something you're not telling me?"

CHAPTER 13

It was an eternity before he spoke. During his silence, Kendall's stomach clutched with dread. Life after her mother left town had been time spent in a perpetual state of limbo— never knowing what action on her part would set her father off— only certain something surely would. One day she was too noisy, clattering in the kitchen. The next . . . she was skulking around— trying to spy on him. Over the years, she'd finally given up trying to please the man who seemed to resent the very air she breathed.

"No . . . of course not," he finally answered, his voice still tinged with anger. "I hate knowing that bastard is getting away. Lance ruins your life . . . and he'll end up walking away with more money."

"If he hadn't ruined my life, I probably wouldn't have met you, right?" Ken forced a smile into her voice, one that didn't match the fingers of doubt beginning to claw her chest. Why was he so angry with her?

"Yeah. I'm a real prize." He shook his head derisively.

His tone sent a shiver down her spine. "Harrison? Tell me what's wrong because you're scaring me." She was glimpsing a side of him she'd never known existed. A side that made her wonder. And doubt. *Had she made a colossal mistake?* Had she traded her peaceful, settled existence for a new life that would mimic the misery she'd spent fifteen years trying to erase? A wave of raw terror swept over her. After all these years. . . after being alone for so long. . . had she given her heart to a man who would never be happy with her?

"I couldn't even protect you."

Relief flooded her, leaving her wobbly in its wake. Crossing the room, she wrapped her arms around him, desperate for the reassurance of his warmth. Resting her head against his back, she closed her eyes, still too upset to admit how frightened she'd been. For several minutes, he'd become a stranger . . . furious with her for reasons she didn't understand. She was again reminded of her father.

She'd learned to placate his anger . . . to swallow the inevitable disappointment when she'd failed his expectations. What she'd never learned to master was the overwhelming sense of dread– *waiting* for his criticism. Kendall had wanted reasons. How could she ever improve if she didn't know what she was doing wrong? Instead, her father hoarded them . . . doling out illogical rationalizations with a stinginess that succeeded in making her more anxious.

Harry isn't Dad. She'd never known a more compassionate and thoughtful man. Releasing a ragged breath, she willed herself to stay in control. "Please, let's not argue, okay? I made a mistake. I've been alone so long . . ." She'd never had someone care what happened to her. "I'll be more careful from now on."

"If anything ever happened to you. . ." Turning from the window, he slipped his arms around her. She went willingly, grateful the strange, tension-filled moment had passed. Still clutching her to him, his lips brushed her forehead before he rested his cheek against the top of her head. For a long time, they stood together in the darkened window, neither willing to break the strange spell.

∞

Harry tightened his hold, wanting to absorb her into his skin. Wanting to place her in a protective bubble until this was over. For the first time– maybe ever . . . he was vulnerable– in a way he'd never imagined possible. This was not how love was supposed to feel. It was supposed to feel great. Instead– he felt weak. Exposed. Defenseless. And most of it– was his fault. For not telling Ken what she had every right to know.

Dammit, he should have told her. She'd opened the door to the truth . . . and he'd ignored it– his cousin's strident voice echoing in his head. *Liar.* His gut knotting with his deception, he would've felt a thousand times better if Ken knew what they faced.

Screw Charlie. Screw the investigation. His skin had crawled as he'd endured her praise. Thanking *him* for helping with her problems. The shards clawing his stomach grew sharper. If Ken knew what he'd really done, he'd be dodging her fists right now.

The irony wasn't lost on him. She'd finally opened up– in a way he'd only dreamed possible. She trusted him. With her heart. With her business. With her very life. And he repaid that faith by lying to her– about everything. About everything he knew to be important to her. And the betrayal was killing him. The kicker was– he sucked at it. Kendall already sensed something was wrong. She could feel the change in him. She just didn't know the source . . . didn't know he was being eaten alive with guilt.

He couldn't even reassure her– that it wasn't about him not loving her. He'd witnessed the fear in her eyes. Her love for him was so new . . . so fragile. Ken's instinct would tell her he'd changed his mind . . . or worse– that maybe he really was a jerk who'd break her heart and leave. And Harry couldn't deny any of it because it would require an explanation. Reasons were the *last* thing he could provide. Dammit, he couldn't even relieve her of the notion that she was imagining the change in him.

You should have told her. Still snuggled against his chest– the opportunity had clearly passed. "Babe . . . you haven't eaten all day. Let's see if those sandwiches are still edible."

Reluctantly he released her, giving her a little nudge toward the table and forcing a smile for her curious eyes. Jesus– he had to do a better job than this.

"I'm sure they're fine." She gave his arm a squeeze. "Let's sit down and eat."

They were seated on the deck, fingers linked, eyes lifted to the heavens, admiring the sweep of stars on the cool, clear night. Lurch flopped contentedly on the deck between their feet. Earlier in the day, Harrison had swept the debris and broken glass away. But just to be safe, he'd watched Kendall slip on a pair of sandals before agreeing to take her around back after dinner. She'd played the violin for him, captivating him with a lyrical, hopeful piece she'd been working on– one she'd actually written down. The realization that she'd taken his suggestion to heart made him smile.

Harry had regained his footing on the slippery slope of his life. Okay, so he couldn't tell Kendall what was happening with the investigation. That didn't mean he couldn't shore up her confidence in him. It didn't mean he wasn't free to use every opportunity to remind her how much he loved her. Which in turn, he hoped, would reassure her that her feelings were accurate . . . that *she* hadn't made a mistake.

In turn, he had to trust Charlie. He had to have faith they would catch Barker. Kendall would be safe. The investigation would end– and all would be right with their world. Smiling in the dark, he brought her fingers to his lips.

"You've still never explained– how did Charlie know to come here? Did you get here first and call him?"

To his credit, Harry didn't startle as the lies surrounded him– closing in. "Yeah. I got here . . . saw the mess . . . and I called him." Cautiously, he repeated her words back. If he didn't embellish much, maybe he'd avoid trouble. "He was the first person I thought of."

"Then what happened?"

He sighed, not wanting to be on guard tonight. "We searched the house then went outside. I heard Lurch bark. . ." Harry paused when the dog raised his head, his eyes questioning. Reaching down, he scratched behind his ears.

"And?"

". . . we headed into the woods. We– I– found you in the clearing. You were unconscious," he recited carefully, aware of his pulse beginning to hammer in his ears. He would never erase the picture of her lying there. "I thought. . . "

"I remember you there."

"We got you out pretty quick." Once he'd started breathing again. "Took you to the hospital."

"So, what happens now?"

"Charlie's leading the investigation." Finally. Something he didn't have to lie about. "I've offered to help."

"Help?" Kendall focused those all-knowing eyes on him and he held his breath. "What can you do to help a police investigation?"

Christ, if she only knew. "Keep an eye on you for one thing. Make sure whoever did this doesn't get the opportunity again."

"Honey, it's not going to happen again. It was a-"

"Fluke. Yeah, I know. You're probably right. But I'm not taking any chances. Not with you."

Ken smiled then, a sweet, sunny smile that hit him squarely in the chest. The burst of warmth radiated outward to his limbs before the liquid heat traveled along his nerves, settling the tension that had begun to take root. When she finally returned her gaze to the stars, he released the breath he'd been holding.

Harry began to relax, lulled by the tranquility of a lush summer night, entranced by the beautiful woman at his side. He'd never felt so connected to anyone– had never known he could experience such an intrinsic satisfaction simply by being with another person. If this—completeness . . . was what Buchanan had experienced with his mother– then he finally understood why his father had stayed through the horrible years of alcoholism. With a certainty that neither shocked nor surprised him– he knew he would do anything for Kendall. No matter what the fates held in store for them over the next several decades . . . he couldn't wait to get started on the life they would build together.

"What's happening with the acquisition? Is the deal finalized?"

"It's close." Reluctantly, he shook off the moonlight-induced lethargy and returned to reality. Back to treading on conversational landmines.

"Do we have a date for the transfer yet?"

"Not yet. Shouldn't be more than a couple weeks." Not that she would be needing it, anyway. By then, Barker would be caught. By then, the insurance carrier would pay her fire claim and the dig for Specialty would be substantially complete. She'd be back on solid financial ground. Even better– he'd discovered while sifting through her computer records that Lance had been bonded by A & R's insurance carrier. Her insurance agent deserved a bonus for keeping such close tabs on his clients. That meant Kendall could make a separate insurance claim for all the money he'd stolen from A & R.

"That's good." She exhaled a noisy sigh. "I went to the bank yesterday and took out a second mortgage on this place."

He froze, his grip tightening. "You– what?"

"I can't let the crew work without getting paid, Harry. The second mortgage gives me cash to make payroll for the next several weeks . . . just until the insurance check comes or the deal goes through."

"Kenny– why didn't you . . . say something? What if something goes wrong?"

"Then I would've lost this place eventually. If I go bankrupt, I won't be able to afford the payments." She sat up straighter in the deck chair. "You know how it is with insurance companies . . . they could jerk me around forever before they finally pay that fire claim."

"Babe . . . we're so close. As soon as you and Lance agree to the terms . . . the deal's good to go."

"Well, why haven't I seen the papers? Hell, I'll sign them right now."

Because Charlie held the reins. Because the damn sting operation was taking too long. Exasperated, Harry tried to stem his temper. He should have known she would take matters into her own hands so no one else got hurt.

Another problem to worry about. If things didn't go according to plan, Ken could lose the home she loved. "Deborah will have the papers ready in another day or so."

"Deborah?" He felt her stiffen beside him. Dammit. Would he ever learn to think before speaking? He'd never been good at synthesizing his thoughts. Trying to withhold information from Kendall felt like lying. And lying made him act defensively.

And Kenny picked up on the vibes like a tuning fork.

"What does Deborah have to do with this? You said the offer was from an outside party."

Lying caused him to make mistakes. "Babe, someone has to handle the paperwork. Deb's firm is already on retainer to Specialty. It seemed like the logical choice."

He was painfully conscious of every sound . . . every breath Kendall drew in the lengthening silence. Her fingers lay still in his hand, but he was too afraid to squeeze them for fear she'd read something sinister in the action.

"All right. It seems a little weird." She finally broke the tension. "I mean . . . you and she- I just wondered . . . that's all." She turned to face him. "But you have to understand why I couldn't let Jimmy and Woody and the crews work for free. Even though they offered,

I can't take advantage of their loyalty. Please don't ask me to do that."

Her strength of character humbled him. Harry couldn't decide which hurt worse . . . the guilt lancing his chest or the pride swelling it. "You're right, love. I'm sorry. I would never want you to trade on their friendship."

"Don't worry about the mortgage. As soon as the money comes in, I'll pay it off, first thing." She raised startled eyes to his when he leaned over to brush her lips. Harry kept it light, careful not to pour the relief flooding him into the kiss. Her faith in him was as steady as her love. He'd known if he were lucky enough to win her, the amazing gift of her love would be given freely. The full force of her loyalty would be thrown behind him, no holds barred. Because once she put her mind to it, Kendall didn't do anything halfway.

He vowed to talk with Charlie again in the morning. There had to be a way to accelerate his investigation because he couldn't last much longer. He wanted his freedom back– to be as honest and trustworthy with Kendall as she was with him.

⸺∾⸺

"What do you mean . . . speed it up? Maybe we could just tell Barker to take another whack at Kendall so we can catch him in the act."

"Seriously– you'd say that to me?" Harry resisted the urge to rip his cousin's head off. He didn't want to imagine Ken getting hurt, never mind joke about it. "Charlie . . . shut up and listen."

He set his coffee cup down with a clang. "What?"

"What if Barker thought he'd won?"

"What d'ya mean?"

"What if he thought Kendall was out of the picture?"

"Like dead?" The cop shook his head impatiently. "We shoulda thought of that yesterday before she left the hospital."

Harry suppressed a shiver of dread. "No– not dead. Stop talking like that. I'm thinking about the fire." Kenny's words replayed in his head. Words that had given him the seed of an idea. *"How can Floyd arrest me? I've got you for an alibi, remember?"*

What would've happened if he hadn't confirmed her story? It would have been Kendall's word against Barker's. He suspected it wouldn't have taken much to convince Floyd of Kendall's obvious motive– her business was in trouble. Everyone knew it. He lifted his gaze to Charlie, the wheels already turning.

"What if the fire marshal had reason to believe she started the fire? If Ken was arrested, it would sure as hell seem real to Barker. And it would keep her out of reach until we catch the bastard."

"Jeez. . . I don't know. She'd be pretty ticked off."

"But she'd be safe," Harry countered.

Charlie's forehead creased in thought. "Barker might buy it. You could play it like you wanted A & R for yourself– real cheap. Might make him think you were on his side."

Harry's betrayal would telegraph a clear signal to Barker he was willing to negotiate. His heart began to race at the possibility. She'd be safely tucked away until the whole thing was over. He wouldn't have to worry about her protection.

"You want me to lock up your girlfriend? In a real jail?"

He shook his head in disgust. "You must have somewhere you can park her that would be comfortable?"

Charlie's expression of disbelief slowly faded. In its place, a slow grin settled over his features. "Man, I wouldn't wanna be you when this is over. She'll beat the hell out of you."

"*If* she ever found out. On the other hand," Harry argued, "if she knew all the facts, she might have agreed to protection in the first place." But that wouldn't happen because Kendall didn't realize the danger she was in. Judging by her reaction last night, she wouldn't have believed it anyway.

Locking up Ken would be a definite setback to their relationship. The fragile trust he'd worked so hard to build would come crashing down if she discovered his role in the plan. But she loved him. Saying the words had made it official. Her words meant everything, because Kendall hadn't made the admission lightly. He could only pray she wouldn't want to take them back.

They mulled over the plan for several minutes, mentally throwing darts to find the weak spots. No matter how he played it, Ken would be seriously ticked at him. But the trade-off was her safety. No one could hurt her in a jail cell. Anger he could handle. Anger could be soothed and stroked away. It was the sting of betrayal that had him second-guessing. She would be devastated. It was the part Harry couldn't bear to think about. Her heart had been trampled on enough to last a lifetime.

"Maybe we should scrap this idea."

"Nah. . . let's do it." His cousin made the decision for him. "I'll get the paperwork going."

"Can you do that? Arrange a fake arrest?"

Charlie snorted in disbelief. "You really are clueless."

"You'd have to make it look believable . . . maybe at the job site?"

"Believe me. . . Barker will buy it. Hell– everyone on that site will buy it." He scratched his head. "From what I've seen, she doesn't strike me as the type of woman who'll go quietly."

Harry winced. She'd be kicking and screaming. "Make sure you warn the arresting officer."

"Warn him?" His eyes grew wary. "She's not registered for a firearm. I already checked."

"No. . . worse. Those boots she wears are steel-toed."

Charlie winced. "She'll be aiming for his jewels."

"Forget the vest . . . your guy better wear a bullet-proof cup."

⸎

"Harrison . . . they've locked me up in jail!"

Holding the phone away from his ear, he nodded at Jimmy. The old man winced, scratching his salt and pepper crew cut when Kendall began shouting again. "Babe, tell me where you are. . . I'm on my way," Harry lied.

"You sure those boys know what they're doin', Traynor?" Jimmy squinted in the glare of the late day sun. "Kenny ain't the most forgiving soul I've ever met."

Releasing a deep breath, he nodded, praying everything would go like clockwork. "I hope so."

Blocking one ear as Woody fired up the end loader, he quickly dialed Deborah's office. He needed the fake transfer papers . . . today.

"Deborah Lawrence, please." Frowning when the line filled with static, Harry impatiently strode away, putting as much distance as possible between himself and the belching earthmovers.

"Deb? Can you hear me?" He winced over the spotty reception. "Kendall's at the courthouse. Do you have the papers ready?" Dammit, why did the line have to give him trouble now? "Deb? You there?"

"What do you mean 'her office just called'? Who called you?" Harry groped to find the meaning in her long-winded explanation. Another clear difference from Kendall, he realized. Deb had never been able to complete a thought in under a thousand words. Catching only every fifth word wasn't helping. He shook his head when he finally caught a full sentence.

"No— *I* need the papers— not Kendall. She's already at the courthouse-"

Despite the buzz of activity going on at the site, despite the heated conversations taking place over a set of blueprints more than fifty yards away, several heads raised to stare at him curiously when he shouted in frustration.

His cell phone had gone completely dead.

∾

Kendall's heart was still racing thirty minutes later. Traynor would move heaven and earth to get her out, she reminded herself. But, Good Lord— she was in jail!

An actual cell . . . and it wasn't like anything she'd ever imagined. Wiping her eyes on her sleeve, she glanced up to take a good look around. Come to think of it . . . the room didn't look anything like the jail cells on TV. It reminded her more of a cheap motel room . . . without windows. Except for the really, really small one on the far wall. Kendall scaled the wall with her eyes. The window was up near the ceiling. To see outside, she'd have to climb on the bed.

And that was another thing— she had a real bed. Shouldn't it be a cot? Rising to her feet, she rubbed her aching ribcage. And found her first smile. She might be sore, but Officer TightAss was likely hurting worse. It had taken two of them to wrestle her into the squad car. Her smile evaporated, replaced by a scowl. When she got out of this place, she was going to kill Floyd. How dare he have her locked up? Without any proof she'd started the fire. Without conducting a damn investigation? Hell— if it hadn't been happening to her, she would have laughed. The situation was like something out of a sitcom.

Only it was real. She took a few steps across the carpeted room. Kendall Adams was in a real jail cell— albeit a clean, carpeted cell. She stuck her head around the corner and flicked the light switch.

The grinding noise of the fan made her jump. A jail cell with a private bath and shower? What the hell-

Crossing the room in three steps, she climbed on the narrow bed and tried to peer out the tiny window. Below her a parking lot stretched across the remaining acre of land. Several cruisers were parked there. Her fingers still clutching the dusty window sill, she turned at the sound of a key scraping.

"How're ya doin'? Can I getcha anything?"

Still standing on the bed, she glared at the officer perched in the doorway. "Yeah. I want to call my lawyer."

"Can't do that, hon." Laughing, he shook his head. "How about something to eat?"

Hands on her hips, she stepped down from the bed. "I was never read my rights by the arresting officer."

He had the gall to chuckle. "I don't think Stanley was capable of speech after you got through with him."

"Who's Stanley?" Taking a step closer to the irritating cop, she was surprised when he retreated, hand on the doorknob, ready to slam it in her face.

"Officer Dillwyn– the one you kneed in the groin? A smirk creased his doughy face. "We were warned about you," he added disapprovingly.

"Who? That bastard Floyd?" Blood pressure spiking, heat swept over her. "You call that an investigation? Why the hell would I burn-"

" No sense gettin' all worked up," he interrupted. "You're gonna be here a while."

"I've never even had a damn speeding ticket before. I want to call my lawyer." It was ironic the first name popping into her head was Deborah– Harry's Deborah. But what was her last name? And where the hell was Harry for that matter? It felt like she'd been locked up for an eternity. Flicking a glance at her watch, she sighed. Only two hours had elapsed since she'd arrived.

The officer glanced over his shoulder before retreating, closing the door with a sharp click. Kendall moved to the door and pressed her ear against it. She tried the knob half-heartedly, knowing it was locked, but testing it anyway. Murmured voices drifted through the wooden door, and she strained to make out their words.

A minute later she jumped when the door jerked open without warning. "You-" He pointed a beefy finger in her direction. "Someone's here to see ya. I'm taking you down the hall." He eyed her dubiously. "Do I gotta cuff you . . . or will you go nice and lady-like?"

With all her heart, Ken wished she could remove his condescending smile. Instead, she folded her arms across her chest, forcing a casual stance. He outweighed her by an easy hundred pounds. It would be like taking on Woody the Redwood and expecting to win. "I don't know about ladylike . . . but I'll go quietly."

⁂

Curiosity won out over defiance as they traveled the tiled, windowless hallway. Kendall scanned the frosted glass in the doors they passed, searching for a clue to her whereabouts. There'd been a few human-sized shadows looming behind several of the doors. The distant sound of phones ringing . . . of keyboards clicking melded together with the faint scent of stale coffee. She must be at the police station.

But she hadn't been fingerprinted . . . hadn't been checked in. Again– she had nothing but cop shows to compare her experience to. And this was nothing like television. She'd been hustled into the building through a back entrance and taken straight to the motel/jail room she'd just left.

"Here's where we part ways." The officer stopped before another frosted glass door. Fingering his key ring, he found the one he was searching for and unlocked it. "After you."

She passed him silently, entering a sparsely furnished conference room, again with no windows to the outside world. How could anyone work in a place like this? Looking completely out of her element, a well-dressed woman was seated at the scarred oak table. Even Kendall, whose fashion sense started and ended with jeans, estimated the woman's suit cost more than her entire wardrobe.

Her heart began tripping once again. Dear God. What had she gotten herself into this time? Warily, she approached the beautiful woman, conscious of her flawless manicure tapping the scuffed wood under her fingertips.

"Kendall Adams?" She rose to her feet, the charcoal suit moving effortlessly with her.

"Yes?" Ken tried to remember whether her hands were clean. The cops had yanked her from the site trailer even as she fought to leave a list of instructions for Claire. At least her assistant had been unflappable. Well– except for her mouth hanging open as her boss swung wildly between two police officers. But she'd reassured Kendall she'd follow up with Harry and Jimmy.

"I'm Deborah Lawrence. Your office said I could find you here. I'm a friend of Harrison."

"You're D-Deborah? You're his attorney." She swayed on legs that had gone liquid with relief. She flopped into a chair before they collapsed underneath her. Bless his heart, Harrison had saved her. He'd sent his beautiful former girlfriend to bust her out of this stinking jail. "Thank God. I thought you'd never get here."'

Frowning slightly, she shook Ken's outstretched hand. "That's odd. . . Harrison only called me an hour ago. Had I known you needed the papers sooner. . . I could have couriered them. But Harrison has been going back and forth so much with changes. I thought we'd never get it settled."

"The papers. . ." She wrinkled her nose in confusion. *The papers?* It suddenly dawned on her that she was referring to the acquisition. "Oh . . . that. No– I'm afraid that's not what he called you about today."

"But I just spoke with him. He said you were at the courthouse." Her perfectly glossed lips pursed delicately. Without looking over her shoulder, Kendall knew Officer Pudge had been completely captivated.

The courthouse. "I knew this wasn't the police station," she muttered. "I do need the papers, Miss Lawrence. It's just that I need bailing out even more." She dragged the chair close enough to lean on the table, disregarding the stunned expression on her attorney's face. "I've been arrested– that's why I need your help."

⁓

"I think we have a problem." Harry's clipped voice matched his strides across the hundred acre site. "I couldn't get through to Deborah . . . and now she's left her office."

"So what? Another ten minutes and I'll have Barker right where I want him," Charlie said. "He's on his way now– meeting with one of my guys. It's perfect."

The lead weight in Harry's stomach lightened with the glimmer of hope Charlie's words brought.

"Barker's expanding the business . . . and I'd bet Miami doesn't know about it.

"Why do you think that?"

"Barker's setting up a little smuggling op on the side. Why not kill two birds with one stone? He can move all kinds of contraband when he rolls the stolen equipment over the border."

"Have you confirmed the. . . Miami thing? You're sure it's him?"

"Yup. Nice piece of detective work there, Cuz."

Damn, he'd hoped he'd be wrong. Swallowing a lump of despair, Harry forced his attention back. "I think Deb might be heading for the courthouse. She thought I wanted her to see Kendall."

"Harry– stop worrying. We're gonna pick up Barker in—like . . . ten minutes."

"Yeah. . . but we didn't want her to sign the papers first, remember?"

"That was only if we needed to use Ken. I didn't want him tryin' to burn her after she signed the transfer papers. The bastard might've assumed he could kill her and inherit the whole company by default."

"You've lost him before, remember? He's not exactly in custody." Harry bit back the edge of temper– knew he was overreacting. But, dammit. The last thing they needed right now was Charlie getting cocky.

"I've got four men at the scene. I've got another six along the route and I've got two in the freakin' room with him. I'm not gonna lose the bastard. Not this time."

"What if Kendall talks to Deborah?"

"That soap opera is all yours. Once I've got Barker– you can tell her everything."

Harry closed his eyes. "Yeah– I'm aware of that. I just didn't want her to find out from someone else." Because once the smoke cleared. . . after Charlie and his crew received accolades for the bust that would surely make national headlines, only he would remain– to pick up the pieces with Kendall. To explain all the lies he'd told. . . the information he'd withheld. He'd have to explain the purchase offer was fake– and that Specialty Construction had been the buyer. He'd have to explain why he'd locked her up in jail– and pray she would understand . . . and forgive him.

And if Harry ever managed to accomplish that series of miracles . . . he'd have to break the news to the woman he loved that she'd been the unwitting pawn in a hundred million dollar stolen equipment ring. Run by a criminal mastermind named Kenneth Adams, Sr.

And if Kenny hadn't tossed him to the curb by then, he'd have to confess that he'd been the one to turn her father in.

$$\infty$$

"Thanks for getting me out." Words couldn't describe the exquisite sense of relief throbbing through Kendall's veins. Deborah was a hero. She'd torn them all to shreds with a lifted eyebrow and an expression of incredulity that had to have been perfected before a mirror. Never once had Deborah raised her voice, with the exception of when Officer Doughboy had explained the lame-assed logic behind her arrest.

"My pleasure. It's all in a day's work." The wind whipping her perfectly coifed hair into a black cloud around her face, Deborah slanted her eyes at her as they flew down the road leading to Kendall's house. "Although I admit to being surprised by the charge of resisting arrest. You neglected to tell me you'd kicked the shit out of two cops when they brought you in, Kendall."

"It slipped my mind. Besides, I was resisting a *false* arrest," she shot back. "They should be grateful I'm not suing." For the first time since meeting the cultured, serious beauty, Deborah Lawrence laughed. The bubbly sound made her shockingly human. And very likable.

"I can see why Harrison is so taken with you. I hope you'll both be very happy together." They were flying toward her home in a sleek BMW convertible that had 'Successful Corporate Attorney' written all over it. Her speed was approaching an eye-popping eighty miles per hour. "Are you all right?"

"Don't look at me. Keep your eyes on the road," she ordered.

"Sorry, I'll slow down. Speeding is my one vice. Speeding and shoes," she amended. "Do you want me to stay with you until Harrison gets home?"

"No, thanks. I called him before we left the courthouse. He'll be home any minute. It's the next street on the right," she directed, trying to keep the relief from her voice.

Deborah nodded, distracted while wrestling the wheel to make the turn into her lane. "Call me if you have any questions when you read through those papers." Kendall glanced down at the folder clutched in her white-knuckled grip. "Technically, I represent Specialty in the deal, but since you and Harrison have worked it out together, I see no harm in answering any questions you might have."

Specialty? "I don't understand- It's the gray Victorian," Ken pointed out, ". . . there on the right." She couldn't have heard her correctly. Why would Specialty be in on the deal? Harrison had made it sound as though Deborah's firm was performing the service as *a favor* to Specialty.

"Aren't we talking about the same thing?" Gravel flying, the BMW screamed to a stop in her driveway. Deborah's hand hesitated on the shift, her pert nose wrinkled in confusion. "The acquisition. . . A & R is being purchased by Specialty Construction."

CHAPTER 14

He was in serious trouble.

Harry knew the moment he pulled up in front of the house. She was sitting on the front steps . . . waiting for him. One look at Kendall's face told him she knew . . . maybe everything. Swallowing hard, he crossed the grassy front lawn. Her molten eyes bored through him with the intensity of sulfuric acid on metal. In his suddenly constricted chest, his heart flopped uncomfortably.

"Let me explain–"

"Deborah took care of that. I think I've heard enough– from everyone but you."

"Kenny, I was terrified for you." There was a finality to the ice in her voice that sent a ripple of fear down his spine. He'd anticipated her fury– ready to smooth it over. Cajole her into understanding his reasons. His fear for her safety.

"You have a funny way of showing it."

"Lance was desperate. He didn't just want A & R. He wanted you dead." Rising to her feet, Kendall showed little reaction. Intent on reaching the door, she would have ignored him, had he not blocked her. Harry realized his fatal mistake. He hadn't prepped for devastation. He hadn't anticipated . . . resignation. As though Kendall had already moved past anger into the arena she knew best. Her default expectation was that she couldn't trust anyone. And he'd played right into it.

"Get out of my way, Traynor." She jerked free of his grasp.

"Ken– I would have done anything to keep you safe."

"You had me arrested and thrown in jail." Her eyes widened with disbelief.

At least it was a reaction. "That was strictly for your safety," he argued. "The bastard wanted to kill you. Did you actually expect me to do nothing?"

The flicker of animation in her eyes died. "I expected you to be honest. I *expected* you to keep me informed. This is *my* life. A & R is *my* company. How dare you decide what's best for me?"

"I tried . . . but you wouldn't listen."

"When was that? When I begged you to tell me what was wrong?" She advanced on him, fury heating her eyes. "I knew you were holding something back."

"Charlie . . . felt it would be best for you not to know-"

"Charlie! You let Charlie decide what was best for me? You're both assholes." She threw up her hands.

Annoyance flared. He'd done it for *her*. "You're so hell-bent on doing everything yourself– you won't accept help. I've offered my help a hundred times . . . but you'd rather wear yourself out than admit you need someone-"

"You're blaming me for this?" Kendall shoved him out of the way and slammed into the house.

"You were in danger." Hot on her heels, he tried to rein in his anger. "He'd already gotten his hands on you once. And he'd tried several times before-"

"What's that supposed to mean?"

"My fall into the pit was meant for you. Barker's already admitted he loosened the safety railing, hoping he'd catch you . . . not me. For God's sake-" Releasing a tortured breath, he experienced a wash of shame when she flinched. "The fire was meant for you, too." The accusation in tear-drenched golden eyes knifed a jagged hole in his heart. If Harry hadn't known better, he would have sworn his chest had been flayed open.

"How do you know that?"

"Charlie connected the stolen equipment ring he was investigating to our job site. I'd spoken to him at the picnic . . . because I knew Lance started the fire."

"That was weeks ago," she shouted. "You've known since then?"

"I didn't like Barker." He shrugged. "I asked Charlie to check him out."

Hands fisted at her sides, she stared at him, her gaze unforgiving. "Is that what you do when you start sleeping with someone? Spy on everyone around them?"

Harry's blood pressure spiked. Damn it, he was willing to grovel if that's what it took to convince her. But he would not be insulted. "The first time I met Lance he was attempting to break your arm. Twenty minutes later he was the prime suspect in the firebombing of your building." He advanced a step closer. "I tried to convince you Barker was dangerous, but you dismissed my concerns. Don't you see? It was a game to him– even at the end."

She smirked. "You told me very little. If you hadn't withheld information, I'm pretty sure I would've been onboard with the plan."

He shook his head. "You would've made yourself the target. You wouldn't have been able to resist throwing it in his face."

Fury flared in her eyes. "Damn straight I would. For six months that bastard has ruined my life-"

"You would have played right into his hands. Lance would've taken off."

An eyebrow quirked. "So? Problem solved."

"Charlie's investigation would've gone up in smoke."

A flicker of anguish crossed her features. "And that was more important-"

He reached for her. "All I knew– was that I had to keep you safe." His heart sank over the finality in her expression. Defending himself was useless. What he'd done was unforgivable.

Kendall studied him, the silence growing thicker with each passing second. Soon the gulf between them would be a yawning chasm of anger and recrimination. And Harry was helpless to close the distance. Because he wouldn't have changed a thing.

∽∾

"The purchase offer . . . that was fake as well?" As her life crumbled before her, a corner of Kendall's brain was marveling over her control. When she wanted to fall to her knees and weep . . . her perverse need for a display of strength held the tears at bay. She would not allow Harrison the satisfaction of seeing her cry.

"Let me explain why-"

"So you admit Specialty is the buyer?" Kendall felt the implosion reverberate through her frame as her heart detonated. It was all true. The doubting voice in her head had been accurate. Why the hell had she chosen not to believe it?

"Sort of. I approached Jake about a financing deal to get you out of trouble."

"You approached Jake? What about me?" she cried, unable to hide her anguish. "Why didn't you consult *me*?"

"You wouldn't let me help you. I-I thought if I could bail you out, you'd get back on your feet and everything would work out for the best."

"The best for who? Me? Or you?" Kendall dragged in a shuddering breath. All this time . . . he'd acted solely on Specialty's behalf– and Specialty wanted A & R. Her head swimming, she sank down on the couch before her legs gave out. She was going to be sick. Thirty years of history, of blood and sweat and devotion. And she'd failed. She'd done everything she could to please her father . . . and he'd never loved her.

And neither, apparently, did Harrison. A & R would be absorbed into Specialty Construction . . . purchased by Traynor for pennies on the dollar and a couple tumbles with the owner. "Was Lance in on this? Or was the acquisition simply a score for Specialty? Pick up a site contractor on the cheap."

"That was *never* the plan and you know it," Harry replied, his voice harsh at her implication. "We did it to catch Barker."

She was cold . . . so very cold. Suppressing a shiver, she absently scrubbed the goosebumps raised on her arms. The trickle of anguish pumping through her veins only added to the pervasive chill washing over her limbs. Her heart had iced over, leaving only a desolate hollow sensation in her chest.

"I don't know anything, remember?" Ken experienced a brief jolt of heat when he visibly winced. Her arrow had struck the mark. "So, what was I? The consolation prize?"

"Don't be ridiculous-"

Ignoring the whiplash of his anger, Ken felt nothing. A thick blanket of desolation protected her from his barbs. "Deborah was right about our relationship. So perfect– mixing business and pleasure. After all . . . the plan might not have worked if you hadn't been sleeping with me."

Harrison's eyes iced over with something dangerously close to violence. She experienced a moment's panic, wondering if she'd finally pushed him beyond the limits of his control. But Harrison Traynor was the master of control. He'd carved her open with the icy precision of a surgeon– taking what he'd wanted and leaving the rest for someone else to clean up.

He shook his head. "We're not going there, babe. Not tonight . . . not ever." His voice was deceptively calm, but his expression seemed to be chiseled from a block of granite. "I'll be damned before you paint me with that brush. I don't use women to get what I want . . . especially not the woman I love."

"Love?" Her voice rose, incredulous. "You don't know anything about love." Loving someone meant trusting them– it meant confiding in them. Her voice broke on a sob that made her cringe. She hadn't wanted to break down in front of him. With a discipline she hadn't known she possessed, Ken forced the anguish back. There would be time enough later to dissolve in a shattered, hysterical mess.

"It never crossed your mind to involve me in decisions that directly affected me." She ignored the stab of pain in her chest. She couldn't possibly love him. This couldn't be love . . . because it hurt too much. This was betrayal at its heart shattering, razor sharp best. "You're just like my father," she whispered. "I wasted my life trying to make him proud of me. And look where it got me. He gave away half of my business . . . and now you're here to steal the rest of it."

"Your father is one of the reasons we're here," he agreed.

It was an effort to keep speaking. "He's fifteen hundred miles away."

"Your dad is the brains behind one of the biggest insurance thefts of the decade."

Her next several breaths were excruciating. Kendall waited . . . for him to gloat over the knowledge he so clearly possessed. But instead of triumph, she read only defeat in his gaze. "What are you talking about?"

"He's been arrested for causing nearly forty million dollars in losses from fourteen different insurance companies."

"You can't be serious-"

"The equipment thefts you experienced? That was his network. Lance worked for him. That was the true reason your father handed over a chunk of A & R." He hesitated. "It wasn't personal, Ken.

Adams and Rey was the perfect cover for the theft ring. He needed a legitimate front to hide their activities. What better company than the one he knew best?"

She lasered him with her eyes. "Is that supposed to make me feel better? My father destroyed me– but that wasn't his intent?" To her horror, hot tears welled up, blurring her vision before spilling over to trail down frozen cheeks. "After all these years, do you think I c-care how he feels?"

"I think it means everything to you." Harrison moved cautiously toward her. "Do you think I wanted to tell you *that* about your father? It was bad enough his actions nearly got you killed."

"All this . . . you got from Charlie."

"He'd been investigating the theft ring for months. When I approached him about Lance– it turned out to be a break for them."

A lightbulb went off over her head. "Him showing up here . . . after the break-in. I questioned how Charlie would know anything about it. Stupid me. . . I thought it was coincidence." The hard knot of anguish had settled in her chest, not as painful now. Almost comforting. "You both must be very proud."

"I'm not proud of lying to you. It's not who I am, Kendall." He dragged a hand through his hair.

Even in despair, she managed to chuckle over the unbelievable statement. "At least you discovered my criminal roots before anything got too serious." The pain was agonizing. No one could hurt this much and not die from it.

"I'm not even going to dignify that with a response." His voice sounded weary. *Of dealing with her.* "He turned himself in, Kenny. When I called him-"

"*You called him*?" Alarm bells clanged in her pounding head. "What right- What possible reason-"

"I suspected-" He eased down on the couch next to her, his expression uncertain. "From the things you said about him– the contract he forced you to sign when he turned over the business . . . it didn't make sense."

"He's a bastard. It makes perfect sense."

"To you, it was one more attempt to control you," he explained, his tone gentle. "But from a purely business perspective, I viewed the contract differently. I saw the terms for what they were."

"And?" She tried not to despise him for sounding so calm and rational when she was slowly bleeding to death– when her heart was suffocating under the weight of his betrayal.

"A business opportunity. If he'd truly wanted to hurt you, he would have sold the company out from under you."

His voice was persuasive, eager to explain everything away– to somehow convince her his actions were justified. Harry may have destroyed her, but her dignity remained intact. She raised a brow in silent question. Why should any of this matter?

"Give me a break, Kenny . . . please? Just let me explain."

Damn him. The agony in his voice reached out to tangle with her own. The anguish she read on his face could only be mirrored in her expression. Defeated, Kendall released a deep breath, hoping for a sense of calm to descend and wash away some of the bitterness. Instead, she felt empty and more desolate than she'd ever thought possible. "Go ahead."

"Your father had already set himself up for retirement when he was approached with the equipment scheme. So, he rewrites your contract and sends his new stepson up to Virginia to oversee the operation."

"Why? He didn't need the money."

Harrison stared at her for endless moments before finally speaking. "I don't know but he said he never wanted you to know about it."

"Because he couldn't trust me?"

"Because he knew you would never agree– because if he were ever caught, he didn't want you knowing anything about it."

She blinked back scalding tears with sheer willpower. If she let them fall, she would never stop. "So what happened with this perfect plan?"

"Lance forgot the real reason he was here. He was supposed to steal equipment . . . not drain the company of cash."

"Why did you call my father?"

"When Lance attacked you. . . I went a little crazy. I picked up the phone and . . . basically accused him of trying to kill you. I asked him what kind of father sacrificed his daughter for money."

"And?" Ken told herself she didn't want to hear the answer. Self-loathing washed over her as she acknowledged how much she needed to hear his explanation.

"He didn't know what Lance was doing. He had *no idea* you were in danger." Cautiously, Harry reached for her hand. "He still wanted to protect you. Your dad hung up the phone and called the police to turn himself in."

She stared at him for several seconds, her brain unable to process another thought. Her stomach churned with questions she would likely never receive answers to. She didn't know what to say to Harrison– how to process what he'd done. All she knew for sure was that she needed time. To sort everything out.

"Well . . . I guess I can read the rest in the papers tomorrow." Her voice sounded as hollow and dejected as her body felt. "You can go now." Shaking her hand free of his, she retraced her steps to the foyer, her vision blurred by unshed tears. But seeing his face one last time wouldn't have mattered. Because her heart was too sick to care anymore.

"Kenny . . . once this settles-"

"We go on as though nothing happened?" She smirked. "I don't think so."

"Kendall-" His voice was sharp. "Don't do this. I love you."

"I don't know what that means," she admitted, her voice small . . . . defeated. He reached for her, his hand tentative when he laid it on her shoulder. Unable to bear the thought of his betrayal, she jerked away. "Please leave, Harrison. I'm begging you."

He flinched, compassion and sorrow in his gaze– as though he could sense her pending meltdown. "I'll go . . . but . . . this isn't how it ends, Kendall. I'm coming back."

Ken managed to hold herself together, tears streaming down her face as he reluctantly left. Whatever tiny scrap of pride she had remaining provided the strength to not break down in front of Traynor. He'd taken everything she'd had to give, leaving only the crushed, lifeless shell of her soul. He couldn't hurt her anymore. *No one* could hurt her anymore. When the door clicked shut, she released the cascading breath she'd been holding. But there was no relief from the pain.

Sinking to the floor, she buried her face in her hands, succumbing to the grief she'd contained for so long. The dams collapsed on endless years of emotional battering she'd taken from her out-of-reach father . . . and for the bruising her castoff heart would now endure as she faced a future without Harrison. As

Lurch flopped down at her side, she let the shaking sobs overwhelm her. Because nothing mattered anymore.

∽

It was funny, she thought later, how life went on . . . through disaster, through pain and even, she discovered, through disillusionment. Kendall rolled the window down, letting the breeze catch her hair as she headed for the jobsite. Harrison had vacated her life almost the same way he'd entered it . . . with a loud, violent thud– similar to a tornado swooping down, before fleeing the scene as quickly as he'd arrived. Leaving her to jumpstart her life from the shattered aftermath.

Ken ignored the irritating voice scuttling through her head– reminding her she'd *ordered* him to leave. But Traynor usually did whatever he wanted. Why would he have listened to her today . . . unless he'd been eager to leave.

Flicking a glance at her watch, she was floored to realize only hours had passed since he'd left. Time had ceased to matter as she'd wandered from room to room. She'd been almost grateful when the phone rang. Anything to break the shattering silence.

Clearly, it was to be a milestone day for her. Like life itself, sometimes you caught a break. As you floundered in the angry seas of despair, God sometimes offered you a lifeboat . . . a single ray of hope that tempted you to stay afloat for one more day. Claire had called, announcing A & R had finally received three badly needed checks– payments that had been delinquent over ninety days. It was too late to visit the bank today, but if she picked them up now, she could deposit them first thing in the morning. Her assistant promised to leave them on her desk before locking up for the night.

The jobsite was already deserted when she parked in the dusty, rutted parking lot. Only an hour earlier, the desolate site had been overrun with workers. But once the job shut down for the night, the scene sometimes reminded her of an abandoned western movie set. The only props missing were a few blowing tumbleweeds. The sun would be gone in under an hour. Trudging across the site, the silence was broken only by the gravel under her feet. Mentally, she took notes. With Harry out of her life, Ken needed to throw herself full force back into work.

Still numb from the events of the day, she was nearly upon the trailer before she noticed the door was wide open. Checking her watch once again, she wondered if Claire had changed her mind and waited.

"Claire? You still here?" For a change, Kendall approached the trailer cautiously, Harrison's safety lectures buzzing in the back of her brain. Too much had happened over the past several days to dismiss the possibility that something might be wrong. Though no sound emanated from the darkened trailer, she hesitated. If someone actually lurked inside, she'd be trapped.

Scrubbing at the goosebumps raising on her arms, she scowled over her sudden case of jitters. "I can't call Traynor." *Jimmy*. Sure, he'd be ticked off over the disruption to his evening, but his stool at the Hickory Pub would still be waiting for him when he returned. Tugging her cell phone from her belt, she punched in his number. As it rang, she took a few steps closer to the trailer. Maybe just poke her head in for a quick peek. That would save Jimmy from driving all the way back– only to rescue her from her stupid imagination.

When his voicemail picked up, she sighed. Damn. Now she'd have to leave a lame sounding message. "Pop . . . I'm at the site. It's about seven. The trailer door's wide open. I think Claire just forgot to lock it . . . I was gonna ask you to swing by and check it out with me, but since I didn't catch you. . . I'll just do it myself. Don't waste your time calling back." She was ready to disconnect when she remembered the good news. Forcing some enthusiasm into her voice, she continued. "Oh yeah. . . Claire said we finally got paid on those three old jobs. Can you believe it? I'm taking you to lunch tomorrow to celebrate. See you in the morning."

Disconnecting her phone, she'd climbed two steps when Ken realized her senses had flared to red alert. Her heart had begun pounding a drumbeat of warning– her neck prickling with an urgent alarm.

Someone was behind her.

Her only hope was surprise. Fists raised, she whirled to face her attacker. "Who are-" Her eyes widened with shock before the person at the bottom of the steps registered in her brain as friend . . . not foe. "Jesus– you scared the hell out of me."

"Yo– Harry– I think we have a problem."

Harry set his beer on Andrea's granite kitchen island. He had several problems right now . . . all of them revolving around the woman who'd just kicked him out of her life. "I don't think my life can get much worse at this particular moment."

Charlie tossed his car keys on the counter and stared at him quizzically. "Christ– are you drunk?"

He couldn't summon the energy to glare at his pain-in-the-ass cousin. "Not yet."

Over his shoulder, Charlie shouted for his wife. "Baby– how long has Harry been drinkin'?" He snatched the bottle from his fingers. "Snap out of it. There's a loose end."

Andrea appeared in the doorway with Mona hot on her heels. Harry had endured enough words of wisdom from his aunt over the past several hours to last a lifetime. How he'd royally screwed up . . . how he had to fight to get Kendall back. Like he didn't already know that?

"He's only had three. I hid the rest out in the garage." Andrea stood on tiptoe to kiss her husband. Harry was forced to endure watching Charlie manhandle his wife. All it did was make him more despondent. He could have had that with Kendall. That's how they would have looked after twenty years of marriage–

"Let me guess. You've already lost Barker? Has he escaped from jail?"

Charlie dragged a chair over to join him at the counter. "It's Kendall's dad. He's been singing to the feds down in Miami. I just got off the phone with them."

Great. More bad news he'd be tasked with delivering. "What now?"

"We need to talk to Kendall. ASAP."

"So, go talk to her. She made it pretty clear she doesn't want to see me for the next several centuries."

Feeling the vibration of his cell phone, Harry jerked it from his pocket. Praying for a miracle, he glanced at before swallowing a rush of disappointment. What the hell did Jimmy want?

"Yeah?" He listened to the old man for several seconds. "Pop– she called you . . . not me." He held the phone away from his ear when Jimmy started shouting. "Okay . . . okay. I'm on my way. I'll meet you there." He slid from his stool, his gaze locking with

Charlie's. "Make this quick. I need to meet Jimmy out at the site. Why do you need Kendall?"

"Ken, Sr. told the feds Lance wasn't working alone up here. He had a partner. Senior didn't know about it until Lance started screwing up. Senior sent someone up here to check on Barker."

"That's not surprising. I never believed Lance had brains enough to handle an operation like this by himself. The embezzlement alone-" Harry's heart lurched into his throat, cutting off his ability to speak. His brain shook off the buzz of alcohol as the pieces fell into place with a clarity that left him reeling. He was halfway out the door before he spoke again. "Hell- I know who it is."

CHAPTER 15

"Claire. . . what are you doing?" Kendall's instinct was to duck, but the muzzle of the gun in her assistant's hands was trained at her chest. She wouldn't get far.

"We were so goddamned close. One more day and those contracts would've been signed. But– you couldn't let up. You and that damn Traynor. It's like you're friggin' indestructible. No matter what we did . . . that bastard would show up and ruin it."

"You? You did this? We . . . thought it was Lance." Her gut screamed 'flee' . . . but logic told her to stall for as long as humanly possible. Sweat gathering at her spine, Kendall's scattered thoughts ran the gamut. It would be dark soon. Maybe she could distract Claire . . . or wrestle the gun away. Run. Get lost in the shadows.

Or maybe it truly would be a landmark day. Her *last* day.

"You're not much smarter than your idiot brother." Claire smirked. "Even without him, I would've been able to bleed you dry. But this place-" She glanced around the site with an air of boredom. "This place was chump change. When I heard about the equipment gig– there's some serious money. I figured . . . what the hell?"

"You'd planned to screw over Lance, too?" More frightening than the gun she held, was the subdued evil emanating from the woman standing before her. Her heart skidded erratically at the realization Claire's anger stemmed from being stymied . . . She wouldn't be content to take the money and run. In fact . . . she would probably look forward to punishing her.

"Honey– we both know he borders on idiocy. The *only* thing Lance had going for him were his connections to your father. He wasn't even good in bed." She shuddered delicately. "Once he received his cut from selling this dump . . . his usefulness would have ended."

"You weren't worried my father would hunt you down?" The sheen of perspiration chilled her skin when the breeze kicked up. Fighting the tremors wanting to charge through her system, Ken groped for any way to prolong the conversation.

Claire laughed, the jarring motion making the gun waver. "I was going to hunt *him* down. With Moron out of the way, I could offer my far superior services. Hell, I could've tripled his operation up here. Besides being stupid, Lance was too friggin' lazy. He didn't want to work."

"I can't argue you on that point," she admitted.

Claire nodded. "In this business, you've got to be ruthless." Her gaze less disparaging, she stared at Kendall. "In the beginning, I really admired you. If we hadn't been ripping you off so well, A & R probably would've had a banner year," she acknowledged. "You work damn hard in a tough business. The guys really respect you," she said. "You weren't afraid to get your hands dirty."

"Thanks. . . I guess. I really liked you, too, Claire." If Kendall lived to talk about it, this conversation would go on record as the weirdest.

"Well– enough chitchat. I've got things to do . . . business to wrap up before I hit the road. Come on." When Claire waved the gun in her direction, she instinctively ducked. And her assistant laughed again, the sound drifting away in the growing darkness. "Hell, Kenny– I'm not gonna shoot you."

She nearly doubled over on a wave of relief. Thank God for sisterhood. She'd misjudged her. Somewhere in the dark recesses of Claire's soul, a shred of humanity remained.

"We're gonna do a little free-falling. I know how much you love swinging on those damn ropes. And this time you don't have Jimmy around to catch the frayed ones before you use them." Leveling the gun at her head, she smiled. "Get moving."

⚯

"Kenny . . . hang on, love."

Kendall panted with the effort it cost to keep her fingers locked around the safety fencing. "Get back, Harry. The fencing is rigged. It won't hold much . . . longer." When he ignored her order, it was raw terror that made her shout.

"Dammit, Traynor . . . get away from the edge." The plea spilled from her lips on a groan of anguish. Her arms felt on the verge of tearing free from her shoulders . . . her muscles screamed with an agony she never would have imagined possible. Her hands were raw and bleeding from the effort to hang on.

It would be a blessing. The voice in her head buzzed a little louder this time. *Let go . . . let go and fall.* When the perspiration dripped into her eyes . . .stinging . . . blinding, she nearly complied. Under normal circumstances, the hand swipe to her eyes was a reflex. Ken pried her fingers free and felt the fence shift overhead.

"No. . . Kenny!"

Her eyes jerked open at the tortured sound of Harrison's voice and she blinked through the pain to find his face. If she could only see his eyes . . . those beautiful, deceitful eyes. She wanted so badly to hate him. He'd betrayed her. But what did it matter now? She'd rather die loving him. "Harrison? Are you there?"

"Honey . . . don't move your hands, love. Please– don't move. Don't give up."

In the faintest corner of her mind she heard him bellow for help and wondered who could possibly be there to offer it. "Traynor . . . I'm begging you– move away from the hole. Please, Harrison. She's rigged the whole thing. Claire . . . You'll fall."

"If you move a muscle I'm *jumping* in there after you," he vowed.

"Where are you?" She had to see him one last time. She had to tell him what was in her heart. Nothing short of a miracle could help her now. But if she fell without telling him the truth, she'd want to die anyway.

"I'm right here, baby. If you look up you'll see me," he coached.

"My neck. . . I can't move." Everything around her was fading black save for the sparks of light at the end of a very long tunnel. Even the agonizing pain in her arms was starting to blissfully fade away. Ken concentrated on one simple movement of her shoulders. If she twisted just a little bit . . . she'd see him one last time. With a groan of agony, she jerked her aching arms.

"Harrison." Closing her eyes, she sighed with relief.

"Open your eyes, love."

Complying, she smiled when she discovered beautiful green eyes pinned to hers. "I love you, Harry. I needed to tell you one last time-"

"Don't let go," he shouted in a voice thick with terror. "Dammit, Kenny. . . I'm ordering you– hang on."

She blew out a breath of exquisite pain as the fencing jolted her arms, sending a waterfall of liquid agony coursing through her muscles. Ignoring his tirade, she continued her one-sided conversation. "I've loved you for so damn long . . . but I didn't want to admit it. I figured you'd get tired of me."

"I'll never be tired of you."

His face swam before her eyes and she ruthlessly blinked back the tears. She wanted his face to be the last thing she saw– her very last thoughts would be of Harrison– of loving him. Of never wanting to leave him. Despite his betrayal, she still loved him. He would be the last vision imprinted in her mind when her arms betrayed her. "I'm sorry I took so long."

His eyes flared with relief and the unmistakable spark of determination. "We have a lifetime to make it right." He turned, shouting to someone over his shoulder.

"Kenny . . . please love, I know you're tired. Just another minute. Don't let go– no matter what happens."

The fence shifted again and her shrill cry of fear reverberated off the walls of the underground canyon. She felt one last jerk on her aching arms before everything shifted, rumbling and shaking as she was thrown into the cavern wall.

"I've got you, love. We won't let you fall." Harrison's hoarse voice tickled her ear. If this was the end, she would latch on to the sound.

"Traynor– you puke on me and I'll kill you."

"Pop?" How had Jimmy landed in her dream? Her nose was pressed into the front of Harry's shirt. His heart thundering against her ear, his glorious scent filling her nose.

"I'm– good. I'm . . . I'm okay." Harry's panting breath ruffled her hair. "It's just . . . oh God. This height."

"Stop lookin' down, you idiot."

Harrison's arm tightened around her waist. Had he fallen, too? He was breathing as though he'd run a long, long way. Maybe he was tired? "Harry?'

"Woody– haul us up. Traynor's turnin' green."

Kendall startled when Jimmy bellowed. Pain sliced through her ribcage and she moaned. As the light began to fade, the last thing she remembered was Harrison. The terrible pain faded. Nothing could hurt her anymore.

∞

"We're almost home, love."

Battered and achingly fragile– but alive. For twelve hours Harry had waited– first for Ken to awaken, then for the barrage of tests before the doctors agreed to release her. He'd spent the night by her side, while she slept through doctors poking and prodding her. Bruised shadows still lurked under her eyes from all she'd endured.

Her slender shoulders stiffened. "I told you I could get a ride home with Jimmy."

An overwhelming floral scent filled his car. The mountain of flowers had provoked the only smile he'd seen in days. But as he pulled into her driveway, Kendall appeared as though she wanted to launch herself from his car.

Harry would be grateful for the opportunity to apologize. No matter the outcome– at least he'd be able to breathe again without feeling the stabbing pain in his chest. But she sure as hell wasn't making it easy. "Jimmy told me to fix it with you or there's a beating in my future." He wished he knew what she was thinking. "Kenny– can we please talk?"

"I think we've pretty much covered everything." Easing gingerly from his car, she winced with pain.

"We haven't begun to cover it." Approaching cautiously, he stifled the urge to gather her in his arms, instead offering his arm to help her up the steps. When she finally raised her gaze to his, the finality in her expression was another blow to his confidence. "I know I've hurt you. But I swear I'll fix it. Please . . . please let me try."

"I don't trust you, Traynor. And I can't love someone I don't trust."

"You love me," he reminded, trying like hell not to sound as desperate as he felt. "Last night you *said* you loved me."

"I thought I was dying."

Harry shook his head resolutely. "Baby, we're not ending it like this. I'm sorry I hurt you, but your life was in danger."

"Would you do it again?" Fathomless golden eyes pinned him.

"I– would protect you. With my life . . . I would protect you."

Temper flared in her eyes, heating the gold until it shimmered. "You would lie to me again?"

"I'll never lie to you again," he vowed. "I was wrong not to tell you what was happening . . . but I was so afraid of losing you– I just wanted to hide you from the danger." He swallowed convulsively. "Instead, I led you straight to it."

"That wasn't your fault. No one knew about Claire."

"It *was* my fault," he insisted, reaching for her. "If I'd confided in you, we might have figured it out sooner. Together."

Her eyes filled with a fresh batch of tears. "I don't think I can do this, Harry. It's too hard. I'm not strong enough." She tugged futilely to release her arms from his grip. "Let me go, Traynor."

"I can't," Harry admitted, and it was so damn true. The pain in her eyes would haunt him for the rest of his days. But he would spend every one making it up to her . . . if she'd let him. He ran a shaking hand down his face, his stomach knotted with the very real fear she would tell him to leave.

"I love you, Kendall. I've never said those words before. You're *it* for me. If you . . . if you don't want me . . ." Harry closed the space between them, his stance resolute. "I'll go. But-" His voice thick with emotion, he swallowed around the pain in his throat. "I'll keep coming back until I make it right again."

Kendall stared at him . . . thinking about what it meant . . . what her life would be like without Harrison in it. And felt the walls slowly close in around her. "Jimmy said you were hanging over the side to rescue me. He and Woody held your feet-"

His grip tightened convulsively on her arm. "I– couldn't let you fall."

"But– it's so high . . . and you don't like-"

Before her eyes, Harrison's complexion turned chalky. "Can we. . . not talk about that?"

"Harry? You need to sit down?"

"I'm good." He blew out a shaky breath. "Will you at least consider giving me a second chance?"

Kendall had lived her life without– so many things. But she'd never lived it without Harrison Traynor. He'd owned a place in her heart since that long ago night in the rain. But her memory of him was one of perfection . . . of a hero– with no human flaws to destroy the girlish image.

Now, she had the chance to live the remainder of her life with the real man standing before her. With all the dents and flaws. Harrison was stubborn and overprotective. A perfectionist. A planner. All the things she would never be. But he was also the most loving, generous man she'd ever known. He was strong and courageous and honorable.

And absolutely perfect. For her.

Reaching out, she twined his icy fingers through hers. "I don't want you to go, Traynor. I've waited my whole life for you to finally get here."

His sharp cry of relief was muffled when he pulled her roughly against his chest. Under her ear, she heard the reassuring thunder of his heartbeat.

"Kenny– I'll never hurt you again. I swear it." As he rained kisses over her face, she snuggled happily against him, the powerful strength of his arms wrapped around her battered body. She lifted an aching arm to squeeze him tight. A life without Harrison would be a life without music, without laughter. But together, they could face anything. Together, they'd smudge his meticulous blueprint into a wrinkled, livable plan. They'd start building a life– one filled with vibrant colors and quiet moments and the noisy symphony of children to bring them joy and chaos for the rest of their lives.

Their wedding was celebrated on a gorgeous autumn day. Harrison had the traditional, romantic ceremony he'd always envisioned. The candlelit church had been fragrant with the spicy scent of harvest. And Kendall experienced the reception she'd always dreamed of . . . a big family gathering in Jake's backyard. No longer the outsider looking in, she was the guest of honor at her very own 'picnic in the park', surrounded by an extended loving family. Harry's relatives blended seamlessly with her motley construction family. Laughter and animated conversations filled the air, mingling with the bluegrass band and the tantalizing scent of barbecue.

She finally belonged.

"Thanks for the great party, Traynor." Ken smiled up at her handsome husband as he tugged her even closer on the dance floor. A moment earlier they'd been stunned speechless when Woody twirled by, dragging Deborah Lawrence by the hand, her flawless cheeks flushed pink with exertion.

"You're very welcome, Mrs. Traynor," he emphasized. "Thanks for marrying me."

"I'm a Traynor now, aren't I?" Burrowing closer to his chest, Kendall released a sigh of perfect happiness. A magical harvest moon hung low in the sky over their heads, the air sharp with the scent of fall. Winter eased closer, waiting around the corner. "Mona and Linc look pretty cozy over there." She nodded to the pair, heads together as they chatted over champagne.

"What— you're a matchmaker now?"

The sudden chorus of tinkling glasses interrupted their conversation. Harrison's answering kiss made her head spin. Once she managed to catch her breath, she found her voice again. "Pretty cool about Jake and Jen."

"He doesn't seem panicked by the thought of twins." Gazing into her eyes, Harrison's smile was conspiratorial. "You know, if we put in some overtime this winter . . . we could maybe catch up with them."

Ken raised a brow, her mouth curving with the irresistible urge to have the last word over her handsome husband. "You know what a dedicated worker I am, Harry. Why wait until winter?"

Please enjoy the following excerpt from Jefferson Traynor's story,

CHASING MARISOL.

Love Under Construction . . .

Construction executive Jefferson Traynor has zero problems attracting women. Until now. It's a serious blow to his ego that the sexy, beautiful Marisol is immune to his superpower charms.

Marisol Ortega is on a mission to build the safest shelter she can negotiate on her shoestring budget. If that means playing along with the gorgeous, cocky stud building it– then game on. A single mom to foster son Hector, Mari can't afford distraction from the crazy hot man pursuing her.

Chasing Marisol was supposed to be a fun, no-strings interlude while building a safe shelter for strong women he has grown to admire. Falling for Mari and Hector wasn't in the blueprint. But can Marisol ever move past old fears to risk building a new life with him?

CHASING MARISOL
Available February, 2016

CHAPTER 1

She had a run in her pantyhose– left leg, inside the ankle. Not usually one to notice such a small detail, Jefferson Traynor momentarily forgot the phone in his hand– fascinated by the shapely limbs transporting his next girlfriend quite ably across the hotel parking lot.

"Earth to Jeff– you still there?"

"I'm here. Wasting time at Dad's charity thing." His slow assessment had yet to reach her face, and in a way, Jeff was reluctant to continue. The rest of her couldn't possibly hold his attention so readily. "Jake, when I said I wanted more responsibility– I meant at work. Can't you stick this charitable stuff with Jenna?"

His brother launched into the *many* reasons why his presence at a charitable board meeting *was* important to Specialty Construction. With a sigh, Jeff resumed his perusal of the lithe body heading toward him, praying her destination would coincide with his.

Wow. He'd been wrong. If possible, the face was more stunning than the body. A Latin supermodel. . . right here in Arlington. Jeff's pulse ricocheted as she drew closer. His presence at the board meeting might be delayed a few minutes while he scored her number.

"So, Dad dumps the homeless shelter gig on you and now you're sticking me with it." The spark of interest he'd experienced as she approached morphed to inferno level awareness. When their eyes finally met over the wobbly stack of files she struggled with, he drew a breath of dismay.

Her eyes were wide-set and shimmering blue. Had they been welcoming, they would have reminded him of the clear turquoise of a tropical sea. Instead, her challenging, *don't-even-think-about-messing-with-me* stare told him what she thought of his perusal. When she turned haughtily toward the hotel entrance, he was left to admire long, chocolate curls that bobbed with every step.

Damn– he should be offering to grab the door for her instead of wasting time arguing with his brother. "Jake– are you gonna pull this four-kids-excuse forever? Because it's getting a little old." Pocketing the keys to his bike, he hustled after the supermodel. Jeff managed to reach the door as she jockeyed her briefcase with the precariously sliding stack of folders.

"We'll argue later. I'm late for this stupid charity thing." In one motion, Jeff stuffed his phone into his pocket and reached for the door handle. Offering her one of his patented Traynor smiles, he winked. History being what it was, Legs would be unable to resist for long. "You look as though you could use some assistance. Allow me to get the door, Miss-"

Ignoring his blatant end run, she responded with a smile, but it was the kind meant to freeze out– not invite in. And it most definitely didn't reach her eyes. "Thank you."

Okay– maybe a little too obvious. Truth was– most women approached him, not the other way around. But her voice held promise– husky, melodic and a touch of an accent. Definitely worth another try. Not the least deterred, he fell into step beside her.

"Can I carry something? I'm on my way to a meeting but I always have time to assist a beautiful woman." Eventually they all caved. The Traynor charm was damn near irresistible.

"Only the beautiful ones merit assistance? What a shame." She eyed him with amusement. "Many women need assistance." She turned for the bank of elevators. "Thankfully, I'm not one of them."

❈

"What is wrong with you?" Marisol Ortega muttered as she rode the elevator to the third floor. Her arms were moments from snapping under the weight of her briefcase and the load of presentation materials she carried. An absolutely stunning man offers assistance and what does she do? Accept gracefully? No– that would be too easy.

Absolutely stunning and completely full of himself, she amended, entering the carpeted hallway. Remembering his expression, she smiled. Gorgeous, hazel eyes had registered something akin to shock. Perhaps it had been worth it after all. Motorcycle Stud wasn't familiar with being rejected– for anything. Despite his disarming smile and the drool-worthy build his expensive suit couldn't hide– everything about him screamed 'player'. Mari had too much experience with that type to ever be tempted again.

Sexy and conceited were only attractive for a short while. Inevitably, the inherent shallowness left her bored. Her next relationship would be with a plain, earnest man. Maybe even a bit dull, Mari decided. No– not dull. She needed someone to laugh with. So– plain, earnest and funny. And gainfully employed, she added– after a brief flashback to Nick. Employed would be a major plus.

A little bitter, Mari? Because that definitely sounded like sour grapes. And what did it matter anyway? She had enough problems to manage without adding a high maintenance man to her list. Besides– she had Hector to think of now.

Annoyed with herself, she shook off the ambivalent mood. It would not serve her well to head into this board meeting with an attitude. She needed cooperation– and lots of money. Otherwise, the shelter would suffer for her bad temper. The wealthy patrons who showed up for these meetings expected to feel noble about the money they parted with. With the exception of a few hardworking board members who truly embraced the mission– most wanted to hear a sad story, learn how their specific donation would make the difference, then write their check and leave.

Setting the stack of PR materials on the table inside the room, she massaged her aching arms. Her practiced eye noted the fine china coffee service, the tray of expensive pastries that would barely be touched by the toothpick-thin wives of the wealthy executives she was courting. Yet, if the trappings weren't there, her shelter would appear less worthy– less photogenic to the corporations she solicited. She continually walked a fine line between wasting valuable donations on the elaborate trappings required to gain more donors and appearing too lowbrow to merit their attention.

Hearing the rustle of footsteps behind her, Mari shelved her thoughts. Pasting on a smile, she turned to face her arriving guests. "Good morning-"

"So, we meet again."

Her smile faltered as she met the discerning gaze of the sexy fratboy from the lobby. What were the odds? "What a pleasant surprise," she lied. "I'm Marisol Ortega from the New Beginnings Shelter. And you?"

"Jeff Traynor, from Specialty Construction. Nice to meet you."

Her hand was engulfed in his. She noticed he took his time before releasing it. It was a nice hand, she admitted reluctantly. Sturdy. Capable. "You're related to Linc and Mona? They're wonderful people." Who couldn't possibly have spawned such a self-indulgent charmer. Perhaps her original impression had been wrong.

"My parents– and they are pretty great. They speak very highly of the shelter. On behalf of Specialty, I look forward to helping in any way we can."

Mari couldn't help her smile. "You realize our shelter is the very one you referred to in the parking lot as 'being stuck with the homeless shelter gig'?"

His expression chagrined, he raised his hands. "Guilty as charged. But try not to let my initial impression sway you."

"You've suddenly realized a previously undiscovered interest in the homeless?" His warm, green eyes sparked with what she could only term mischief. How could a man his age have the capacity to appear as though he'd been caught with his hand in a cookie jar? "Perhaps you had an epiphany in the elevator?"

"Go figure." A slow grin flashed. "Seriously, the shelter means a great deal to my parents. Therefore it means a great deal to me."

"Where is Mr. Traynor? He's well, I hope?"

"Dad's out of town this week, so he asked me to sit in for him. Something about an addition you're planning?"

"Yes, we've been working together for months on the final plans." She chewed her lip at the realization there would be yet another delay. With Linc out of town, she would make little progress. "I'd hoped to spend a few minutes with him after this meeting to finalize the outstanding issues we still had-"

"I'll be happy to review the plans with you," he interrupted.

Jeff's smile revealed perfectly even white teeth and a dimple in one cheek. It truly was unfair that one man could be blessed with such amazing features. She hesitated– knowing the flare of interest in his eyes was more of a personal nature than a sudden fascination with the city's homeless population. "Perhaps I should wait for Linc-"

"I insist," he interrupted. "He'll be ticked if he thinks I'm the reason your project is delayed. He assured me I should do whatever you asked."

Thankfully, a sudden cluster of new arrivals crowded the doorway. The tall, likeable man standing before her was a little too charming. Nodding to Jeff, she drifted to the door. "Very well. I look forward to working with you."

Nodding as introductions were made, Jeff tried to contain his smile. A private meeting with a gorgeous woman– a project that would keep them in close contact. He owed the old man big-time. He couldn't have planned the situation better himself. Marisol. An unusual name for a beautiful woman. She'd be charmed. Grateful for his assistance. By the time the project was ready to break ground– she'd be his for the taking.

"As most of you are aware– the homeless population in Arlington has only grown since the downturn in the economy forced people further outside the District-"

Jeff had every intention of paying attention. But each time she passed his table, her scent drifted over him, tantalizing him with the spice of cinnamon and something else– something exotic and sensual that had his senses prickling with awareness. She was making it very difficult to concentrate.

Discreetly checking his phone, he rearranged his schedule for the next several hours. They would review the plans . . . flirt a little. Invite her to lunch. Easy enough to extend their *work* discussion over a meal. Then shift their conversation to the personal side-

"Despite having seven homeless shelters in this area– over one hundred people are turned away each night for beds. That number will more than double or even triple when the weather gets colder."

Glancing up, he discovered Marisol staring at his phone as she spoke. Damn. What had she just said? That last statistic sounded ridiculously high. Sliding his phone into his pocket, he vowed to pay closer attention.

"At New Beginnings, we serve over three hundred meals each day– not including those that are prepared for the residents at the shelter."

"Is this shelter unisex?"

Marisol acknowledged the woman with a gracious smile. The simple act sent his pulse into overdrive. "The shelter is for women and their children only. But our daily meals are open to anyone. We serve breakfast, lunch and dinner to the area homeless. At night we have a separate living area that serves as short term housing for women in transition."

Transition? Jeff raised a brow. He smiled a moment later when someone asked the same question.

"We offer temporary housing to women who are experiencing domestic violence and must make a quick escape-"

"How often do those situations occur?" Jeff surprised himself with the question. Her beautiful eyes shifted their focus to him and he experienced a punch of heat.

"At New Beginnings we receive at least three calls a week from agencies asking to place women– sometimes alone– but usually mothers with children. Typically, they have escaped their situation with only the clothes on their backs." Marisol's voice grew husky, her expression serious. "Currently, those are hard for us to accommodate. We have limited space and we don't have separate apartment units for mothers to care for their children."

Wishing he'd taken the time to review the plans his dad had dropped off earlier in the week, Jeff frowned. "Is that what this addition is all about?"

She nodded. "We hope to expand the homeless shelter to better provide an appropriate setting for mothers to care for their children– somewhere they will feel safe from harm– safe from being discovered– as they work to get back on their feet."

Nodding his thanks, he jotted notes as others asked detailed questions about the expansion and the financing. He had several construction-related questions– most of which would be answered once he took a good look at her drawings.

Her voice washed over him as she calmly answered each question, at times, her sexy accent more pronounced. Had she been raised in the States? Marisol was painstaking in her answers– yet unvarnished. He was left with the impression of a woman would not couch the truth in pretty words. Nor would she paint an extremely dire picture– even though making the situation appear worse might be helpful in securing donations. From what he'd heard so far, she was straightforward. Her eyes sparkled with intelligence and compassion for the women she assisted.

Jeff glanced around the room. She had them eating out of her hand. Hell– after thirty minutes in her presence, she had him hooked, too. He'd entered the room resentful about having to waste his time. Now– he was eager to review the plans– see what changes needed to be made. Research what engineering could be accomplished to shave costs without hurting design. She'd won him over to the challenge– just as she'd won over several others in the room. He watched as several heads nodded, agreeing with the point she was making.

His thoughts drifted back to their conversation by the elevator. When he'd been busy launching a standard pick-up line, her response had been decisive. *Many women need help. But I am not one of them.* Marisol was tough. He'd bet she was protective of her clients at the shelter. She'd probably seen just about everything humanity had to offer.

Jeff allowed himself a grudging smile. Marisol represented an interesting challenge. His usual game plan would require tweaking. She wasn't a typical one-and-done pushover. She would demand effort. Well-planned and highly coordinated. Though subtlety was a tool he'd rarely been called upon to utilize in the past, he was smart enough to realize he would need it now. But with a little Traynor elbow grease– and maybe some advice from his sisters-in-law– he could pick up a few pointers. By the time he was finished, Marisol Ortega wouldn't know what hit her.

∞

Mari sank back in her chair, resisting the urge to kick off her pumps. Soon enough she could slip back into the jeans and sneakers that were her uniform at the shelter. The men and women she served didn't care how she dressed to assist them. They worried about the roof over their head and the hot meal in their belly. They cared whether they would be privy to the same luxury the next day. And the one after that.

Checking her watch, Mari waited for Jefferson Traynor to return. For a part of her job she did not enjoy performing, she was rather adept at soliciting donations– of both time and money to assist the New Beginnings Shelter. About to undertake her biggest challenge, it was fortunate she performed so well. Adding a wing to the shelter had been her dream for nearly five years. She was down to the last half million they needed to complete the addition. But—more importantly, they finally had enough money to get the project started.

The remaining hurdle was securing the contractor who could make it happen for the lowest price, in the shortest amount of time. The shelter had been overcrowded for months. Every night, people were turned away. That situation would only intensify by the time winter rolled around again.

Marisol rose when she saw Jeff in the hallway, wrapping up his conversation with a colleague. It was the ultimate irony that the annoying man she'd met in the lobby was the unlikely savior who would be the catalyst to make her dreams for the new wing happen. But if she could parlay his interest in her into lower prices . . . a shorter schedule . . . better equipment. Mari smiled. She didn't mind using sexual attraction to get what the shelter needed.

He re-entered the room with as much energy as he'd shown earlier. Shrugging free of his suit jacket, he tossed it on the chair. "Okay - let's take a look at these plans."

"How about back here?" She cleared one of the tables, unable to contain her frown as she noticed the mountain of untouched pastries on the tray.

His gaze followed hers. "You hungry? I'll get the waiter to bring us more coffee."

She shook her head. "No, thanks. I was thinking of the waste. To you, that pile probably doesn't mean much." Meeting his attentive gaze, she smiled. "Just a billion calories."

Rolling up his shirtsleeves on tanned, strong . . . capable looking forearms, he paused. "What does it mean to you?"

She turned to survey the room. "To me, this represents three hundred dollars that could have been spent on meals at the shelter." Turning back, she found him watching her expectantly. "Care to take a guess how many meals that would provide?"

He shrugged. "To be honest– three hundred bucks doesn't sound like a huge amount of money, but when you put it that way-" His expression changed, indicating he was performing some serious mathematical calculations in his head. "I'd guess if you were careful you could make about fifty meals with three hundred bucks?"

She smiled over the flare of interest in beautiful, green eyes. "Actually we can do a little better than that. With three hundred dollars, the fantastic volunteer chefs at New Beginnings can stretch that to cover closer to two hundred meals."

Jeff emitted a low whistle. "Seriously?" When she nodded, he held up a finger. "Don't move. I'll be right back."

When he disappeared through the double doors once again, she wondered where he possibly derived so much energy. She was leafing through her construction notes when he returned five minutes later– an army of waiters following closely on his heels.

His wink made her stomach flutter. Shocked, she met his gaze. The cocky smile told her Jeff knew it, too. He pointed out the pastry. "I'd like all of this sliced into smaller portions and wrapped so Miss Ortega can take it with her. We'll be leaving in forty minutes."

It was her turn to stare as the waiters scurried around to load up the pastries. "Why are you doing this?"

"The money's not totally wasted if everyone at the shelter gets to enjoy a billion calorie dessert, right?"

Why hadn't she thought of it? Jeff Traynor's eyes sparkled when he grinned– reminding her of an overgrown kid who was having way too much fun. He'd taken her lemons and gifted her with lemonade. Mari's smile was genuine when she thanked him. "You're absolutely right."

∽

Jeff was pretty sure he deserved a medal. He glanced at his watch to confirm his award-winning abilities. Yeah. He was damn sure. The last hour and fifteen minutes had been spent inhaling the intoxicating scent of Marisol Ortega. He'd observed– at close range– how her eyes changed from one bewitching Caribbean blue to another– depending on her mood and the light in the room. Her hair– long, chocolate strands that whispered for his fingers to run through each curl had remained untouched. He'd noticed– yet miraculously refrained from confirming, what he suspected was the softest, honeyed skin he'd ever seen.

All of this herculean effort had taken place while he'd been required to speak coherently about the numerous changes she wished to make. She'd hit him with question after intelligent question– how much would this change cost? Would they still have room for this other feature? Where would it go? Would it add days to the schedule?

Releasing a gusty sigh, he watched her gather her briefcase. Marisol had been pleasant. She'd been polite. She'd been persistent– damn persistent about what she wanted for her shelter. She'd grilled him steadily– yet by all accounts, she'd been completely unaffected by him. When he'd asked her to lunch, she'd paused for so long, Jeff figured she was trying to think up a plausible excuse. When she finally answered, she'd asked if she could decide later. Apparently if their current meeting ran too long, she'd shoot him down again. Not exactly the situation he'd painted for himself.

What the hell was going on? He was charming, damn it. He was persuasive. *Plenty* of women had made it abundantly clear they found him attractive. Seriously . . . it was a shitload.

He worked out. He showered daily. So– what was he doing wrong with her?

"Jefferson? Did you still wish to have lunch?" Marisol set her briefcase near the stack of pastry boxes that still needed to be loaded into her car.

His gloom-laden thoughts scattered as his brain skidded back to reality. "Do you have time?"

"I don't mean to be forward, but I would have time if you let me pick our lunch spot." She smiled, a question in her mesmerizing eyes. "Would that be okay?"

Hooyah. *Hell, yeah.* He contained his grin with effort. And the high-five. Definitely not cool. "No problem."

"I want to take you to one of my favorite places."

Jeff's stomach tilted. She could choose the most expensive place in town for all he cared. Marisol had offered a genuine smile– the first one directed solely at him. "Lead the way. I'll carry these boxes to your car."

CHAPTER 2

Mari parked in the alley behind the building, forced to wedge her car between a delivery truck and a volunteer's sedan. Confirming in her rearview mirror that Jeff was still with her– she crossed her fingers she wouldn't embarrass herself when she parallel parked in the tight space. With parking at a premium, he definitely had it easier with his motorcycle.

Pulling up next to her, Jeff parked his bike on the sidewalk in an effort to keep the alley clear. She opened the passenger door, intent on pulling boxes of pastry from her backseat when he approached, a concerned expression in his eyes. "What's wrong?"

He scanned the deserted street, frowning. "You shouldn't be parking here– this isn't safe."

She waved a hand to dismiss his worry. "I've parked here before. We'll be fine."

"Where are we? I don't think I've ever been here before."

Before she could respond, he quickly moved in front of her– putting himself and the car door between them. "What are you doing?"

"Stay behind me," he ordered, his voice suddenly tense. "There's a very large, very scary looking guy approaching us. Whatever happens– if I tell you to run– just go."

Mari stole a peek over a broad, solid shoulder and smothered her laughter. Brushing his arm, she felt the muscles contract under his shirt. "Jefferson– it's not what you think."

Determined, he kept his gaze on the massive man approaching. "We're *not* about to be attacked by a giant who looks as though he walked off the set of a James Bond movie?"

Still clutching his arm, she moved into the alley. "Jeff– this is the shelter. We're having lunch at New Beginnings. And this-" She stepped forward to greet the man approaching them with a scowl on his scarred face. "This is Pete Shea." She nodded at the man towering over her. "Pete? I'd like to introduce you to my friend, Jeff Traynor."

To her relief, Jeff immediately relaxed, his guarded expression dissolving in a smile. "Nice to meet you, Pete."

Pete continued to glare down at Jeff from his six foot seven height. His expression indicated he'd slipped into his world of military scenarios. She made a mental note to discuss the increasing lapses with his counselor at the V A Center.

Mari sensed Jeff closing the gap between them. "Pete?" She tried again to defuse the tension. "Jeff is building our addition for us. Maybe after lunch– you can walk with us for a few minutes and share your suggestions with Mr. Traynor."

Her words had the hoped-for effect. Like a magic charm, Pete's brooding face split with a smile of welcome and he extended his hand to Jeff. "Nice to meet you. I've got lots of ideas on the addition– lots of stuff that will make the perimeter safer," he explained. "We need to protect the flank. Right now–we're exposed."

"Exposed?" Jeff's gaze shifted to her.

"Yeah, man. It's hard to sleep at night knowing we could be attacked from the south. I don't like it. I don't like it one bit."

Mari ignored the question in Jeff's eyes. "Pete– could you help us carry these pastries inside? If you've already eaten lunch, you could set these out on the dessert table in the back."

"Yes, ma'am. I'll be happy to accept that duty." Walking past Jeff without a second glance, Pete gathered the boxes from her seat and headed to the back door of the shelter.

Beautiful eyes reflecting curiosity, Jeff stared at her for a moment before smiling. "I have a feeling this will be the most interesting lunch I've had in a long time."

CHASING MARISOL, February, 2016

DEAR READER:

Thank you for reading FALLING FOR KEN. I hope you enjoy the Traynor family as much as I enjoyed creating them. If you liked this book, please consider leaving a review on Amazon or Goodreads. Now that you've read Harry and Kendall's story, I hope you'll return for Jefferson. The third installment of Blueprint To Love is CHASING MARISOL, when perpetual player Jefferson meets Marisol Ortega– a rare woman who has zero interest in his overwhelming charm. CHASING will be available February, 2016. The first book, TRUSTING JAKE, is available at all retail sites. Other books include my traditionally published novel, a romantic suspense, FOR HER PROTECTION released in 2010. Another four- book series will be on its way to readers in late 2016.

Blueprint To Love Series
Book 1: Trusting Jake
Book 2: Falling for Ken
Book 3: Chasing Marisol (February, 2016)
For Her Protection

To learn about upcoming books, please visit me at www.laurengiordanoauthor.com or at Lauren Giordano Amazon page. Visit Lauren on Goodreads, follow Lauren on Twitter or Facebook.

Happy reading!
Lauren Giordano

ABOUT THE AUTHOR

Lauren Giordano is an award-winning author of eight novels ranging from contemporary romance to romantic suspense. She also writes a blog exploring the endless, troubling encounters she experiences on the journey to 'create' in her kitchen. Her Cooking Disasters blog can be found at www.laurengiordanoauthor.com. Originally from the Northeast, Lauren makes her home in the Mid-Atlantic with her husband, two daughters and two vacationing cats who never seem to leave.

Printed in Great Britain
by Amazon